The "ever-exciting"* Stone Barrington has a beauty
of a problem . . .

KISSER

After a harrowing sojourn in Key West, Stone Barrington
is back in New York, working on some simple divorce and
custody cases for Woodman & Weld. But when he crosses
paths with a fetching Broadway actress—and sometime lip
model—Stone gets a little more deeply involved with show
business than he'd expected.

Then the fleecing of a wealthy art dealer's daughter
leads him into the world of financial fraud, "Big Art," and
Manhattan's Upper East Side, where opulent co-op apart-
ments are hung with multimillion-dollar paintings, and
where family scandals never remain hidden for long. No
stranger to high society or the foibles of the rich, Stone
soon realizes he must uncover the truth in a world where
wealth and beauty sometimes come at an unusually high
price. . . .

Praise for Stuart Woods's Stone Barrington Novels

Indecent Exposure

"[An] irresistible, luxury-soaked soap opera."
—Publishers Weekly

Fast & Loose

"Another entertaining episode in [a] soap opera about the
rich and famous . . ." —Associated Press

Below the Belt

"Compulsively readable . . . [an] easy-reading page-
turner." *—Booklist*

Sex, Lies & Serious Money

"Series fans will continue to enjoy this bird's-eye view of
the high life." *—Booklist*

Dishonorable Intentions

"Diverting." *—Publishers Weekly*

Family Jewels

"A master of dialogue, action and atmosphere, the Key West resident has added one more jewel of a thriller-mystery to his ever-growing collection."

—*Florida Weekly* (Fort Myers)

Scandalous Behavior

"Woods offers another wild ride with his hero, bringing readers back into a world of action-packed adventure, murder and mayhem, steamy romance, and a twist you don't see coming."
—*Booklist*

Foreign Affairs

"Purrs like a well-tuned dream machine . . . Enjoy this slick thriller by a thoroughly satisfying professional."

—*Florida Weekly*

Hot Pursuit

"Fans will enjoy the vicarious luxury ride."

—*Publishers Weekly*

Insatiable Appetites

"Multiple exciting storylines . . . Readers of the series will enjoy the return of the dangerous Dolce." —*Booklist*

Paris Match

"Plenty of fast-paced action and deluxe experiences that keep the pages turning. Woods is masterful with his use of dialogue and creates natural and vivid scenes for his readers to enjoy." —*The Sun-News* (Myrtle Beach)

Cut and Thrust

"Goes down as smoothly as a glass of Knob Creek."
—*Publishers Weekly*

Carnal Curiosity

"Stone Barrington shows he's one of the smoothest operators around." —*Publishers Weekly*

Standup Guy

"Stuart Woods still owns an imagination that simply won't quit. . . . This is yet another edge-of-your-seat adventure." —*Suspense Magazine*

Doing Hard Time

"High escapist suspense."   —*Mystery Scene*

Collateral Damage

"Undoubtedly a hit. It starts off strong and never lets up, building to an exciting showdown."   —*Booklist*

Severe Clear

"Stuart Woods has proven time and time again that he's a master of suspense who keeps his readers frantically turning the pages."   —*Bookreporter*

Unnatural Acts

"[It] makes you covet the fast-paced, charmed life of Woods' characters from the safety of your favorite chair."
—*Code451*

D.C. Dead

"Engaging . . . The story line is fast-paced."
—*Midwest Book Review*

Son of Stone

"Woods's vast and loyal audience will be thrilled with a second-generation Barrington charmer."   —*Booklist*

Bel-Air Dead

"A fast-paced mystery with an inside look into Hollywood and the motion picture business. Barrington fans will enjoy it."   —*The Oklahoman*

Strategic Moves

"The action never slows from the start."
—*Midwest Book Review*

Praise for Stuart Woods's Other Novels

Barely Legal (with Parnell Hall)

"Woods and Hall have crafted a fast-moving tale with a light touch. . . . Crime fiction doesn't get much more entertaining than this."   —*Booklist* (starred review)

Smooth Operator (with Parnell Hall)

"Fans are sure to welcome this action-packed start to a separate series within the larger Stone Barrington story arc."   —*Publishers Weekly*

BOOKS BY STUART WOODS
FICTION

Quick & Dirty[†]
Indecent Exposure[†]
Fast & Loose[†]
Below the Belt[†]
Sex, Lies & Serious
  Money[†]
Dishonorable
  Intentions[†]
Family Jewels[†]
Scandalous
  Behavior[†]
Foreign Affairs[†]
Naked Greed[†]
Hot Pursuit[†]
Insatiable
  Appetites[†]
Paris Match[†]
Cut and Thrust[†]
Carnal Curiosity[†]
Standup Guy[†]
Doing Hard Time[†]
Unintended
  Consequences[†]
Collateral
  Damage[†]
Severe Clear[†]
Unnatural Acts[†]
D.C. Dead[†]

Son of Stone[†]
Bel-Air Dead[†]
Strategic Moves[†]
Santa Fe Edge[§]
Lucid Intervals[†]
Kisser[†]
Hothouse Orchid[*]
Loitering with
  Intent[†]
Mounting Fears[‡]
Hot Mahogany[†]
Santa Fe Dead[§]
Beverly Hills Dead
Shoot Him If He
  Runs[†]
Fresh Disasters[†]
Short Straw[§]
Dark Harbor[†]
Iron Orchid[*]
Two-Dollar Bill[†]
The Prince of
  Beverly Hills
Reckless Abandon[†]
Capital Crimes[‡]
Dirty Work[†]
Blood Orchid[*]
The Short Forever[†]
Orchid Blues[*]

Cold Paradise[†]
L.A. Dead[†]
The Run[‡]
Worst Fears
  Realized[†]
Orchid Beach[*]
Swimming to
  Catalina[†]
Dead in the Water[†]
Dirt[†]
Choke
Imperfect Strangers
Heat
Dead Eyes
L.A. Times
Santa Fe Rules[§]
New York Dead[†]
Palindrome
Grass Roots[‡]
White Cargo
Deep Lie[‡]
Under the Lake
Run Before the
  Wind[‡]
Chiefs[‡]

COAUTHORED BOOKS

Barely Legal[††]
(with Parnell Hall)

Smooth Operator[**]
(with Parnell Hall)

TRAVEL
*A Romantic's Guide to the Country Inns of
Britain and Ireland* (1979)

MEMOIR
Blue Water, Green Skipper

[*]A Holly Barker Novel
[†]A Stone Barrington Novel
[‡]A Will Lee Novel

[§]An Ed Eagle Novel
[**]A Teddy Fay Novel
[††]A Herbie Fisher Novel

KISSER

STUART WOODS

G. P. Putnam's Sons
New York

PUTNAM

G. P. PUTNAM'S SONS
Publishers Since 1838
An imprint of Penguin Random House LLC
375 Hudson Street
New York, New York 10014

First Signet printing / September 2010
First G. P. Putnam's Sons premium edition / November 2017
G. P. Putnam's Sons premium edition ISBN: 9780451229632

Printed in the United States of America
1   3   5   7   9   10   8   6   4   2

This is a work of fiction. Names, characters, places, and incidents either are the
product of the author's imagination or are used fictitiously, and any resemblance
to actual persons, living or dead, businesses, companies, events, or locales is
entirely coincidental.

This book is for Bob and Liz Woodward.

I

Elaine's, late.

Stone Barrington and his former NYPD partner, Dino Bacchetti, were dining in the company of herself, Elaine, who, as usual, was making her rounds. "So?" Elaine asked as she joined them.

"Not much," Dino replied.

Stone was deep into his *spaghetti alla carbonara*.

"Nice, isn't it?" she asked. Elaine had a good opinion of her food.

"Mmmmf," Stone replied, trying to handle what he had stuffed into his mouth and speak at the same time.

"Never mind," Elaine said. "Enjoy."

Stone swallowed hard and nodded. "Thank you, I am."

The waiter came with the wine and poured everybody a glass.

Stone began to take smaller bites, so as to better participate in the conversation. As he took his first sip of wine, he froze.

Dino stared at him. "What's the matter? Am I gonna have to do a Heimlich?"

Stone set down the glass but said nothing. He was following the entrance of a very beautiful woman. She was probably five-eight or -nine, he thought, and closer to six feet in her heels. She was dressed in a classic Little Black Dress that set off a strand of large pearls around her neck. Fake, probably, but who cared? She had honey-blond, shoulder-length hair and a lot of it, cascades of it, big eyes, and plump lips sporting bright red lipstick. Dino and Elaine followed Stone's gaze as the woman turned to her left and sat down at the bar.

"She can't be alone," Dino said.

"Who is she?" Stone asked Elaine.

"Never saw her in here," Elaine replied, "but you'd better hurry; she's not gonna be alone long."

Stone put down his glass, got up, and walked toward the bar, straightening his tie. Normally, the people at the tables didn't have much to do with the people at the bar; they were different crowds. But Stone knew when to make an exception.

"Good evening," he said to her, offering his hand. "My name is Stone Barrington."

She took the hand and offered a shy smile. "Hello, I'm Carrie Cox," she said, and her accent was soft and Southern.

Stone indicated his table. "My friends Dino and Elaine agree with me that you are too beautiful to be sitting alone at the bar. Will you join us?"

She looked surprised. "Thank you, yes," she said after a moment's thought.

Stone escorted her back to the table and sat her down. "Carrie Cox, this is Elaine Kaufman, your hostess, and Dino Bacchetti, one of New York's Finest."

"How do you do," Carrie said. "Finest what?"

"It's a designation meant to describe any New York City police officer," Stone said, "without regard for individual quality."

"Stone should know," Dino said. "He used to be one of New York's worst."

Carrie laughed, a low, inviting sound.

"You must be from out of town," Dino said.

"Isn't everybody?" Elaine asked.

"I've only been in New York for three weeks," Carrie said.

"Where you from?" Elaine asked.

"I'm from a little town in Georgia called Delano, but I came here from Atlanta. I lived there for two years."

"And what brought you to our city?" Stone asked.

"I'm an actress, so after a couple of years of training in Atlanta, it was either New York or L.A. Since it's spring, I thought I'd start in New York, and if I hadn't found work by winter, I'd move on to L.A."

Stone was fascinated by her mouth, which moved in an oddly attractive way when she talked.

"And have you found work yet?"

"Almost immediately," she said, "but not as an actress. I've been working as a lip model."

"I'm not surprised," Stone said.

"A *lip* model?" Dino asked.

"I've been modeling lipstick," she explained, "in the mornings. In the afternoons I've been making the rounds, looking for stage work."

"That's tough," Elaine said.

"Well, I've had one very attractive offer," Carrie said, "from a man called Del Wood."

Stone knew him a little, from a couple of dinner parties. Wood was a king of Broadway, who composed both music and lyrics and who owned his own theater. "The new Irving Berlin," Stone said, "as he's often called."

"Unfortunately," Carrie said, "the offer came with some very unattractive strings."

"Ah," Stone said. "Del Wood has that reputation. He is also known as Del Woodie."

Carrie laughed. "I can believe it. Do you know what he said to me?"

"I can't wait to find out," Dino said, leaning forward.

"He said—and please pardon the language; it's his, not mine—'I want to strip off that dress, lay you on your belly, and fuck you in the ass.'"

"Oh," Dino said.

Stone was speechless.

"I was thinking of suing him for sexual harassment," Carrie said.

"Well," Dino said, indicating Stone, "meet your new lawyer."

"Oh, are you a lawyer?" Carrie asked Stone.

"Yes, but I'm not sure you'd have much of a case."

"Why not?"

"Did he force himself on you?"

"No. I got out of there."

"Were there any witnesses?"

"No."

"Then I'm afraid it would be your word against his," Stone said.

"Well," Carrie said, "I did get him on tape."

2

S tone nearly choked on his wine. "That was pre-
  scient of you," he rasped.

"Well, I had heard a little about him," Carrie
replied. "A girl has to protect herself."

"Certainly," Stone replied.

"Too fucking right," Elaine added.

"And by what means did you record him?"
Stone asked.

"Small dictator in my open purse on his desk,"
Carrie replied. "So, shall I retain you as my attorney and sue the son of a bitch?"

"First things first," Stone said. "What may I get
you to drink, and will you have some dinner?"

"Thank you. A Knob Creek on the rocks, please,
and no, I'm not hungry, having already dined—
partially, anyway."

Stone ordered the drink. "And what do you mean by having dined 'partially'?"

"Well, a friend, a stage manager, invited me to a very nice dinner party being given by a well-known actress. We arrived a little late, and to my surprise, I found myself seated next to Mr. Del Wood, who couldn't keep his hands to himself. Having fought that off in the afternoon—something the other diners seemed to be aware of—I tried to make conversation, but then Mr. Woodie interrupted me and announced for all to hear that the offer he had made me that afternoon was still open. He was beginning to explain to everyone what the offer was when I tipped his dinner plate into his lap—we were having *spaghetti Bolognese*—then I got up, offered my thanks to my hostess, and left."

"Wow," Dino said. "I wish I'd been there for that."

"So do I," Stone said. "Perhaps you'd like dessert, Carrie?"

"Thank you. Perhaps I would."

Elaine grabbed a passing waiter and ordered up the dessert tray. Normally, she would have moved to another table by then, but she seemed to be enjoying the conversation.

The waiter appeared, and Carrie chose a crème brûlée.

"How many people were at the dinner party, and were they all theater people?"

"Twelve, and yes, they were actors, composers, producers, the works. I was rather looking forward to doing myself some good there, but Old Woodie spoiled that."

"Well," Stone said, "by lunchtime tomorrow you will be famous among a certain level of the Broadway cognoscenti; people will be dining out on that story for weeks, and I wouldn't be surprised if it made the gossip columns."

"Would that be a good thing?" Carrie asked.

"Good for everybody but Mr. Woodie," Stone replied. "You'll be immediately famous, as long as they spell your name right."

"Oh, good."

"What part did he offer you?"

"The lead in his new musical."

Stone was stunned. "The *lead*? What sort of audition did you do?"

"I sang 'I Loves You Porgy' from *Porgy and Bess* and a Sondheim tune, 'I'm Still Here,' and I danced a little. This was in the theater."

"And he let you get all the way through the two songs?"

"Yes, and there were a dozen or so people sitting in the orchestra seats who all stood up and applauded. That's when Mr. Wood invited me up to his office to talk."

"That sounds like something out of a movie about a Broadway show," Stone said. "Small-town girl shows up in the big city and wows everybody at her first audition."

"Well, it wasn't my first audition," Carrie said. "I had to audition for the lip modeling, too."

"And who did you have to kiss?" Dino asked.

"A mirror. I didn't mind that; a mirror has no hands." Her crème brûlée arrived, and she did it justice.

"Coffee?" Stone asked

"A double espresso, please."

"No trouble sleeping?" Stone asked.

"No trouble at all," she replied, giving him a little smile that made those beautiful lips enchanting again. "The benefit of a clear conscience."

"Always a good thing to have," Stone said. "Tell me, do you remember the names of the people at the dinner party?"

"Most of them. My date, Tony, will know them all."

"And have their addresses?"

"Yes, I think so. They were all his friends."

"First thing tomorrow morning you should write little notes to those people, expressing your regret for having to depart the party and say how sorry you were that you didn't have time to get to know them better. Start with your hostess."

"Just to remind them who I am?"

"Exactly, and please be sure your address, phone number, and cell number are clearly printed on your letterhead. If the letters don't get you other auditions, they will, at least, get you some dinner invitations—dinners Mr. Wood will not be attending."

"What a good idea, Stone," she said. "Now, will you be my attorney so that I can sue Mr. Woodie?"

"I'm afraid I have a serious conflict of interest that would prevent my representing you. However, I'd be happy to give you some free advice and to recommend an appropriate attorney."

"What's the conflict of interest?" Carrie asked.

"I am so impressed with your beauty, your intelligence, and your quick wit that I would much rather take you out to dinner than take you to court."

She laughed. "I think I would like that, too," she said. She opened a tiny purse and gave him a beautifully engraved card, and Stone reciprocated.

"Now, give me the free advice."

"I don't think you should sue Mr. Wood—at least, not right away. I think the dinner party incident will show up in tomorrow's papers, and with nearly all the details. Mr. Wood can't hold you responsible for that; he has only himself to blame. And who knows? You might even end up working for him some day, but under more favorable circumstances. Do you have your Equity card yet?" This referred to Actor's Equity, the union representing stage actors.

"No, but all I need is one job to get it."

"I think you are more likely to get that first job, if you don't have a reputation for suing producers for sexual harassment. Anyway, having drawn a very firm line in the sand with Mr. Wood, you will henceforth have a reputation as an actress who does not brook unwanted advances from potential employers, and you will be treated with some respect."

"A good point," she admitted. "I will take your advice."

"And, should you feel receptive to an advance at some point in the near future," Stone said, "I will be around to fulfill that need in an entirely nontheatrical setting."

She smiled broadly at him. "We'll see," she said.

3

When Stone arrived at his desk the following midmorning, the *New York Post* was lying on his desk, open to the "Page Six" gossip column, which was not on page six. His secretary, Joan Robertson, had left it there and had conveniently highlighted the passage:

> Last night at dinner at the home of theater diva Gwen Asprey, the composer/producer Del Wood, whose reputation as a casting-couch Lothario is richly deserved, was given his comeuppance after having previously made advances on (including, we hear, a request for anal sex) and been rejected by a new girl in town, the beautiful and talented Carrie Cox. When Woodie, as he is known to some, began to tell the table of his

thwarted attempt, Ms. Cox, who had, unaccountably, been seated next to him, dumped his own plate of red-sauce pasta into his lap and made a grand exit. The evening was greatly enjoyed by everyone present, except Mr. Wood. Incidentally, only that afternoon Carrie Cox had performed a brilliant audition for Mr. Wood and his backers that resulted in an offer of the lead in his new musical. Unfortunately, Woodie considered the transaction a trade instead of an offer, so the lovely Ms. Cox remains at liberty. (Other producers, take note!) Later in the evening, she was seen at Elaine's in the company of local lawyer Stone Barrington. Out of the frying pan and into the fire!

Stone thought that the piece was a remarkably accurate account of events, for a gossip column, and he was surprised to see a very good photograph of Carrie Cox, in balletic flight, accompanying it. He wondered where the paper had found it on such short notice.

His phone buzzed. "Carrie Cox on line one," Joan said.

He picked up the phone. "Is this the beautiful and talented Carrie Cox?" he asked.

"That's what it says in the papers," she replied, giggling. "You were right!"

"I've seen the *Post*," Stone said. "How did they get it so accurate?"

"There was a message from them on my answering machine when I got home," she said, "and I played the tape for them."

"If the tape should ever be mentioned again, deny its existence and tell them you took notes after the conversation."

"All right," she said, "but I made them promise not to mention that, and they didn't."

"You're a lucky woman, as well as a smart one."

"Thank you, kind sir."

"How about dinner this evening?"

"I've been invited to a dinner party," she said. "Another prediction of yours come true. Why don't you come with me?"

"You're on. Where shall I pick you up?"

"I'm downtown, and you're closer to the dinner. Why don't I pick you up? You can make me a drink around, say, seven?"

"You're on again. Is this a necktie party?"

"Well, I hope I'm not going to be hanged."

"For me, not you."

"My mother always said a gentleman can't go wrong by wearing a necktie, and tonight you're supposed to wear a black one along with a dinner jacket."

"Then wear one I shall. You have my card; see you at seven."

"Bye-bye." She hung up.

Joan was leaning against his doorjamb. "I don't believe this," she said.

Carrie arrived at seven on the dot, and Stone met her at the door.

"Oooh," she murmured, looking around the living room. "I want the tour! How many bedrooms?"

"Five, and as many baths, with three powder rooms scattered around the place."

"How long have you owned it?"

"Since I inherited it from my great-aunt. I did most of the renovation myself. Come on. I'll show you this floor." He took her through the living room, the dining room, and a garage. Finally he sat her down in the study and produced a half-bottle of Schramsberg champagne from the wet bar.

"Such wonderful woodwork and bookcases," she said.

"My father built all of them. In fact, you could say that this house saved his career and his marriage. He was going door-to-door in Greenwich Village, doing whatever carpentry work he could find. This house bought him his shop and equipment and made him feel that he could earn a living at what he did best."

"That's a wonderful story," she said.

"I haven't heard your story yet," Stone said, "except the part about Delano and Atlanta."

"Ah, well, there is a bit more," Carrie said. "After Agnes Scott College I went to the Yale Drama School for a master's, then went back to Atlanta and married my college sweetheart instead of going to New York when I should have. That went bad pretty quickly, but I did last a few years before I divorced him."

"How long ago?"

"Three years, when his property development business was at its peak. That improved my settlement. Now he resents me because he's nearly broke."

"Wasn't your fault," Stone pointed out.

"Tell him that!"

"I hope I don't have to."

"Don't worry; he's well in my past."

"So, after the divorce . . ."

"I danced with the Atlanta Ballet and worked in local theater and studied acting. I enjoyed it, but I wanted to try a bigger arena."

"I'm glad you chose New York instead of L.A.," Stone said.

She raised her glass. "So am I."

"Tell me, where did the *Post* get the photograph?"

"I directed them to the *Atlanta Constitution*, which had done a piece on me last year."

"I think you're going to do well in this town."

"From your lips to God's ear," she said. "I Googled you and read some of your old press."

"Not all of it favorable," Stone said.

"Oh, I don't know. Like you say, they spelled your name right. I was confused about your connection to a law firm."

"Woodman & Weld. I'm of counsel to them, which means I handle the cases they don't want to be associated with publicly. They're far too prestigious to be representing people who are involved in nasty divorces or have been accused of drunk driving or spousal abuse. Once in a while they throw me a nice personal-injury suit to settle, but I also generate a good deal of my own business."

"Well, if I'm ever in terrible trouble, I'll call you," Carrie said.

"Don't wait until then," Stone replied. He looked at his watch. "Perhaps we'd better move along."

"Yes, we're already fashionably late," she said, jumping gracefully to her feet.

They walked out into the spring night, hand in hand.

4

The party was a ten-minute cab ride away, in a large apartment on Central Park South, overlooking the park. A uniformed maid answered the door, and the glitter began.

Stone didn't know anybody there, but he recognized a few faces from the Broadway stage. There were at least forty people for dinner, so he reckoned it would be a buffet, and he was right.

They worked the room slowly, and they could just as well have stood still and let the crowd come to them, such was Carrie's new fame. Stone admired the way she met people, not as an equal, but as the new girl. One or two of the young women seemed to be looking her over enviously, but most people seemed impressed with her. Some of them were agents who offered their cards.

"I wish I could recommend somebody," Stone

said, "but this crowd is not part of my world. I'm a theatergoer, but I'm no insider."

"I think that's refreshing," Carrie said. "I love theater people, but it's nice to know people from other worlds, too."

They sat on the big terrace with the park views, and a waiter brought them plates. When they had finished dining and were on brandy, a middle-aged man pulled up a chair in front of Carrie, turned and spoke briefly to Stone, then turned his attention back to Carrie.

"I'm Mark Goodwin," he said, "and I'm one of the two or three best theatrical agents in this town. I'm not going to tell you who the others are." He gave her the names of half a dozen clients, and it was an impressive list. "I want you to talk to everybody you can, then come and see me." He gave her his card. "You've made a splash already," he said, "and I'm not talking about the columns, though that doesn't hurt. I heard about your audition for Del Wood less than an hour after you finished it, and so did a lot of other people."

"If I were your client," Carrie asked, "how would you handle me right now?"

"The first thing I would do would be to heal the breach with Del, though not in a way that would put your virtue in jeopardy. Del is an important man in this business, and the part he offered you is the best thing to come along in years. I've read the script and heard the score, and you're perfect for it."

"How are you going to get him to apologize?" Carrie asked.

"Oh, he's never going to apologize," Goodwin said. "The best you can hope for is that he will deign to forget what he did in his office and what you did at the dinner party. If you can forget it, too, he might be willing to call it a draw. I've known him a long time, and I know how to handle him."

"Mr. Goodwin," Carrie said, "I'm well aware of who you are and how good you are. Get me the part, and I'll be your new client the same day."

"It won't be that hard," Goodwin said. "After all, you've already aced the audition. Come see me tomorrow afternoon at three." He shook her hand, then Stone's, and then wandered off into the crowd.

"That sounds promising," Stone said.

"If I could have picked anybody for an agent, it would have been Mark Goodwin," Carrie said. "The day before yesterday, I couldn't have gotten in to see him."

"Your movie continues," Stone said. "Next, we'll have some shots of rehearsals, then a triumphant opening-night scene, then trouble of some sort—alcohol or drugs or an awful man, then recovery and . . . well, you know the rest."

"I'm not inclined toward addictions," Carrie said, "and especially not to bad men. I've had one, and that was enough."

"I'm glad to hear it."

Carrie stood up. "Let's get out of here. I want to show you something."

Stone followed her downstairs and into a cab, and she gave the driver an address in the West Fifties, between Fifth and Sixth avenues. Once there, they got out of the cab in front of an elegant building. Taking a key from her purse, she led him up the front steps, opened the front door, then another door.

Stone found himself standing in the large room that had, apparently, been the living room when the building had been a single-family house. It was empty of furniture, but it had recently been painted and seemed in very good condition.

"It's a duplex," Carrie said, pointing to a balcony at one end of the room. "The bedrooms are up there, and I signed the lease this afternoon."

"That was quite a leap of faith," Stone said. "Maybe you'd better slow down a little."

"No need; I told you that I got a good divorce settlement and that my ex was a rich man then. I've been living downtown with a friend, and when I've furnished this place, it will be a good leading lady's apartment. The lease is for two years, and after that I'll buy something grander on the East Side."

"A woman with a plan," Stone said.

"I've learned to make my plans happen," Carrie replied. "It's something I'm really good at."

"What other plans do you have?" Stone asked.

"If I had planned better, I would have had a bed delivered this afternoon," she replied, standing on her tiptoes and kissing him. "I guess we'll have to make do with one of your bedrooms." She took his hand and trotted him out to the street and into another cab.

Stone did not offer any resistance.

5

Stone woke slowly to the sound of Carrie on the phone, speaking quietly but urgently. She had been a transcendent lover the night before, and in the middle of the night, too, and he felt a little worn out.

Carrie finished her conversation and hung up. "Oh, you're awake. Good morning. Your house-keeper made me tea and toast." She began pulling on clothes. "I've got a dance class in half an hour. Then I'm meeting my designer at the apartment. I'd like you to attend my three o'clock meeting with Mark Goodwin, if you're available."

Stone pressed the button on the remote control that raised his bed to a sitting position. "Good morning, Carrie," he said. "I should tell you that I have no experience with theatrical work, so I'm not sure what use I'd be to you."

"I just want you to represent me in dealing with Goodwin. I'm told he has a boilerplate client contract that isn't entirely client-favorable, and I think I need some help with my negotiations with him."

"Okay. What time?"

She handed him a slip of paper with the address. "Three o'clock. Be five minutes early, will you?" She bent over and kissed him. "You were just great last night; now I've gotta run."

"You're going to a dance class in an LBD?"

"I've got dance clothes in my locker at the studio. Bye-bye." Then, with a wave, she fled downstairs.

Stone shaved and showered, got dressed, had some breakfast, and went down to his office. Once again, "Page Six" in the *Post* awaited him:

Last night at a black-tie dinner for fifty at the home of Broadway angels David and Shirley Medved, Carrie Cox, the new girl in town, continued her sweep through Broadway circles by signing with superagent Mark Goodwin on a handshake. We hear that, before the day is out, he'll have her signed to her first major role.

My God, Stone thought. How does she do this? His phone rang. "Hello?"

"It's Dino. You seen the *Post*?"

"Yeah, just now."

"How does she do this?"

"I was just wondering the same thing. I was with her continuously from seven last evening until about an hour ago, and I never saw her make a phone call until this morning. She must be communicating psychically with 'Page Six.'"

"Don't get knocked down in the whirlwind."

"I'll try not to."

"Dinner?"

"See you at eight thirty."

"Are you bringing the girl?"

"I don't know yet." Stone hung up.

Mark Goodwin's suite of offices was upstairs over a big Broadway theater and reached by a tiny elevator. Carrie was sitting in his reception area, flipping through a fashion magazine.

"Oh, hi," she said. She turned to the receptionist. "Now you can tell Mr. Goodwin we're here."

The woman spoke on the phone. "You can go right in," she said.

Stone followed Carrie into a large office overlooking Schubert Alley. Mark Goodwin kissed Carrie, shook Stone's hand, and waved them to a sitting area with a sofa and chairs.

"I had lunch with Del Wood," he said. "My girl is typing up the contract now."

"Contract?" Carrie asked.

"Two contracts, actually," Goodwin replied. "One between you and Del and one between you and me."

"Tell me about the one between Woodie and me."

"Oh, we sorted things out over lunch and worked out what may be the best deal for a first-time starring role in the history of the Broadway theater."

"Tell me about it," Carrie said.

"It's a one-year contract with an option for another three months. He wanted a run-of-the-play deal, but I nixed that; you may be getting even better offers after the West Coast crowd sees you onstage. Hollywood is going to be interested, I can promise you." He ran through the salary and other conditions.

"That does sound good," Carrie said.

"Listen, I already know Del's production costs, the number of seats in his theater, and the kind of money he's paying the rest of the cast, some of whom are my clients; believe me, this is a good deal."

"Wonderful," she said. "Now tell me about my deal with you."

A young woman walked into the office and handed him a file folder. "Here's my standard client contract," he said, handing her two sheets of paper, which she turned over to Stone without looking at them.

Stone read quickly through the agreement while Carrie and Goodwin sat silently, waiting. "Two things," Stone said. "There's a paragraph in here that says you take a commission on anything she ever does involving somebody you introduced her to. That won't do."

"It's standard," Goodwin said.

"The other thing is, you can fire her as a client whenever you like, but she has to give you a year's notice. That won't do, either. We want termination on thirty days' written notice by either party, and the other paragraph comes out."

"Can't do it," Goodwin said.

"I'm so sorry we couldn't reach an agreement, Mark," Carrie said, "but I think Stone's points are valid." She got to her feet.

"Sit down, sit down," Goodwin said. "For you, I'll do this." He made some notes on the contract and buzzed for his girl. "Make these changes pronto," he said, and then turned back to Carrie. "Here's your contract with Del Wood." He handed it to her, and she signed it without reading it.

"You don't want your attorney to read it first?"

"Not necessary," Carrie said, handing the contract back to him. "You represent me to others."

The secretary returned with the other contract,

and Stone looked it over and handed it to Carrie. "Looks fine with me," he said.

Carrie signed it and handed it to Goodwin. He signed both contracts and handed copies to Stone; then he handed Carrie a script and another thick booklet. "Carrie, here are your script and score. You start rehearsals Monday morning at Central Plaza, ten o'clock sharp. You should learn the first act by then, and you should run through the score with a pianist, so that you're familiar with it."

"Who's directing?" she asked.

"Jack Wright," he replied.

"Oh, good." She stood up. "Thank you so much, Mark. I look forward to working with you. By the way, I don't need my hand held; I'll call you if I have any problems with Woodie."

Goodwin stood up. "Remember not to call him that," he said. "He doesn't like it."

"I'll be nice to him, if he's nice to me," she said.

"If he gets mad and fires you for any reason, don't worry about it—just call me." He handed her a card. "Here's my BlackBerry number. Memorize it, then eat the card." He offered Stone his hand. "Nice working with you, Stone. I take it you'll be Carrie's personal attorney from here on."

"That's correct," Carrie said, not giving Stone a chance to reply. "Bye-bye, Mark."

They left the office. Stone looked at his watch: They had been there for twenty-seven minutes. "You do business briskly," he said to Carrie.

"You have no idea," she replied. "Please bill me for this and any other work at your usual hourly rate. Now come with me."

They hailed a taxi, and five minutes later they were at Carrie's new address. "I want you to see this," she said, getting out of the cab.

"I saw it last night, remember?"

"No, you didn't," she said. She let them into the building. The double doors to her apartment were already open, and some men were carrying boxes upstairs.

Stone's jaw dropped. The living room was completely furnished, down to small objets d'art on side tables, and there was a Steinway grand piano in a corner. It looked as though Carrie had lived there for a year.

"Like it?" she asked.

"It's gorgeous. How did you do it so fast?"

"A friend of mine is the best theatrical designer in town. I told him to do it fast, with the best stuff he could find on short notice. I had the pictures and some smaller things in storage."

"It took me two years to get my house to this state," Stone said.

"As you said, I do things briskly. What time is dinner?"

6

Stone and Dino were on their second drink, and Carrie still hadn't arrived. It was nearly nine o'clock.

"She didn't strike me as the late type," Dino said.

"She's had a busy day," Stone replied, "and she's just moved into her new apartment; she probably couldn't find what she wanted to wear in the boxes." Stone told Dino about the instant furnishing and decoration of the new apartment.

"Here we go," Dino said, nodding toward the door.

Carrie, dressed in slacks and a sweater, was walking toward the table, limping.

Stone stood and held a chair for her, and it was not until he sat down and looked at her closely that he realized something was wrong. He waved at a waiter, pointed at his drink, then at Carrie.

"I'm sorry I'm late," Carrie said, trembling.

The drink came, and Stone handed it to her. "Big swig," he said, and she complied.

"Now tell me what's wrong."

She gulped. "I was leaving my building, and as I came down the front steps I saw a man coming down the street from the direction of Fifth Avenue."

Stone waited while she took a couple of deep breaths.

"He was backlit by a streetlight, so his face was in shadow. To get a taxi I had to walk toward Sixth Avenue for a little bit, because the parked cars were so close together that I couldn't squeeze between them without getting my clothes dirty. As I walked I could hear his footsteps getting quicker and realized he was running toward me. I saw a cab coming from up the street, and without even looking back, I just threw myself over the hood of a parked car and in front of the cab. As soon as I got inside, I screamed at the driver to get out of there, and I locked the door, because I saw the man reaching for the handle. There was a knife in his other hand."

"Did he hurt you?" Stone asked. "You were limping when you came in."

She reached down, took off a shoe, and held it up. The heel was missing. "This was the only wound," she said. Calmer now and breathing more slowly, she took another big swig of the bourbon.

"Describe him," Dino said.

"Tall, over six feet, athletic-looking, wearing a raincoat and a felt hat."

"Any distinguishing features?" Dino asked. He was taking notes now.

"Small scar at the corner of the left eye, another scar on the inside of the right wrist—childhood injury—and a broken nose from football that never healed properly."

"You saw all that?" Stone asked. "How?"

"I've known him since college; he's my ex-husband."

"Did you ever see his face?"

"No, but I know how he walks. I know his fascination with knives; he has a collection. It was Max."

"What's his last name?" Dino asked.

"Long."

"Address?"

"It used to be on Habersham Road in Atlanta, big house. He's living in an apartment now. I don't know where; it's just what I've heard. Maybe one of his own developments."

"But in Atlanta."

"Yes. He wouldn't go any farther from Habersham Road than he had to." She was perfectly collected now.

Dino produced his cell phone. "I'll get the precinct looking for him now."

"No, don't," Carrie said, putting her hand over the cell phone. "I can't have this in the papers."

"Carrie," Stone said, "if you know Max was the guy, then we have to get him off the street. He knows where you live."

"Monday morning I start rehearsals, the biggest break of my life," she said. "I've been all over the papers for two days; they would just love this."

Stone looked at Dino and shook his head. "Do you have an alarm system in your apartment?" he asked Carrie.

"No."

"Is there another entrance besides the front door?"

"Yes. There's a rear door from the kitchen and stairs down to a garden."

"Excuse me for a minute," Stone said. He walked into the empty dining room next door and made a call to Bob Cantor, an ex-cop who did many jobs for him.

"Cantor."

"Bob, it's Stone."

"Hey, Stone. What's up?"

"I need a bodyguard for a woman first thing tomorrow morning at my house. Her name is Carrie Cox; she's at Elaine's with me. Are you free right now?"

"Yeah, but I'll put somebody else on guard duty."

"She needs a security system: double front door, kitchen door leading to a garden, the usual windows, front and rear."

"You got a key?"

"You can pick it up here."

"I'm on it."

"Listen, on the bodyguard, not too much of a gorilla—she travels in polite circles—but somebody who can handle a man with a knife and deal with an angry ex-husband."

"Gotcha. I'll be there in half an hour." Cantor hung up, and Stone returned to the table.

"What did you do?" she asked.

"Tomorrow morning there will be somebody with you, and they will be until it's no longer necessary. Give me the key to your apartment."

She took a small ring from her purse, took off one of two identical keys, and handed it to him. "What for?"

"My friend is going to install a security system; it's probably going to take all night, because he does these things right, so you should come home with me tonight."

"All right."

Stone handed her a cocktail napkin and his pen. "Make a list of what you need from your apartment for the weekend; my friend will put it together and bring it to you."

Carrie began writing and filled up one side of the napkin, then the other.

Bob Cantor walked into the restaurant and stood at the front, waiting. Stone waved him over and introduced him to Carrie.

"Hi, Bob," she said. "Let me explain this list to you, where everything is in the apartment." She took him through it, item by item, and told him where to find a suitcase.

"Got it," Cantor said, pocketing the list. "Do you have a photograph of your ex-husband?"

"No, I threw all of them away."

"What's his name and address?"

"Max Long, Atlanta. I don't know his street address."

"Your protection is named Willie Leahy. He'll be at your house with his brother Jimmy at nine tomorrow morning. You want them to rent a car? I think it's best; you can be a target while trying to get a cab."

"They can use my car," Stone said.

"Good idea, with the armor and all."

"You have an armored car?" Carrie asked.

"Lightly armored," Stone said. "It came that way, and it'll stop a bullet."

"You," Carrie said, putting her hand on his and squeezing, "are the second-best thing to happen to me in a long time."

7

Carrie slept in Stone's arms for most of the night, and neither of them was much interested in sex. Stone took a handgun out of his safe and kept it in the bedside drawer.

Carrie didn't wake up when he gently disengaged from her. He put on a robe, went down to the kitchen, and made them bacon and scrambled eggs, English muffins, coffee, and orange juice, then sent it upstairs in the dumbwaiter. He got the *Times* and went back upstairs to find Carrie sitting up in bed with a breakfast tray in her lap, bare-breasted, which was all right with him.

"Your dumbwaiter woke me," she said. "A little bell went off."

Stone took his own tray from the dumbwaiter and got in bed with it, adjusting the back with the remote control. "I'm glad you're feeling better this

morning," he said. She was digging into the breakfast with enthusiasm.

"I am, and I'm starved," she said.

Breakfast finished, he put their trays back into
the dumbwaiter and sent it downstairs. He poured
them both some more coffee and got back into
bed. "I need to know a lot more about your
ex-husband," he said, "if I'm going to be able to
help."

"What do you want to know?" she asked, sipping her coffee.

"How long were you married?"

"Nine years."

"What was the character of the marriage?"

"At first, okay, then increasingly distant, then
finally violent."

"You beat him up?"

She laughed. "I got in a couple of good licks,"
she said, "but I got the worst of it. I moved in with
a girlfriend and got a lawyer."

"Tell me about the settlement."

"He wouldn't settle, so it was really an award by
the judge. I got the house on Habersham, which I
sold immediately; half his brokerage account, which
I put into a municipal bond fund; and one million
dollars in cash, most of which I invested con-
servatively."

"Did the house have a mortgage?"

"No; times were good when he bought it. He

paid a million two, and I sold it for four and a half million."

"So, you've got several million dollars squirreled away."

"Winter always comes," she said.

"What is he so mad about?" Stone asked.

"The fact that I left him and the size of the award. It amounted to half of what he had."

"He was surprised that you divorced him after he beat you up?"

"Not surprised, I think, just angry. It made the papers, and that made him look bad. He's angry about the award, because he wouldn't have given me a dime, unless he had been forced to. He's mad, too, because he knows that he could have settled for less than the judge gave me. That *really* got him angry. That and the fact that, in the real estate crunch, he's lost most of what he had left."

"Does he have anything to gain by killing you? Insurance, maybe?"

"No."

"So, it's just irrational anger?"

"That's what he's good at."

"You said you don't know his address in Atlanta?"

"That's right."

The doorbell rang on his phone, and Stone pressed the SPEAKER button. "Yes?"

"It's Bob. I've got Carrie's luggage, and the Leahys are here."

"Take the Leahys to the kitchen. There's coffee already made and Danish in the fridge. We'll be down in a few minutes." He pressed the button again and turned to Carrie. "We'd better get dressed; Bob is going to want to brief you about your security."

They found the three men sitting at the kitchen counter, drinking coffee and eating pastries.

"Morning, Carrie," Cantor said. "This is Willie and Jimmy Leahy."

The two husky men waved.

"Tell her what she needs to know," Stone said, and they both sat down.

Bob handed Carrie his card. "Your security code is written on the back: 1357. I tried to make it easy. You've got a keypad in your living room, next to the front door, another in the kitchen, next to the back door, and another upstairs, next to your bed." He handed her a bunch of keys. "I've changed the locks on your front and rear doors; the old ones were worthless. All the exterior windows are alarmed."

"Got it," she said. "Can I change the code?"

He handed her an instruction book. "Easily. The instructions are in here."

"Thank you, Bob. Send me your bill."

"Will do. Now, let me explain Willie and Jimmy. One of them drives the car; one sits in the back with you. The car doors will be locked at all times. When you get somewhere, say to the theater, one opens the door for you. Don't ever, *ever* open your own door. He comes inside with you and remains close, while the other deals with the car and then joins you inside or just sits in the car, depending on the circumstances.

"One of them stays in your apartment at night, near the stairs up to your bedroom. They'll take turns. They're both armed, and they're very good at dealing with assaults without killing the perpetrator, but they may have to. You'll have to leave that to their judgment."

"I'm happy to do that," Carrie said.

"If you go to someone's home, say a dinner party, one will stay outside their door; there'll be no intrusion into your privacy unless it's necessary to protect you."

"Thank you."

"Carrie," Stone said, "does your husband own a handgun?"

"Yes, at least a dozen. He collects them, along with knives."

"He's not going to get a handgun from Atlanta to New York on an airplane," Bob said.

"Maybe not," Stone admitted, "but if he's a

planner, he could send one to his hotel by an overnight shipper."

"Right," Bob said. "We'll keep that in mind. Any questions, Carrie?"

"No, I don't think so."

Stone spoke up. "Bob, we need to locate Max Long in Atlanta; Carrie doesn't know his address. You know somebody down there?" Cantor had a network of ex-cops who handled this sort of thing.

"Sure thing. Last known address?"

Carrie gave him the Habersham address.

"I want to know if somebody in Atlanta can place him in New York last night, besides Carrie," Stone said. "Could be important later."

"What's wrong with me?" Carrie asked. "I can place him here."

"You said you didn't see his face," Stone replied. "It wouldn't hold up in court. We need copies of a plane ticket or a hotel reservation or a credit card record. Somebody who drove him to the airport would help."

"I'll deal with it," Cantor said. "What's your schedule like today?" he asked Carrie.

"I've got an accompanist coming to my place at one o'clock," Carrie said. "I have a score to learn."

"Willie and Jimmy are ready when you are," Cantor replied.

"Now is good," she said.

Stone put his keys on the counter. "You know how to get into the garage, Bob." He turned to Carrie. "There's a house key there, too. Remember, you're sleeping here tonight," Stone said, "just in case he's still in town."

"Her suitcase is in the living room," Cantor said, tossing the keys to Willie, "and so is a cardboard box she wants to send to her ex-husband."

"Bob, you keep the box for when we find out his address," Stone said. He turned to Carrie. "I think you're in good shape now."

"I feel very safe," Carrie replied. She kissed Stone and followed Cantor and the Leahys to the garage.

8

Stone took Carrie's suitcase upstairs and put her things in a closet and chest of drawers. As he was about to get into the shower, the phone rang. He noticed that the caller ID showed the call as being from area code 404: Atlanta. He grabbed a pen and wrote down the number; then he pressed a button on the phone to have the conversation recorded.

"Hello?"

"Is this Stone Barrington?" A male voice, deep, the accent Southern, the words a little slurred.

"Hello, Max," Stone said.

There was a moment's silence. "So you know who I am?"

"I don't know all that many people in Atlanta. Are you back home now?"

"Maybe."

"I have some things to send you," Stone said. "What's your mailing address?"

Max Long gave him a post office box number.

"No. I'm sending the package FedEx; I need the street address and phone number."

"What are you sending?"

"Some things that Carrie thought you might like to have. She found them when she unpacked."

"What things?"

"I don't know; I haven't opened the package."

"I'm not giving you my address," Long said.

"Whatever. I don't really care whether you get this stuff. I'll put it out with the garbage. Why did you want to speak to me?"

"I want to speak to Carrie."

"She isn't here, and she doesn't want to talk to you. After the encounter last night, she wants nothing further to do with you."

"So you're the new boyfriend, then?"

"I'm her attorney."

"Why does she need an attorney?"

"I'm also a retired police detective with excellent contacts in law enforcement."

"So you're going to protect her?"

"You can count on it, and let me give you some free advice: The New York Police Department takes a very dim view of a person carrying any sort of weapon on the streets of the city, gun or knife. Anyone caught with a weapon can count on jail time, and you wouldn't enjoy our penal system."

"So you're threatening me?"

"Certainly not. I'm just giving you good advice. Here's another good piece: Stay away from Carrie. She's taking out a protection order, barring you from coming within a city block of her. Violate that, and you'll do jail time. You see, there'll be lots of opportunities for you to go to jail."

"Tell her to give me back my money, and I'll leave her alone," Long said.

"Ah, now, that's extortion. Did I mention that I'm recording this conversation?"

"You can't do that."

"It's already done," Stone said. "Now tell me if you want this package, because I'm tired of talking to you."

"Go fuck yourself," Long said.

"I'll take that as a 'no,'" Stone said. "Tell me, are you always drunk at this hour of the day?"

Long hung up. Stone called Bob Cantor.

"Hello?"

"I've just had a phone call from Max Long. Here's the number." Stone recited it. "He wouldn't give up his address, but if it's his home number you can trace it back. It may be a cell phone, in which case he could still be in the city, and he's drunk."

"That prefix is a cell phone," Cantor said. "If it's not a throwaway I can get an address for it."

"He gave me a PO box number," Stone said, giving it to him.

"That's harder, because it's federal, but one of my Atlanta contacts might be able to do something."

"I'll get Dino to trace the location of the cell phone," Stone said.

"Anything else?" Cantor asked.

"Not at the moment." Stone hung up and called Dino.

"Lieutenant Bacchetti."

"I just got a call from Carrie's husband, from a cell phone. He may still be in town; will you run the number for a location?" Stone gave him the number.

"I'll get back to you," Dino said, then hung up.

Stone shaved, showered, and dressed; then he took the *Times* down to his study with a second cup of coffee. He had finished reading the paper and was on the crossword when the phone rang.

"Hello?"

"It's Dino. Your guy was calling from LaGuardia, at a gate that a Delta flight is scheduled to depart from in five minutes. He may have already been on the plane."

"Thanks, Dino."

"Dinner?"

"Sure. See you then." Stone hung up and called Bob Cantor.

"Cantor."

"Bob, Max Long called from LaGuardia, and he's apparently on a Delta flight to Atlanta, leaving now."

"I'll have somebody pick up on him there and follow him home. You want my guy to say anything to him?"

"You might have him give Long the impression that he's under constant police surveillance, without using those words."

"Give me a description."

"Get that from Carrie," Stone said. "I've never seen the man. I just know that he's tall and slim."

"Will do," Cantor said. He hung up.

Stone went back to the crossword. It was a bitch, as it often was on Saturdays. He was still working on it nearly three hours later when Cantor called back.

"Hello?"

"It's Cantor. My guy met your guy and imparted your suggestion to him. He's tailing him now. I ran his license plate, but it's still registered to the

Habersham Road address; he didn't bother to change it after moving. I'll call you back when I get an address."

"Good going," Stone said. He went to the kitchen, made a ham and mozzarella sandwich on whole grain, toasted it, and brought it back to the study with a Diet Coke. He finished it and was down to the last couple of impossible words on the crossword when Cantor called again.

"Got a pencil?"

"In my hand."

"Max Long drove to an apartment complex in northeast Atlanta called Cross Creek. Nice place, with a golf course. My guy couldn't follow him past the guard at the gate, but fifty got him the address: 1010 Cantey Place. His phone is unlisted, but I'll have it for you later. You want my guy to surveil?"

"For a couple of days."

"I can put a watch for his name on the Delta reservations computer," Cantor said.

"Great idea. That'll give us some notice if he decides to come back, and we can have him met at LaGuardia."

"Consider it done," Cantor said. "By the way, Max Long is six-three, two hundred pounds, long-ish dark hair going gray, broken nose. I'll do a search for a photo; shouldn't be hard to come up with one."

"Sounds like we've got the guy just about boxed," Stone said.

"We're getting there."

"Talk to you later." Stone hung up and attacked the last two words on the crossword. They took another half hour.

9

Stone and Dino had been at Elaine's just long enough to order a drink, when Carrie came rushing in, flushed and excited. Stone signaled for a drink for her. "You look happy," he said.

"I feel happy," she said. "I've got two very good solos in the show and one absolute, solid-gold showstopper."

"I look forward to hearing them," Stone said.

"Not until opening night; I want you to get the full effect."

"I'm already getting the full effect," he replied. Their drinks arrived, and they clinked glasses.

Dino spoke up. "It's nice to see you both so happy."

"If you'd had my day," Carrie said, "you'd be happy, too."

"I *am* happy," Dino said. "Can't you tell?"

"He always looks dour," Stone said. "You could know him for years before seeing him smile."

"Do you have a wife, Dino?" Carrie asked.

"Had. Don't want another."

"A girl?"

"Until recently."

"What happened?"

"I got tired of obeying. Stone and I spent a little time in Key West, and I discovered I didn't miss her."

"He smiled more then," Stone said.

"If I goose him, will he smile?" Carrie asked.

"If you goose me in the right place," Dino said.

Carrie laughed, a healthy, unrestrained sound. Dino smiled a little.

"There, I knew I could do it," she said.

"So, do you know your script and score?" Stone asked.

"I will by Monday morning," she said.

"How'd it go with Bob and the Leahys?"

"Bob showed me how to work the security system, then left with Max's box to take it to FedEx. The Leahys are sweet and made me feel very safe. They dropped me off here, and I've dismissed them until Monday morning."

"I think we've got Max pretty boxed in now," Stone said, "so you shouldn't have to worry. I wouldn't go back to Atlanta any time soon, though, or if you do, don't tell anybody who might tell him."

"How long will we have to deal with this?" she asked.

"It could go two ways: Either he'll mellow with time, like most people, or he'll obsess about it until he can't stand it anymore, and then make a move."

"Knowing Max, it's going to be the latter," she said. "He's the obsessive type, believe me."

"Then we'll just have to be ready for him," Stone said.

"Am I going to have to have bodyguards for long?"

"Hard to say. Cantor and I may feel better about it in a week or ten days, but when the show opens, that's when we'll have to watch ourselves."

"You mean, watch me."

"Well, yes. In the meantime, I'll cultivate his dislike for me. I'm already off to a good start, after only one phone conversation."

"Why?"

"We'll see if we can deflect him from you to me. By the way, on Monday morning we're going to get you a protection order from the court and have it served on him in Atlanta."

"If you say so," Carrie replied, "but I have to warn you, he has a broad antiauthoritarian streak. I used to have to pay his speeding tickets to keep him from getting arrested, and he missed a couple of court appearances during the divorce process."

"Still, if he violates it, it's an excuse to put him behind bars, and that's where I'd like him to be."

"So would I," Carrie said.

"What was in the box you sent him?" Stone asked.

Carrie sighed. "Two guns he gave me, and some small things of his that somehow got packed with my stuff—neckties, cuff links, socks, things like that."

"Maybe you should have kept the guns," Stone said.

"I still have one."

"Don't take it out of the house; New York City has a very rigid licensing law, and they turn down everybody who applies, unless you're carrying around a briefcase full of diamonds or large sums of cash. The city believes that protecting property is more important than protecting life."

"But you have a gun," she said. "I saw you put it in the bedside table."

"I have several guns, but retired cops get licenses. Dino's packing right now, but he's still on the force, so he has to."

"The one I have is small enough to put in my purse," she said.

"Have you had any firearms training?"

"I fired a .22 rifle at camp when I was twelve."

"Then you're more likely to hurt yourself or an innocent bystander than Max."

"You underestimate me."

"Maybe so, but here's the sort of thing that happens. Maybe you're injured in a taxi accident, and the EMTs come. At the hospital they go through your purse, looking for ID and an address, and they find your gun and call the cops. Then we're in court, and believe me, you wouldn't want to go through that."

"So I'm vulnerable."

"You have the Leahys, Dino and me, and Cantor. You have your security system and a phone to call 911. If you have to do that, tell the operator that someone has broken into your house and you're hiding. That will get immediate attention."

Dino gave her his card. "Put my cell phone number into your speed-dial list," he said. "You can always get my immediate attention, even though you're not in my precinct."

She took out her cell phone and entered the number. "Thank you, Dino."

The waiter came with menus, and they talked about other things.

10

On Monday morning the Leahys picked up Carrie and took her to her first rehearsal, and Stone went to work in his office, as usual. Shortly after ten o'clock, Joan buzzed Stone. "Bob Cantor on one."

Stone pressed the button. "Good morning, Bob. Did you have a nice weekend?"

"I did until a minute ago," Cantor said.

"What's up?"

"I had my people in Atlanta on Max Long all weekend. They found a cooperative guard on the apartment complex gate who let them in for a hundred. He was in and out until yesterday afternoon, and then he seemed to hunker down for the evening. Then, this morning, FedEx delivered the box I sent him, and nobody answered the door. Since it required a signature, the guy put it back on the truck.

"My guy got suspicious when this happened. He called Long's phone number, but there was no answer. Finally, he looked in some windows, and there's nobody home. His car is still parked outside."

"So, he got past your guy?"

"His place is on the ground floor; he could have left by a back window and called a cab, I guess. This is not good."

"No, it's not. Did the airline's reservation computer alarm go off?"

"Nope."

"If he booked under a false name, he'd have to show ID at the ticket counter, wouldn't he?"

"Yes, but he could have made a reservation under another name and had an e-ticket e-mailed to him."

"Have you warned the Leahys?"

"Yep, and that's about all we can do for the moment. Carrie is rehearsing at the theater, isn't she?"

"Yeah. Since Del Wood owns the theater, they didn't have to go to a studio."

"How many ways in?"

"Front doors are locked, so the stage door is the only way. There's a guard there, and we've alerted him, but he's an old guy, and it might not be too hard to get past him."

"Keep in touch." Stone hung up.

*   *   *

Ten minutes later, Joan buzzed him. "Carrie Cox on one."

"Hello?"

"What's going on?"

"What do you mean?"

"I mean, the Leahys are all over me."

"That's their job."

"Has something happened?"

"Am I interrupting your rehearsal?"

"No. I'm in the ladies' room on a break."

"Max has disappeared from his apartment, and we don't know where he is."

"Wasn't somebody watching him?"

"Apparently, he went out a back window."

"Is he on his way to New York?"

"There was no Delta reservation in his name, but he could already be here, so listen to the Leahys."

"How's the weather?"

"What?"

"Between here and Atlanta," she said.

"Jesus, I don't know. When I got up this morning the national forecast was for good weather for the entire East Coast."

"Then he's in his airplane."

"He has an airplane?"

"Yes."

"Why didn't you mention that before?"

"It didn't come up."

"What kind of airplane?"

"It's a King something or other."

"A King Air?"

"Yes."

"With two engines?"

"Right."

"What's the tail number?"

"N-something," she said.

"Every airplane in the United States is N-something."

"I don't remember the rest."

"Does he often fly to New York?"

"Sometimes."

"Where does he land?"

"I don't know, exactly."

"Did you ever fly to New York with him?"

"Yes."

"Where did he land?"

"I don't remember."

"How did you get from the airport to New York?"

"In a limo."

"Did you go through a tunnel?"

"No, we went over a bridge, the big one."

"The George Washington Bridge?"

"That's the one."

"Did you land at Teterboro?"

"Yes, that's it!"

"When you got out of the airplane you were at an FBO. Do you remember its name?"

"You mean, like a terminal?"

"Like that, but for private aircraft."

"What are some FBOs?"

"Jet Aviation, Meridian Aviation, Atlantic Aviation, Furst Avia . . ."

"Atlantic, that's it!"

"Is that where he always lands?"

"I guess so."

"Is there anything else you haven't told me about how Max travels?"

"I don't think so."

"How's your rehearsal going?"

"We're just reading through the script right now. Gotta run!" She hung up.

Stone got on his computer and went to the FAA aircraft registry, then typed in "Max Long" in the search engine. Nothing. Must be owned by a corporation. Stone called Cantor.

"Cantor."

"It's Stone. Carrie forgot to mention that Max Long owns an airplane, a King Air."

"I thought he was broke."

"Me, too. He usually lands at Teterboro, at Atlantic Aviation."

"Got a tail number?"

"That would be too easy."

"I'm on it." Cantor hung up.

Stone was left, tapping his foot. Twenty minutes later, Cantor called back.

"I'm here."

"He landed at ten fifteen last night. Teterboro Limousine took him to the Lowell Hotel, on East Sixty-third Street."

"You may need more than the Leahys," Stone said.

"What, for a guy with a knife?"

"There's nothing to stop him from carrying a gun on a private airplane."

"Oh. Okay, I'll get up to the Lowell now, see what I can see. I don't think we'll need more people. I'll let the Leahys know that he may be packing, but I think the two of them can handle him."

"If you say so," Stone said.

Half an hour later, Bob Cantor walked into the Lowell, a small, elegant Upper East Side hotel, carrying a box from a florist's shop. He approached the front desk. "Good morning," he said.

"Good morning," the desk clerk replied. "May I help you?"

"Do you have a Max Long registered here?" Cantor asked.

The man consulted his computer. "Yes, we do." He reached out for the box. "He's out just now; I'll take the flowers."

"Just tell Mr. Long that Stone Barrington says, 'Hi,'" Cantor said. He turned and walked out of the hotel, dumped the empty box in the trash can on the corner, and called Stone.

"Hello?"

"It's Cantor. Long is registered at the Lowell but he's on the loose."

"Swell."

II

Bob Cantor drove his van down to the theater district, parked fifty yards from the Del Wood Theater, and turned down the sun visor with the NYPD badge on it, so as not to be bothered. He sat there through the morning, lunching on a sandwich he had packed before leaving his apartment downtown. In his pocket he had the protection order Stone had obtained over the weekend from a friendly judge.

He opened a book of *New York Times* crossword puzzles and began his routine: read a definition, then look outside while thinking of the answer. This was not his first stakeout. He had finished two of the puzzles, occasionally peeing into a bag designed for use on small airplanes, and was working on a third puzzle when he saw the tall man approaching the theater from the direction of Eighth

Avenue. He popped open his cell phone and pressed a speed-dial button without taking his eyes off the man.

"It's Willie," one of the Leahys said.

"It's Cantor. Guy coming toward the theater, answers the description. He's wearing a raincoat, hands in his pockets, so watch out."

"I'm on it," Willie said, then hung up.

Cantor hopped out of the van and pressed the LOCK button on his remote key. He had a quarter of a million dollars' worth of electronic equipment in the van, and he was taking no chances. He had to wait for a procession of cars to pass before crossing the street, and he made it to the alley down which lay the stage door just as the man did.

"Mr. Long?" he said. "Is that you?"

The man turned and looked at him. "Do I know you?"

"I've got something for you," Cantor said, handing him the envelope.

The man stared at it but did not take his hands out of his raincoat pockets.

With his left hand, leaving his right in his own coat pocket, Cantor tucked the envelope into the top of the man's raincoat. "You've been served," he said.

"Served with what?"

"A protection order from the Supreme Court of New York State," Cantor said. "It orders you to remain at least a hundred yards away from Ms. Carrie Cox at all times, and you're violating it at this very moment."

"That's ridiculous," Long said, ripping open the envelope and looking at the document.

"I'm afraid it's very serious," Cantor said. "As you can see at the bottom, the penalty for violating the order is thirty days in jail and a thousand-dollar fine. Oh, and did I mention that New York State has a very effective antistalking law? You could get a lot more time by violating that." Cantor reached up and took the taller man's arm, high under the armpit, and gently steered him down the street toward Broadway. "There will be people watching you every moment you're in New York or Atlanta," he said, "so don't give Stone Barrington an opportunity to put you in jail."

Cantor had not lied about Long's being watched, because as he held his arm, he had attached a tiny bug to the armpit of Long's raincoat that emitted a radio signal. Cantor stopped walking. "Bye-bye," he said. "Enjoy your stay in our city." He turned and walked back toward the theater, then stopped at the entrance to the alley and looked back. Long was moving quickly toward Broadway.

Cantor ducked into the alley and went to the stage door. When he opened it Willie Leahy was standing there. "I served him the order," Cantor said, "and warned him off. I got a bug on him, too, so we'll know if he's within five hundred yards." He handed Willie a small, black object that looked like a pager. "If this beeps, he's around. A distance in yards will appear on the display."

"Gotcha," Willie said, looking at the thing. "He's two fifty and moving away."

"Okay," Cantor said. "You don't need me anymore, so I'm outta here."

"Thanks, Bob," Willie was saying as Cantor closed the stage door.

Cantor went back to his van and called Stone.

"Hello?"

"I caught up with our friend Max outside the theater. I served him, gave him a little talk about the antistalking law, and attached a bug to his raincoat at the armpit, where he's unlikely to notice it. Willie Leahy has a pager thing that gives him a distance on Max if he's within five hundred yards."

"Good day's work, Bob."

"I mentioned your name, since you apparently want him pissed off at you."

"Better me than Carrie," Stone said. "Let's hope he makes a move, so Dino can fall on him from a great height."

"Yeah," Cantor said. "I'd feel a lot better with him in jail. Oh, I also left him a message from you at the front desk of his hotel. He's gonna feel surrounded by you."

Stone laughed. "I like it."

"Listen, you watch your ass," Cantor said. "It wouldn't do to underestimate this guy. I did a background check, and in his youth he was a marine. Those guys don't lack confidence."

"I'll keep that in mind," Stone said. "Thanks, Bob." He hung up and called Carrie's cell phone, got voice mail, and left her a message.

She called back an hour later. "What?" she said.

"Max is in town. Bob Cantor served him with the protection order. He's now wearing an electronic bug that will let the Leahys know if he's near."

"Wow, how did you do that?"

"It's the sort of thing, among many other things, that Bob Cantor does."

"Why don't you come over to my place tonight, and we'll order in some Chinese?"

"Sounds good. You're sure you're not going to be too tired?"

"No. I'm wired, but you can give me a back rub."

"I'll rub anything you like," Stone said. "See you at seven."

Stone arrived on Carrie's doorstep at the same time as the deliveryman from the Chinese restaurant. He paid the man and rang the bell.

"Yes?" Carrie said on the intercom.

"Chinese delivery," Stone said, and was buzzed in.

Carrie met him at the door. "Very funny, Chinese guy," she said, laughing and taking the food from him. She went into the kitchen and made a little buffet of the containers, and they served themselves. They had dinner on the floor in front of the living room fireplace and shared a bottle of wine, while a Leahy waited outside her apartment door.

"I'm in love with Bob Cantor," she said. "How do you know him?"

"From when I was on the NYPD. He and Dino and I were in the same detective squad. By the time Bob retired and went into business for himself, I was practicing law, and he's been invaluable to me ever since."

"How come you stopped being a policeman?"

"Because I stopped a bullet with my knee, and when my captain and I had a little disagreement over the conduct of a case, he used that to force me into medical retirement."

"That's shitty," she said.

"Not entirely," Stone replied. "When you retire because of an in-the-line-of-duty disability, you get a pension of seventy-five percent of your pay, tax free. If you've got to be forced out, it's a nice good-bye kiss."

When they finished dinner, she took away their dishes and then came back and sat between his legs.

"I believe you were going to give me a back rub," she said.

"That's how we're going to start," Stone said, starting.

12

When Stone got to his desk the following morning, there was a note on his desk from Joan. "Bill Eggers wants to see you ASAP," it read.

Stone walked over to the offices of Woodman & Weld, the law firm to which he was of counsel. Bill Eggers was its senior attorney and managing partner. When Stone had been forced out of the NYPD, Eggers, an old friend from NYU Law School, had taken him to lunch and suggested that Stone put his law degree to work for Woodman & Weld. Stone had taken a cram course for the bar and passed, and Eggers had started feeding him cases, the sort that the firm didn't want to be seen handling. The work from Woodman & Weld amounted to well over half of Stone's income, and when Eggers called, Stone answered.

Bill Eggers waved him to a chair. "How are you, Stone?"

"Very well, thanks, Bill."

"I had a call this morning from an old friend of mine who's a top guy in the biggest law firm in Atlanta," Eggers said. "It seems you're representing the ex-wife of an important client of his, and I use the word *representing* loosely."

"You would be referring to Carrie Cox, former spouse of the creep Max Long? And I use the word *creep* expansively."

"That I would."

"From what I've heard I'm surprised to hear that Mr. Long can afford to retain an attorney who doesn't advertise on late-night television," Stone said.

"My friend brought me up to date on Mr. Long's affairs, so I'll bring you up to date. After his divorce he went through a bad patch, complicated by the shortage of money from the banks, and he lost a bundle. Shortly after that he acquired copious financing from a Saudi prince who keeps a house in Atlanta, and whose poker buddy he is. He used the money wisely, buying up prime parcels of land that were going at foreclosure prices and selling chunks of it to other investors at a handsome profit. His company is now earning money, and Mr. Long's personal fortune has been recovered well into eight figures."

"I'm sorry to hear it," Stone said.

"I wanted you to hear it, because I suspect that you've been operating on the assumption that Mr. Long did not have the resources to be much of a problem to you."

"I confess I was operating on that assumption," Stone said. "I'm also operating on the assumption that Mr. Long is a real and proximate danger to Ms. Cox and that he is obsessive about her."

"It's clear," Eggers said, "that you are relying on the testimony of Ms. Cox."

"I am. She seems a smart and sensible woman."

"My friend's firm in Atlanta represented Mr. Long in his divorce, and he formed a somewhat different opinion of Ms. Cox."

"That's not surprising," Stone said. "Divorce attorneys often adopt the opinions of their clients; they represent clients better, if they believe them."

"He tells me that, on two occasions, Ms. Cox made attempts on Mr. Long's life, once with a gun and once with a straight razor, which I thought was a quaint choice of weapon."

"Then why isn't she in prison?"

"Because Mr. Long would not bring charges against her and because he managed to keep the police out of it, even to the extent of having his personal physician come to his home and repair the damage from the razor, to the tune of more than a hundred stitches. Mr. Long required a transfusion, as well."

"If that is true, one would think that Mr. Long would be giving Ms. Cox a wide berth, would one not?"

"Apparently," Eggers said, "the man still loves her, and we know how that is. He gave her an inordinately generous divorce settlement without complaint, and if that isn't love, I don't know what is."

"Those things generally arise from necessity, not love," Stone observed. "It's my understanding that a judge allotted the marital assets. After all, they had been married for nine years."

"It was less than three years," Eggers said. "My friend's view is that his client, besotted, spent a fortune on Ms. Cox's training as an actress and dancer, not to mention her wardrobe and jewelry, before and during the marriage, and that she returned the favor by sleeping with her acting teacher, her dancing coach, and whoever else was handy. My friend described her as sexually wanton."

"A trait I've always admired in a woman," Stone said.

"Though not necessarily in a client," Eggers pointed out.

"Bill, do you have some suggestion about my course of action in this case?"

"I do, though I know you are unlikely to accept any such suggestion."

"I'll try to be broad-minded," Stone said.

"I suggest that you extricate yourself from this woman's clutches as quickly as you can politely do so, because if my friend's opinion is of any consequence, she will eventually turn on you, and she may still own that razor."

"I must say that I hadn't noticed that I was in her, as you put it, 'clutches,'" Stone said.

"Perhaps 'clenches' would have been a better word," Eggers said.

"Perhaps, but that is not a bad place to be."

Eggers sighed. "All right, I suppose the only other thing I can do is to exhort you to be very, very careful in your dealings with her and to keep your physician's number in your pocket."

"All right, I'll do that," Stone said.

"That said, I have something for you."

"Oh, good. Wayward wife? Wayward son?" A good deal of Stone's work for Woodman & Weld had involved one or the other.

"Wayward daughter," Eggers said.

"Uh-oh."

"Exactly." Eggers wrote something on a slip of paper and handed it to Stone. "Her name is Hildy Parsons, and this is her address and phone number."

"What is her particular problem?" Stone asked.

"How much time do you have?"

"I'm at your disposal."

"All right, it began in high school, when she had an affair with one of her teachers that resulted in his firing and her transferring to an institution operated by nuns. Her father managed to keep this business fairly quiet, and the girl is very bright, so she actually got into Harvard and earned her degree in the usual four years, though she formed a number of other inappropriate attachments along the way."

"And what sort of inappropriate attachment has she now formed?" Stone asked.

"An artist," Eggers said, "or so he styles himself. He has a studio downtown somewhere, from which he is alleged to be operating a dealership in drugs. Her father is concerned first that he might persuade her to partake and second that when the authorities finally nail him, she will be charged as an accessory—before, during, and/or after the fact."

"Is her father Philip Parsons, the art dealer on East Fifty-seventh Street?"

"He is, and I think it a good idea if you visit with him." Eggers consulted the eighteenth-century clock in the corner behind his desk. "You won't need an appointment; he's expecting you in ten minutes."

"And what, exactly, does Mr. Parsons expect me to do?"

"I'm sure that will emerge in your chat with him," Eggers said.

Stone got to his feet. "You did tell him that I don't do contract killings, didn't you?"

Eggers shook his hand. "I don't believe I mentioned that," he said. "Good day, Stone, and please, please be careful."

Stone left, still feeling unendangered.

13

S tone walked from Eggers's office in the Sea-
gram Building, up Park Avenue, and took a left
on East Fifty-seventh Street. On the way he pon-
dered his friend's information about Carrie and
decided to discount ninety-five percent of it as the
rant of a rejected husband, but he was not entirely
sure of which five percent to believe.

His reverie was interrupted when he arrived at
the Parsons Gallery, a wide building with a gorgeous
Greek sculpture of a woman's head spotlighted in
the center of the window. Stone approached a very
beautiful and impossibly thin young woman who
was seated at a desk thumbing through a catalogue.

"Good morning. Can I help you?" she asked.

"My name is Stone Barrington. I believe Mr.
Parsons is expecting me."

She consulted a typed list of names on her desk. "Yes, Mr. Barrington," she said. "Would you take the elevator to the fourth floor?" She pointed. "Someone will meet you."

Because she was so beautiful, Stone thanked her and did as he was told. He was met on the fourth floor by an equally beautiful but less bony woman in her thirties, he judged.

"Mr. Barrington? I'm Rita Gammage. Good morning. Please come this way."

Stone followed her down a hallway to an open door, where she left him. Inside the office a man who was talking on the telephone waved him to a chair on the other side of his desk.

Before sitting down, Stone made a slow, 360-degree swivel to look at the walls. He recognized a Bonnard, a Freud, a Modigliani, and two Picassos among the works hanging there. He sat down and turned his attention to the man on the phone.

He appeared to be in his early sixties and was handsome in a tweedy sort of way. He was wearing a cashmere cardigan over a Turnbull & Asser shirt, and he needed a haircut, or, perhaps, he had had it cut in such a way as to seem to need a haircut.

The man hung up and stood, extending his hand. "I'm Philip Parsons," he said. "I expect you're Mr. Barrington."

Stone stood and shook the hand, then sat down

again. "It's Stone, please." He waved a hand. "I think this is the most extraordinary collection I've seen in someone's office."

"Thank you," Parsons said, seeming pleased with the compliment.

"Are these part of your inventory or your own collection?"

"These are all mine," Parsons said. "Occasionally, I tire of a piece and sell it, but most of these things I bought many years ago, when an ordinary person could still do that."

Stone wondered how Parsons defined *ordinary*. "You're fortunate to have them."

"Yeesss," Parsons drawled, but then went quiet.

"Bill Eggers suggested I come and see you," Stone said unnecessarily, but somebody had to get to the point. "How may I help you?"

Parsons gazed out the window at the facade of the Four Seasons Hotel across the street and finally mustered some words. "I'm sorry if I seem halting," he said, "but I find it difficult to speak about my daughter."

"Tell me a little about her," Stone said.

"She was a beautiful child, looked extraordinarily like her mother, who died when she was six. I'm afraid I may have relied too much on help to raise her."

"I expect being a single father is difficult," Stone said.

"Well, I was building this gallery, and it took nearly all of my waking hours traveling, searching for good work; cultivating artists and buyers; evenings spent at openings, my own and others. You seem to have a good eye. Do you know art?"

"My mother was a painter," Stone said. "I spent a good deal of my youth in museums and galleries."

"What is her name?"

"Matilda Stone."

"My goodness, what a fine painter. She's not still alive, is she?"

"No, she's been gone for many years."

"Twice I've had paintings of hers to sell, and they both went very quickly. I think I must have asked too little." He turned and looked at Stone. "Do you have any of her work?"

"I have four oils—village scenes."

"She was renowned for her Washington Square pieces."

"Yes, we lived near the square."

"I'd love to see them sometime."

"I'd be happy to show them to you," Stone said. "You must come for a drink."

"Where do you live?"

"I have a house in Turtle Bay."

"I will make a point of it," Parsons said, then turned to gaze at the hotel. "Hildy's troubles began, I suppose, with the onset of puberty. I don't know if all girls have such a hard time with the transition, but she certainly did. Her grandmother, who never really thought I should have been allowed to raise her, was scandalized, and she found that Catholic school to send her to. It was far too rigid an environment for a free spirit like Hildy, but I didn't know what else to do."

"How old is Hildy now?" Stone asked, hoping to bring him to the present.

"Twenty-four. She'll be twenty-five in three months, and she will then have free access to her trust, which came to her from her grandmother through her mother. I fear that three months after that, it will all be gone if she continues to see this man."

"What is his name?" Stone asked.

Parsons rummaged in a drawer and came up with a single sheet of paper. "Derek Sharpe, with an *e*," Parsons said, "né Mervin Pyle, in some squalid border town in Texas, forty-six years ago. No education to speak of; four marriages, three of them wealthy, though not when they were divorced. One of society's leeches, born to the task— trailer trash with a thin veneer of sophistication. I was appalled when I met him." He shoved the paper across the desk to Stone.

Stone glanced at it. "May I have this?"

"Yes. It was put together by a fairly seedy private detective for only twelve thousand dollars."

Stone scanned the document. "He got virtually all of it from the Internet; it cost him less than a hundred dollars. Is the man still on the case?"

"No, something about Mr. Derek Sharpe frightened him, I think. He took his money and ran."

"You should know that I'm not a private investigator but an attorney," Stone said. "However, I have access to good people who provide more and better value than this." He held up the paper.

"Yes. Eggers told me that," Parsons said.

"What would you like done?" Stone asked, and he steeled himself for the reply."

"If I could hire you to shoot him in the head, I would," Parsons said. "Forgive me, I know you're not in that business, and I would probably shrink from the task, if I met someone who was."

"Of course."

"I suppose what I want is for him to go away," Parsons said, "out of Hildy's life, never to see her again. But I don't know how to accomplish that. I've thought of trying to buy him off."

"I think that effort might be fruitless," Stone said, "unless you offered him a great deal—more than Hildy's trust fund—and maybe not even then. Does he know about her impending wealth?"

"I'm sure he does," Parsons said. "Hildy is not the sort to be closemouthed about anything."

"Perhaps we could begin by my meeting Mr. Sharpe," Stone said.

"Perhaps so," Parsons replied. He pushed a card across his desk. "I have an opening this evening on the second floor for a painter named Squires, who is *very* good. Hildy will be there, and I'm certain Mr. Sharpe will be tagging along."

Stone stood and put the invitation and the information on Sharpe into a pocket. "Then I'll come," he said, "and we'll see where we go from there."

The two men shook hands, and Stone departed the gallery. Why, he wondered as he walked home, had most of the women he knew been abused by men?

14

As he entered his house through the office door, Joan waved a message at him. "Carrie Cox called," she said. "She wants you to call while she's on her lunch break."

Stone went into his office, buzzed his housekeeper, Helene, in the kitchen, and asked for a sandwich. Then he sat down at his desk and returned Carrie's call.

"Hello?" she said, and by the sound of her voice she seemed to be eating something.

"Hi, it's Stone."

"Oh, hi."

"How are your rehearsals going?"

"Just great!"

"That sounds delicious."

"It's something called a falafel," she said. "Exotic New York food, not bad. Are we doing something this evening?"

"I have to go to an opening for a painter," Stone replied. "Would you like to come?"

"No, I called to beg off whatever you had in mind; I have to learn the second act. Who's the painter?"

"Someone called Squire. I've never heard of him."

"I have," she said. "He's *very* good."

"That's what the gallery owner says."

"Who is he?"

"Philip Parsons."

"He's *very* big," she said.

"How do you, being from Atlanta, know all this New York stuff?"

"I am conversant with most of the arts," she said. "And besides, I read magazines."

"Aha. Tell me, do you own a straight razor?"

"Aha, yourself. You've been researching me."

"Do you?"

"No, but Max does. We were having an argument in the bathroom once, while he was shaving, and I threw a bar of soap at him. He ducked, and in the process nearly cut his throat. I had to call the doctor."

"Oh."

"I suppose you've somehow heard Max's version of that story, in which I attacked him with the razor and murderous intentions."

"Something like that."

"Well, believe me, it's a lie."

"I believe you," Stone said, and he meant it. "Things uttered in divorce court sometimes take on too much color."

"You're *very* right," she replied.

"Call me tomorrow, when you get a break," Stone said.

"Wilco," she replied, then hung up.

Stone walked into the Parsons Gallery half an hour after the time on the invitation and joined the crowd walking up the stairs to the second floor. He lifted a glass of champagne from the tray of a passing waiter and was surprised at how good it was.

"We don't serve the cheap stuff at openings," said a female voice at his elbow.

He turned to find Rita Gammage standing there. She was really lovely, he thought. Tall, slim without being skinny, with long, dark hair, and breasts that looked real in spite of her slimness. "You certainly do serve the good stuff," he said. "What is it?"

"Schramsberg. Philip feels it's the best California stuff and the patriotic thing to serve."

"The man is truly a patriot," Stone said. "Can I fetch you a glass?"

"No, thanks; I've already had my single allow-able glass at an opening. Come let me show you Squire's work."

"What's his first name?" Stone asked.

"He doesn't use one, just Squire."

"Easier to remember that way, I guess." Stone walked slowly along a wall, taking in the work. "An American impressionist," he said. "I like that."

"So does the market," Rita said. "We sold half the stuff before tonight, and we've already sold half a dozen. There won't be anything left at the end of the evening."

"It's a big show," Stone said, "and I'm glad to hear of an artist getting a big paycheck. What's the price range?"

"Thirty to eighty thousand," Rita replied.

"That makes for a very nice paycheck indeed, even after the gallery's cut."

"A good paycheck for us, too, especially in this economy."

"A lot of people in this city don't have to cut back when the economy goes sour and the market is down."

"I guess half of a hundred-million-dollar port-folio is still fifty million," she said. "A person could scrape by on that."

"Indeed," Stone said, looking around. "Is Hildy Parsons here?"

"Behind you, just getting off the elevator," Rita replied.

Stone turned and looked. Hildy Parsons was an attractive young woman, blond and athletic-looking. The man with her was a different thing entirely.

"Is that Derek Sharpe?" he asked Rita.

"I'm afraid so," she said.

Sharpe was wearing a white suit a size too small for him, white shoes, no socks, and a black T-shirt. His hair was graying, greasy, and down to his shoulders.

"Good God," Stone said.

"My sentiments exactly."

"Grotesque," he said.

"I'm afraid that, in the art world, not everyone dresses as immaculately as you do," Rita said.

"Or gets a haircut," Stone added. "Would you introduce me to them?"

"I will, if you'll take me to dinner when I'm done here," she said.

"You've got a deal."

The couple moved into the room, and Stone followed Rita toward them.

"Hello, Hildy," Rita said, and the two women exchanged air kisses."

"Hi, Rita. You know Derek, don't you?"

"Of course," Hildy said without acknowledging the man. "And this is Stone Barrington."

Stone shook Hildy's hand and looked into her eyes. She seemed smarter than her choice of companion would indicate. "How do you do?" he said.

"This is Derek Sharpe, the painter," Hildy said.

Stone shook his hand and found it soft and damp. "How do you do?"

"I do very well," Sharpe replied.

"I'll bet you do," Stone said tonelessly. He turned back to Hildy. "You're Philip's daughter?"

"Sometimes," she said.

"He speaks fondly of you."

She looked at him in surprise. "When?"

"As recently as this morning."

"Well!" she breathed.

Rita jumped into the conversation. "Stone is a prospective client," she said. "Philip especially wanted him to see Squire's work."

"Oh, you must come downtown and see Derek's paintings," Hildy said.

"I'd like that."

She took a card from her purse and handed it to Stone. "Be sure and call first; he doesn't like to show people around when he's working."

"I'll certainly do that. Will you excuse me, please? I want to see the rest of Squire's pictures."

"Of course," Hildy said.

Stone nodded at Sharpe and peeled off toward

another wall of paintings, glad to be increasing his distance from Sharpe. Rita went to greet some new arrivals.

Ten minutes later he heard a hubbub from the other end of the room and turned to see a knot of people gathered around a picture. He wandered over to see what was happening and saw that the picture had been slashed from one corner to another. Apparently, straight razors were coming back into vogue, he thought.

He looked around and saw Hildy Parsons and Derek Sharpe on the other side of the room, studiously looking away from the damaged painting.

15

They sat at Stone's favorite corner table at La Goulue, on Madison Avenue, sipping their drinks and looking at the menu. The waiter, a young Frenchwoman with a charming accent, came over, told them about the specials, and stood ready to take their order.

Rita ordered sweetbreads and Dover sole, while Stone went for the haricots verts salad and the strip steak. He picked a bottle of Côtes du Rhône, the house red.

"I know you want to know more about Derek Sharpe," Rita said.

"I'd like to hear anything you can tell me," Stone replied. "I confess I don't understand why women are attracted to him."

Rita sipped her wine while she thought about

that. "I think it's a combination of the bad-boy thing and the art, and I should place quotes around that."

"Not good, huh?"

"He's an abstract painter, the sort who looked at Jackson Pollock's stuff and thought he could do that. Do you remember a little documentary film called *The Day of the Painter*?"

"Refresh my memory."

"A fisherman lives in a shack on the shore. He sees some Pollocks in a magazine, so he buys some buckets of paint and a big sheet of plywood, puts it on the foreshore next to his shack, and paints it white with a roller. Then he stands on his deck a few feet above the plywood and spills dollops of paint onto the white surface of the plywood. Finally, he goes down to the foreshore with a power saw and cuts the plywood into smaller squares, then he sells them as abstract paintings."

"That's a funny idea."

"That's the kind of painter Mr. Sharpe is. If someone criticizes the work, then they just don't have the artistic taste or mental capacity to appreciate it, and he raises the price."

"He actually gets galleries to show this stuff?"

"No. When everybody turned him down, he hired a publicist to plant stories in the papers about him and then started selling out of his studio. He gets a prospective buyer down there, and he's quite a good salesman, spewing gobbledygook about passion and genius, and people fall for it."

Their dinner arrived, and Stone tasted the wine.

"Tell me about the drug rumors," Stone said. "I suppose that's what they are—rumors."

"Well, yes, but not entirely. I know someone who bought half a kilo of marijuana from him, and I've heard secondhand stories about his dealing in coke: not little bags, nothing smaller than an ounce, but as much as a kilo."

"Why has no one put the police onto him?"

"The buyers are not going to turn him in—he's their connection—and the nonbuyers don't know about it, I guess."

Stone found Sharpe's card in his pocket and looked at it. "That's a pretty expensive part of SoHo these days, isn't it?"

"Yes, it is. Since I've been aware of him, he's moved twice, both times to a bigger and better place. He bought the building he's in now; he has a garage on the ground floor, his studio on the second, and his apartment on the third. He rents out the two floors above him."

"How did Hildy become involved with him?"

"I'm not sure, but she probably met him at an opening much like tonight's. That's the sort of event where he does his trolling."

"What can you tell me about Hildy's relationship with her father?"

Rita sighed. "I love Philip, and I wish I could say that he's the sweet, adoring, indulgent father and that Hildy is an ungrateful little shit, but it's not really like that. Philip is an enclosed man, and he doesn't let much into his life that isn't art or people associated with it."

"He told me that he thought he had left too much of her upbringing to help," Stone said.

"That's an understatement. After his wife died, he hardly saw Hildy. I doubt they had a meal together when she was between the ages of six and sixteen. Her grandmother hired the governesses, chose the schools, and complained about his parenting or lack thereof, but she never hauled him into court and tried to take Hildy. I don't know why. By the time Hildy started fucking her teacher it was too late, I guess. She was acting out big-time to get back at Philip for his neglect, and I think she still is, with Sharpe."

"And he has a low opinion of Sharpe?"

"It wouldn't work for Hildy if he didn't. She got him to look at some slides of Sharpe's work once, and he reduced it to the visual drivel it is in a few pointed sentences. Then he pissed off Hildy by refusing to go down to Sharpe's studio and look at his stuff."

"The relationships are circular," Stone said.

"Hildy hates her father for ignoring her, so she chooses a man like Sharpe to annoy him. Then Philip hates the guy's work to belittle him, and that reinforces Hildy's opinion of her father."

"Neat, isn't it?"

"Yes, except for the drug sales and the fortune at risk. If Sharpe got busted while Hildy was there, she could be charged as an accessory. I mean, she must know what he's doing."

"I don't see how she couldn't, but who knows?"

"Then there's her trust. I suppose Hildy has no regard for money."

"About the same regard as most young people who've never had to give money a thought, because it was readily supplied by parents who used it to keep them from underfoot."

"And Hildy knows about his background, the name change and the four marriages?"

"Oh, yes. Did Philip tell you that Sharpe was trailer trash?"

"Yes."

"He doesn't even know what that means. He says it only because he knows it's contemptuous. Actually, Sharpe's father made a fortune in the scrap metal business, and they lived in a nouveau riche house in one of San Antonio's better neighborhoods. Sharpe's mother, who knew nothing about art, imbued him with artistic pretensions, even though he exhibited no discernible talent. I hear he can't even draw."

Stone thought about it all for a minute while he finished his steak. "God, what a mess," he said finally.

"I take it Woodman & Weld sent you around to fix it," Rita said.

"Something like that."

"What are you going to do?"

"I don't know. I don't think there's much point in having an avuncular chat with Hildy—older man/young girl."

"Not really. Her only use for older men is to fuck them. Of course, it's a bonus if they annoy Philip."

"What sort of father did you have?" Stone asked.

Rita chuckled. "My father, bless his heart, is everything Philip should have been but isn't."

"Sweet, adoring, and indulgent?"

"Pretty much, and my mother supports him in all those things. They're peaches, both of them."

"You're a lucky woman."

"I am, indeed."

"Dessert?"

"Not on my diet, thanks."

Stone signaled for the check. "Where do you live?" he asked Rita.

"Park and Seventy-first," she said.

Stone signed the credit card slip. "Come on. I'll drop you."

"It's early," she said. "Where are you off to?"

The waiter pulled out the table and freed them. "I'm going to see a man who might be able to do something about Derek Sharpe," Stone replied.

16

Stone got to Elaine's by ten o'clock and found Dino having dinner with a cop about their age, Brian Doyle, who had served with them in the 19th Precinct detective squad years before. Stone shook his hand and sat down. A waiter appeared with a Knob Creek and a menu.

"I'm not dining," Stone said and then turned to Doyle. "You're looking pretty good for an old fart," he said.

"And you're looking as slick as an otter," Brian replied. "I hear you're making more money than Donald Trump."

"I heard Trump was broke," Stone said.

"Not anymore; he found some more hot air to inflate the balloon," Brian said, laughing.

After Dino and Brian finished their dinner, they ordered brandies. Then the three old buddies sat back and began telling each other stories they'd all heard before, until, finally, Stone got to the point. "I've got a heads-up for you," he said, handing Derek Sharpe's card to Brian.

"I've read about this guy somewhere," Brian said. "I know a lot of what's called art ought to be illegal, but I don't think the city council has gotten around to passing the law yet."

"This guy churns out the kind of art that ought to be illegal and sells it briskly to the artistically clueless."

"I guess you can make a living doing that," Brian said.

"From what I hear, that's not how he makes his living," Stone replied. "If he had to rely on his art for money, he'd be living in a garret in the East Village instead of owning a five-story building downtown and living in three floors of it. He rents the top two."

"So what's his dodge?" Brian asked.

"Pretty simple: He's moving quantities of drugs from his space."

"What kind of quantities are we talking about?" Brian asked.

"I don't know that he's wholesaling, though I've heard he's sold up to a kilo of coke, but it's more likely he's moving larger than usual quantities to individuals for personal use."

"Sounds boring," Brian said. "Can't you give me something sexier?"

"Brian," Stone said, "when this hits the *Post* and the *News* it's going to be sexy enough to knock your eye out. This guy is plugged into the art scene from one end of this town to the other. He's very well-known, and the press is going to love it, if he gets busted."

"Like Julian Schnabel?"

"Yeah, but without the talent, the work to prove it, or his following. Schnabel is the real deal; Sharpe is ersatz."

"And you want me to bust him? Tell me why."

"He's glommed on to a young woman who's about to become wealthy, and if he isn't stopped, he's going to get her hooked on something bad, steal her money, and throw her into the street if she doesn't actually do time for being close to him."

"About to be wealthy? What's she going to do, win the lottery?"

"She's about to become twenty-five, and when she does, a fat trust is hers to do with whatever she wants, and what she wants is Derek Sharpe. By the way, his real name is Mervin Pyle, and he's from San Antonio, Texas. He's skinned three or four wives already, and it might be interesting to run his names and see if he has a record back home."

"You know anything else about him?"

"His old man made big bucks in the scrap metal business. Anything else you want to know you can learn by just meeting him. He's a real lizard."

"Look," Brian said, "instead of wasting resources on this guy, why don't I just send a couple of people over there who'll beat him to death and throw the corpse in the East River?"

"That's too easy," Stone said. "Be a cop instead."

Brian took a notebook, wrote down Sharpe's particulars, and pushed the card back to Stone. "Okay, I'll put somebody on him."

"Might be a good idea to insinuate some young detective into his crowd and see what happens."

"How about a girl detective?" Brian said. "I've got a hot one on the squad, young and gorgeous."

"Add rich to that, and she'll attract Sharpe like flies to honey."

"Is he dangerous?" Brian asked.

"He doesn't appear to be but cornered, who knows? That's why I think it would be good to wander around in his background and see what turns up."

Brian looked at him closely. "Come on, Stone, there's more to this than what you're telling me. You got something else against the guy?"

"Brian, I never heard of him until this morning

and never met him until this evening at a gallery opening. I've got absolutely nothing against the guy, except for hating him on sight and hearing bad things about him."

"Well, I guess that's enough."

"Who's the lady cop?"

"Her name is Mitzi Reynolds. She's midthirties, been on the squad for two years, and she's from North Carolina—still has the accent."

"She anything to do with the tobacco family?"

"Nah, her father's a shrimper out of Charleston. She went to a nice school, though. I forget what it's called."

"Well, she can use her own name, and I'll bet Sharpe will think she's from cigarette money. Charleston is far enough away that he won't be able to check her out easily. Use some budget to buy her some clothes."

"Yeah, she'd love that, but don't worry; she dresses good, has a real sense of style."

"I might be able to fix her up with a Park Avenue address," Stone said, "on a temporary basis. I'll make a call tomorrow morning and see." The building where he had dropped Rita Gammage was said to be the best address in the city; it would certainly impress Derek Sharpe.

"I'll have Mitzi call you tomorrow morning. You should get together with her and tell her what you know. If you can get her into this apartment, that'll keep down the budget, which ain't going to be big for a small-timer like this Sharpe guy."

Stone gave him a card. "Tomorrow morning's good."

Brian stood up. "Well, I've got to go out and work for a living tomorrow," he said, "unlike you guys. You buying, Dino?"

"Nah, Stone is," Dino said.

They all shook hands, and Brian left.

"I hope you're not jerking Brian around," Dino said.

"Certainly not. I think this is a bad guy; he'd fit right in at Attica."

"Yeah, Attica is a real artist's colony."

"Don't think artist; think con man, and you'll be closer to the mark," Stone said.

"What's in this for you?" Dino asked.

"Eggers asked me to do what I can; the girl's old man is a client of the firm."

"Who is he?"

"Philip Parsons."

"Gallery on Fifty-seventh?"

"One and the same. How the hell would *you* know?"

"I know a lot of stuff," Dino said.

17

Stone was sitting up in bed the following morning with a cup of coffee and the *Times* crossword when the phone rang.

"Hello?"

"It's Rita Gammage."

"Good morning."

"I just wanted to thank you for dinner last night."

"You're very welcome. Let's do it again."

"Love to. Did you talk to your man last night?"

"Yes, and I've been able to interest the downtown cops in Mr. Sharpe's business dealings. In fact, I'm supposed to have lunch today with a lady cop who's going to be leading the effort."

"Wonderful!"

"Say, why don't you join us?"

"Sure, where and what time?"

"How about my house at noon?"

"Sounds good. I've got your card, so I'll know where."

"See you then."

Stone had hardly hung up when the phone rang again. "Hello?"

"Mr. Barrington?" spoke a honeyed woman's voice.

"Yes."

"This is Mitzi Reynolds. Brian Doyle asked me to call you."

"Yes, we talked about you last night. Can you come to lunch at my house at noon? A lady with some knowledge of the man in question will be here, too."

"Surely."

Stone gave her the address, then hung up and pressed the PAGE button on the phone. "Helena?" He waited a moment; then she picked up.

"Mr. Stone?"

"I have a couple of people coming for lunch today. Could you fix us something?"

"I will be happy to."

"Will it be warm enough in the garden to sit out there, do you think?"

"Oh, yes. Lots of sun, too. What would you like?"

"You decide. They're invited for twelve, so let's sit down at twelve thirty."

"I will do this." Helene hung up.

Stone went back to the puzzle.

He was working in his office when the upstairs doorbell buzzer rang. He picked up the phone. "Yes?"

"Your luncheon guests," Rita said.

"I'll buzz you in and meet you there in just a moment." He pressed the buzzer and then called Joan.

"Yep?"

"I have guests for lunch, so I'll be a while," he said, and then he hung up and walked upstairs.

Rita Gammage and Mitzi Reynolds were standing in his living room, looking around. Mitzi, in what appeared to be an Armani business suit, was shorter than but just as good-looking as Rita, who was dressed in slacks and a cashmere sweater.

Stone gave Rita a peck on the cheek and introduced himself to Mitzi.

"We've already met each other," Mitzi said. "We arrived simultaneously."

"Follow me," Stone said, then led them through the house and down to the kitchen, where Helene was working away. He introduced her to the two women.

"Anybody for a glass of champagne?" he asked, opening the fridge.

"Why not?" Mitzi said, and Rita nodded.

He took a bottle of Veuve Cliquot from the fridge, picked up three crystal flutes from a cabinet, and then led them outside to a group of chairs around a teak cocktail table. Helene had already set the lunch table with the good china. Stone poured them all a glass, and they sipped. Stone was having the problem he always had when meeting two beautiful women: which one to pursue?

"Rita, why don't you tell Mitzi what you told me about Derek Sharpe last evening?" he said. He sipped his wine while Rita talked.

"That's about all I know," she said, finally.

"You make him sound repellent," Mitzi said.

"Then I've done my work," Rita replied.

Helene bustled out with two platters and set them on the table. "Lunch is served," she said.

They took their seats at the table and served themselves from the Greek salad, *taramasalata*, hummus, and dolmades Helene had made.

"Mitzi," Stone said, "did Brian give you some idea of what you're supposed to do?"

"He pretty much left it up to me," she said, "but I think the idea is that I will appear on his social radar and get him interested in the Reynolds fortune."

"Oh, you're from the Reynolds tobacco family?" Rita asked.

"No, I'm from the Reynolds shrimp family—no relation," Mitzi said.

"Mitzi's father operates a shrimp boat," Stone explained.

"No," Mitzi said, "he operates thirty shrimp boats, up and down the coast, from an office on the Charleston waterfront. Brian tends to get confused about my roots."

"Ah," said Stone, "and how . . ."

"Did a girl like me get to be a New York City cop? It was easy. I had a boyfriend for a couple of years who was a detective. I didn't have any real work, and I was fascinated by his, so he suggested I take the police exam. I did well on that and joined the force. I got my gold shield six years later."

"Brian said you went to a good school down there somewhere."

"Agnes Scott College, in Atlanta."

Stone blinked. "I know someone who went to school there, Carrie Cox—do you know her?"

"She was a year behind me," Mitzi said, "and she was a piece of work."

Stone wanted to ask exactly what she meant by that, but Rita interrupted. "She's the actress with the lead in the new Del Wood musical, isn't she?"

"That's the one."

"Yes, I read about her on 'Page Six.'"

"So did I," Mitzi said, "and I can't say I was surprised. How do you know her, Stone?"

"I've done some legal work for her," Stone replied, and hoped she would leave it at that. "Tell me," he said, "do you have a regular partner?"

"Tom Rabbit," she said. "He's due back from vacation tomorrow."

"Good, because I think you'll need some backup."

"What's he going to pose as?" Rita asked.

"Not as anything," Mitzi said. "He wouldn't fit into Derek Sharpe's crowd. He'll watch my back; he'll be the cavalry that rides in if something goes wrong."

"You make this sound dangerous," Rita said.

"That's unlikely," Stone said, "but an undercover cop has to operate on the premise that he—or she, in this case—is in danger at all times. These things tend to have a happier ending if you think that way. Shall we have another bottle of champagne?"

They did.

18

They had finished lunch and the second bottle of champagne and were on coffee.

"Rita," Stone said, "I need your help on something else."

"What's that?"

"I need to find Mitzi a temporary place in a good building on the Upper East Side, somewhere she can operate from. Her address will be the first thing Derek Sharpe will learn about her, and it has to impress him."

Rita turned to Mitzi. "Mitzi, why don't you just bunk with me? I live in my parents' apartment in a nice building. They spend most of their time at their house in the Hamptons, and there are comfortable guest rooms."

"Thank you, Rita," Mitzi replied. "That's very kind of you."

Stone relaxed; that had gone just the way he had hoped. He heard the phone ring in the kitchen.

Helene stuck her head out the back door. "Phone for you, Mr. Stone!"

"Will you ladies excuse me?" Stone said. He took the call so they would have an opportunity to get to know each other better in his absence. He went into the kitchen, sat down at the counter, and picked up the phone. "Hello?"

"Stone, it's Brian Doyle."

"Hey, Brian. Thanks for putting Mitzi on this. I've introduced her to a woman who can help her get to know the scene, and she now has the best address on Park Avenue."

"That's good news," Brian said. "I have some of my own."

"Shoot."

"Mr. Mervin Pyle, aka Derek Sharpe, does not have a record under either of those names."

"I'm surprised to hear it," Stone said.

"Don't be too surprised; he has records under three other names. Apparently our boy took to identity change as a way of life in his youth. He lived in Dallas, L.A., and San Francisco, where he managed an art gallery for a while."

"What sort of stuff?"

"Burglary, embezzlement, battery, attempted murder, all under different names."

"Did he do time?"

"Only while awaiting bail. His IDs were so good that each time he pled out, and as, supposedly, a first offender, he got no jail time."

Rita and Mitzi came into the kitchen, and Stone asked Brian to hang on.

"Do you mind if we have a look around your house?" Rita asked.

"Not at all. Explore to your heart's content."

She handed him a card. "You might have your secretary have some cards like this printed for Mitzi."

Stone took the card: "71 East Seventy-first Street? I thought you lived on Park."

"It's the side-door address for those who want to be discreet. Maybe you should use 740 Park on her cards for Sharpe's edification."

"Sure." The women wandered off, and Stone went back to his call. "I'm back."

"I was particularly interested in the battery and attempted-murder charges," Brian said, resuming. "I got hold of a San Francisco detective who worked the latter case, and he told me that Sharpe has a very bad temper, especially when drinking, and he has a propensity for violence. The attempted murder case arose out of a fight between him and another guy he nearly beat to death. It took four cops to pull him off."

"What was the battery charge about?"

"He beat up a girlfriend, and she called the cops."

"Mitzi tells me her partner is out of town until tomorrow," Stone said.

"And she won't start until then," Brian replied. "Her partner, Tom Rabbit, is a big Irish guy who can handle anything and who is very protective of her."

"Brian, can you get her a car to be driven around in? Rabbit could be the chauffeur."

"Good idea. Let me check the pound and see what we've confiscated lately."

"You were right," Stone said. "She's a very bright lady. Oh, here's her new address: 740 Park Avenue." Then he read out the phone number.

Brian let out a low whistle. "How'd you swing *that* building? I read a book about that place."

"It's where Rita Gammage lives; Rita works for Philip Parsons."

"Then she's a very rich lady."

"Or her parents are."

"Same thing," Brian said. "I gotta run. Tell Mitzi to call me later today, and I'll check on a car."

"Nothing too flashy," Stone said. "Let's not overdo it."

"Gotcha." Brian hung up.

Stone walked to his office, then down the hall to Joan's room. "Can you get some of these printed in the name of Mitzi Reynolds? 740 Park Avenue? Same zip and phone. It's a rush job."

"Sure," Joan said. "I'll run them over to our printer and wait for them." She grabbed her coat.

"On nice stock," Stone said.

"I get it." Joan was gone.

Stone walked back to the kitchen, where Helene was washing the champagne flutes by hand. "Where are the ladies?"

"Haven't seen them," Helene replied.

"That was a delicious lunch," Stone said, and Helene beamed at him.

He walked up to the living room and had a look there and in his study: no sign of the women. He walked upstairs and looked into a couple of guest rooms, then continued on to the master. As he approached, the door was ajar, and he heard giggling. He opened the door and stood there, transfixed.

The two women were in his bed, and, judging from the pile of clothing on the floor, they weren't wearing any. He didn't know what to say.

Rita took up the slack. "Join us?" she said.

19

Stone woke slowly in a champagne-induced haze. He was in the middle of his bed, and the women were nowhere to be seen. Then he heard a laugh from his bathroom and heard the shower go on. He drifted off again.

He awoke to a pair of lips attached to each of his cheeks.

"We're off," Rita said.

"I'm off, too," Stone replied sleepily.

"You were just great, Stone," Mitzi said.

"Yes," Rita said, "but for a moment I thought you were too shocked to accept our invitation."

"Only for a moment," Stone said

"We'll be in touch," Mitzi said, and the two women moved toward the stairs. Stone drifted off again.

*   *   *

The phone woke him a couple of hours later, and he reached for it.

"Hi, it's Carrie."

"Hi, there."

"You sound sleepy."

"Yeah, I had an afternoon nap," he managed to say.

"Will you and Dino be at Elaine's?"

"Sure, eight thirty."

"May I join you?"

"Of course."

"See you then."

Stone hung up, turned on his side, and went back to sleep. He woke in the dark, switched on the bedside lamp, and stood up. He staggered a little before he caught himself; he felt as if he had just run a marathon. Well, he thought, he had, in a way. The bedside clock said almost eight, and he ran for the shower.

Carrie was already at the table with Dino when Stone walked in. He waved for a drink and sat down.

"You look different," Carrie said, kissing him.

"Different?" He didn't know how to respond to that.

"Completely relaxed," she said. "It must have been a good nap."

"It certainly was," Stone replied.

"I talked to Brian," Dino said. "Sounds like you got what you wanted."

"It does, doesn't it?"

"What is he talking about?" Carrie asked.

"Just a little police operation downtown."

"Is it a secret?"

"Yes."

"I hate secrets; tell me."

"Can't. Lives are at stake."

Carrie turned to Dino. "That's a lie, isn't it?"

"Nope," Dino said. "Lives are at stake."

"Oh," Stone said, "I met someone who knew you at Agnes Scott College."

"Who?"

Stone backtracked. "I can't remember her name; she was from Charleston."

"Mitzi somebody?"

"That sounds right."

"She was a year or two ahead of me. She was very pretty."

"She still is."

Carrie's eyes narrowed. "And how did you meet her?"

"I had lunch with a business associate, and she came along."

"I'd love to see her. Did you get her number?"

"She went back to Charleston this afternoon, I believe."

"Good."

So much for changing the subject, Stone thought. He hadn't seen Carrie jealous before, and it was a little scary. He remembered the straight razor. "How are rehearsals going?"

"I had a little contretemps with the choreographer today," she said. "He wanted me to do a move that would have broken my back."

"And how did you handle that?"

"With a flat refusal, a display of temper, and a couple of bad words."

"How did that work out?"

"He removed the move from the routine," she said with some satisfaction. "I mean, I might have managed it when I was eighteen, but I know my body better than he does."

"I'm glad to hear it."

"*You* know it better than he does," she said with a sly smile.

"*Harrumph,*" Dino sputtered. "Too much information."

"Oh, Dino, you're sweet," she said, laughing.

"Was that the only problem?" Stone asked.

"There was an unwelcome twist," she said. "He asked my understudy to demonstrate the move for me. Her name is Melissa Kelley, and she's in the chorus, and if he weren't gay I would suspect something between them."

"And she was able to do the move?" Dino asked, now fascinated.

"Perfectly," Carrie said, "the bitch. I could have throttled her."

"It's probably better if you don't throttle any-body," Dino said. "Then I'd have to get involved."

Carrie laughed. "It's okay, Dino; she tried to apologize after rehearsal, but it came out all wrong. I mean, what was she going to say—'I'm sorry I could do the move and you can't'?"

"I can see how that could be awkward," Stone said.

"She watches me all the time," Carrie said. "It's unsettling."

"Maybe she's just working very hard to learn your part," Stone offered.

"No, it's more like *All About Eve*. You know the movie? The young actress wants everything the star has, including her lover?"

"I remember it well."

"You'll meet her eventually," Carrie said. "When you do, watch yourself."

"I'll be very careful," Stone said solemnly.

"So, what's Mitzi up to?" Carrie asked.

"She didn't say a lot."

"She has a rich daddy, I recall."

"She said he was in the shrimp business."

"That sounds right. You're sure she went back to Charleston?"

Stone shrugged. "I believe so. She had to leave lunch early to catch her plane."

"What did she say about me?"

"She said you were a piece of work."

"And what did she mean by *that*?"

"I don't know, and somebody changed the subject before I could ask."

"It's just as well," Carrie said.

Stone allowed himself to think, just for a moment, about what Carrie might do if she knew how he had spent the afternoon.

Carrie dabbed at his forehead with a cocktail napkin. "You're perspiring," she said. She put two fingers on his throat. "And your pulse is up."

"Isometric ab exercises," he said. "I do them at dinner sometimes."

"By the way, I think you can send the young Irish gentlemen home. Not a peep out of Max. I think he's been subdued."

"Are you sure?"

"Yes. In fact, I sent them home when they dropped me off here. They said they would return your car tomorrow morning."

Stone signaled for a menu, but he had trouble concentrating on it. He was still thinking of all those limbs.

20

Stone was at his desk the following morning when Willie Leahy rapped on his doorjamb.

"Good morning, Willie," Stone said.

Willie tossed him his car keys. "It's in the garage," he said. "I filled it up with the premium stuff."

"Thanks," Stone said.

"Listen," Willie said, "I don't know if we shouldn't be watching her for a while longer."

"Why do you say that? She's feeling safe now."

"Just a feeling," Willie said. "That and a phone conversation I overheard."

"What was that about?"

"Well, there's a pair of restrooms in the wings of the theater—ladies' and gents'—and there's some sort of vent, and you can hear the girls talking sometimes."

"You been eavesdropping, Willie?"

"Look, I was having a splash, and I heard Carrie on the phone."

"Yes?"

"She was talking to Delta Air Lines."

"Yes?"

"She was making a reservation to Atlanta this weekend."

"*Atlanta?*"

"I kid you not," Willie said, "and I don't know why the fuck she would want to be in the same city as that ex-husband of hers."

"Neither do I," Stone said. "I mean, she lived there a long time, and I suppose she could have some business there."

"On a weekend?"

"You have a point," Stone admitted.

"Well, let us know if we can be of further service," Willie said, and, with a little wave, he left.

Stone was still thinking about this when Joan buzzed him. "Brian Doyle on one."

"Hello, Brian."

"Morning. I found Mitzi a car: a Bentley, would you believe?"

"How did you come to confiscate a Bentley?"

"Drug bust, what else? It's an Arnage, a few years old, but it looks good."

"I guess it would," Stone said.

"Listen, Mitzi's new friend Rita found out there's a party at Derek Sharpe's studio tonight.

She wangled Mitzi an invitation, but she doesn't want to go with her, figuring that her connection to Parsons might affect the way Sharpe sees Mitzi. Will you take her to the party?"

"Sure, I guess so."

"Great. A Bentley, chauffeured by a cop, will pick you up at six thirty."

"Sounds good."

"Some guys have all the luck." Brian hung up.

Joan came into his office and put a box on his desk. "Sorry, the printer couldn't get them done yesterday."

Stone opened the box and removed one of Mitzi's new cards. "Very nice," he said. "That should do the trick."

At six thirty sharp Stone's bell rang. When he opened the door, it was filled by about six feet four inches of Irish American, dressed in a black suit with a black tie.

"Evening," he said. "I'm Tom Rabbit."

Stone shook the extended paw. "Good to meet you, Tom."

"You ready?"

"Yep."

"She's in the car already."

Stone set the alarm and locked the door, then walked to the car. Tom had the door open for him.

He slid in beside Mitzi and kissed her on the cheek.

"Don't say anything about yesterday afternoon when Tommy is around," she whispered, before the driver could get into the car.

"Right." He handed her the box of cards. "Your credentials."

She opened the box and inspected the contents. "Hey, very good," she said, tucking some of them into her small purse. "Makes me feel like I really live there."

"Is it a nice place?"

"Haven't you seen it?"

"Nope."

"It's a fucking palace," she said. "Sorry, I'm talking like a cop. Got to get over that."

"I'm glad you're comfortable there."

"My room is better than anything at any hotel in this city," she said.

"I wouldn't talk about that tonight," Stone said. "The card will say everything that's necessary to impress Sharpe."

"What's Sharpe like?" she asked.

"Reptilian," Stone replied, "but women seem attracted to him."

"Oh, we love reptiles," Mitzi said, laughing. "They can always be relied on to slap us around and steal our money."

"I'm sure Derek Sharpe won't disappoint," Stone said.

They drove downtown and arrived at Sharpe's building to find half a dozen drivers waiting outside in their cars, mostly black Lincolns, the preferred transport for New York's affluent, who don't like to arrive at a party in a taxi.

The building looked like a factory, except for the huge murals splashed on the outer walls.

"Ugh," Mitzi said.

"Be sure to compliment Sharpe on them," Stone said.

The elevator held a dozen arriving guests without crowding any of them and opened into a huge space filled with big canvases and many people. Some sort of pop music Stone didn't recognize was blaring from a sound system.

"His paintings are worse than I expected," Mitzi said.

"Sharpe may be, too," Stone replied. He steered her to a bar and collected two plastic flutes of champagne. "This is as bad as the paintings," Stone said, sipping his.

"Shall we hunt down Mr. Sharpe and introduce me?"

"No, let's look at the pictures and pretend to appreciate them," Stone replied. "That should bring him to your side."

They walked along a wall, stepping around people and gazing at the big canvases, stopping before a particularly awful one.

"He's looking our way," Stone said. "Nod and smile a lot."

"I'm nodding and smiling," she said, pointing at a corner of the canvas. "Look, he had the guts to sign it."

"Well, good evening and welcome," a deep, Texan voice said from behind them.

Stone turned and tried to look surprised to see Derek Sharpe accompanied by Hildy Parsons. "Hello, Derek, Hildy," he said. "May I introduce Mitzi Reynolds? She's recently moved to New York from Charleston, South Carolina."

"Well, hey, sugar," Sharpe said, taking her hand, draping an arm over her shoulder and leading her back the way they had come. "Let me show you some of my work."

"I'd love to see more," Mitzi said. "I particularly liked the murals on the building."

"Everybody likes those," Sharpe said. "It's a pity I can't peel 'em off the building and sell 'em."

Mitzi laughed becomingly. "Oh, I like your composition here," she said, framing a canvas with her hands.

Then, from behind them, came a female voice. "Well, hello, Mitzi," it said.

The two couples turned around to find Carrie Cox standing there with a willowy young man.

"Carrie!" Mitzi said, and a big air kiss was exchanged. "What on earth are you doing here?"

"I live here," Carrie said.

"Isn't that funny!" Mitzi replied. "So do I!"

"That *is* funny," Carrie said. "It was my information that you returned to Charleston yesterday." She glared at Stone.

"Oh, shit," Stone muttered to himself.

21

Mitzi looked inquiringly at Stone. "Excuse me for a moment," he said, stepping forward, taking Carrie by an elbow and steering her away from Mitzi and the others. She tried to snatch her arm away, but he held on tightly.

"Don't say anything," he said, marching her across the room toward an unoccupied corner.

"I'll say whatever I damn well please," Carrie spat.

"Not until you've heard me out." He stopped and turned her so that her back was toward the group across the room. "Remember that police operation Dino and I were talking about last night?"

"Sort of," she said petulantly.

"It's happening right now, and Mitzi is a part of it."

Carrie brightened. "Oh, she's going to be arrested? This I want to see." She tried to turn around, but Stone stopped her.

"Mitzi is a New York City police officer," he said.

Carrie screwed her face into an incredulous glare. "*That* is the most preposterous thing I've ever heard! You're going to have to come up with a better story than that."

"No, I don't," Stone said firmly, "and unless you can accept the fact and keep your mouth shut I'm going to throw you out of here right now."

"And how does a shrimper's daughter get to be a New York cop?" Carrie demanded.

"Some years ago, she took the police exam, was accepted, and graduated from the academy. She served as a street cop for several years before she was promoted to detective. That's how it's done."

"I don't believe you."

"I haven't formed the habit of lying to you or anybody else," Stone said, "and if you repeat any of this to anyone, you will put Mitzi's life in danger, and that is no exaggeration."

Carrie stood there smoldering, avoiding Stone's gaze.

"Do you understand me?" Stone demanded.

She wheeled on him. "Yes!" she said. "And now, if you don't mind, I'll be going." She turned and yelled across the room, "Paco!!!"

The willowy young man came trotting across the space.

"We're leaving," she said to him.

"But we just got here," Paco protested.

"I don't care. We're going."

"Well, I'm not," he replied. "There's somebody I want to meet." He gazed across the room at another young man.

Stone guided Carrie toward the elevator. "Downstairs there's a black Bentley Arnage, driven by a very large man. Tell him I said to take you wherever you want to go and he's to be back here in no more than an hour."

"I'll make my own arrangements," she said, then marched into the elevator.

Stone rejoined the others. "I'm sorry about that," he said. "A misunderstanding."

"Not to worry," Mitzi said.

"Do you have a cell number for Tom?"

She pressed a speed-dial number and handed Stone the phone.

"It's Tom," he said.

Stone stepped away. "Tom, it's Stone. There's a beautiful blonde named Carrie on her way down. Put her in the car, take her somewhere else, then come back as soon as you can. Don't be more than an hour."

"I'll call you when I'm back," Tom said. "Here she comes now." He hung up.

Stone handed Mitzi her phone. "That's taken care of." At least for the moment, he thought.

"Oh, good," Mitzi said. "Derek was just telling me about how he does his work. It's fascinating."

"I'll bet," Stone said, trying to keep the irony out of his voice.

An hour later, Mitzi answered her phone. She listened, then hung up. "My driver is back," she said.

"The party seems to be winding down," Sharpe said. "Why don't we get some dinner?"

"I'd love to," Mitzi said brightly.

"Sure, why not?" Stone said. He noted that Hildy didn't seem to have any objections.

They rode down in the elevator with the last of the celebrants, and Tom was waiting out front with the Bentley.

"We'll take my car," Mitzi said.

"I'll take the front seat," Stone said, and got in while Tom held the door for the others.

"Where to, Ms. Reynolds?" Tom asked when he was in the car.

"Derek," she said, "we're in your hands."

Sharpe gave directions, and soon they were stopping outside a chic-looking restaurant. Stone hardly ever came downtown, so he didn't know it.

They went inside, where Sharpe was fawned over by the manager and the reservations lady before they were shown to a big table in the center of the room. Sharpe ordered a bottle of expensive wine and menus.

"I hope you like sushi," Sharpe said to the group.

"Love it," Mitzi said.

Stone detested sushi but said nothing. The menus came, and he began looking for something cooked. He was relieved to find a shrimp teriyaki and ordered that, while the others chose raw things.

"So, Mitzi," Sharpe said. "How long have you been in town?"

"A few weeks, off and on. I bought an apartment uptown, and I've been seeing to the decorating."

"Oh," Hildy said, "let me have your address and number."

Mitzi fished a card from her purse and handed it to her.

Sharpe took it from her, looked at it, froze for a moment, then handed it back to Hildy. "Nice neighborhood," he said.

"I like it," Mitzi replied.

"How did you ever find it?" Hildy asked. "You never see anything listed in that building."

"It was a private sale," Mitzi said smoothly. "A friend of my family owned it."

"That's the best way," Hildy said. "Did you

have any problems with the co-op board? I hear they can be tough."

"None at all," Mitzi said. "In fact, they were rather sweet."

Stone admired how, in a few words, Mitzi had told them that she came from money, serious enough to impress a board made up of people with serious money.

"Are you all settled in now?" Hildy asked.

"Perfectly," Mitzi replied. "My decorator brought over the last pair of lamps today."

"And who is your decorator?" Hildy asked.

"Ralph Lauren," Mitzi replied.

"Who at Ralph Lauren?"

"Ralph."

"Ralph who?"

"Lauren."

Stone nudged her under the table. Ralph Lauren did not deliver lamps. Mitzi was going too far.

"I've never heard of Ralph personally doing decorating jobs," Hildy said.

"He and Daddy are old friends," Mitzi replied. "Daddy was one of Ralph's first backers many years ago, when he was still in the necktie business."

This, Stone thought, was a high-wire performance. He hoped to God that Philip Parsons and Ralph were not old friends.

Hildy answered his question. "How interesting.

My father and Ralph are old friends, too. Ralph has bought a number of pictures from him."

"Oh, is your daddy in the art business?" Mitzi replied.

"The Parsons Gallery," Hildy said.

"Oh, of course. I didn't make the connection. A lovely gallery it is, too. I bought a Hockney there."

"Oh? Whom did you deal with?"

"Rita Gammage."

"Oh, yes."

"Your father was busy with something else that day."

This was out of control. Stone tried desperately to think of a way to change the subject. Fortunately, dinner arrived.

22

The teriyaki was good. Stone tried not to watch the others eating raw animals. As soon as he had finished his main course, Stone asked to be excused and left the table. He found a quiet corner of the restaurant and called Rita Gammage.

"Hello?"

"Rita, it's Stone. We've got problems."

"Did something go wrong?"

"If anything, it's all gone too well," Stone said.

"What do you mean?"

"I mean that Mitzi has gotten a little too much in the swing of things. She's impressed Sharpe and, incidentally, Hildy, too much. Among other things, she has told them that she bought a Hockney from you, and the way things are going, next she'll be inviting them over for drinks."

"Oh, God."

"Does Philip have a Hockney in the gallery?"

"Yes, he does."

"Borrow it, will you? And will you please call him right now and tell him that Mitzi bought it? I have the feeling Hildy is going to call her father tonight and ask him."

"I'm sure he'll loan it to me for a few days when I explain why," she said. "I'll get right on it."

"Another thing," Stone said. "Mitzi has told them that Ralph Lauren personally decorated her apartment."

"That's outrageous!"

"I know, but she did it."

"Fortunately, most of my upholstered furniture is from Mr. Lauren's store."

"That will be a big help," Stone said, "but there's a further complication."

"Now what?"

"When Hildy questioned whether Lauren personally does decorating jobs, Mitzi told her that Lauren and her father are very old friends and that he was one of Lauren's early investors."

"Oh, shit. If I know Hildy, she'll find a way to track that down."

"That's what I'm afraid of. Do you know Lauren?"

"I've met him a few times, but I don't think he'd recognize my name."

"Does Philip?"

"I think he sold him a picture once, a few years back."

"Do you think Philip would call him and try to get him to back up this story?"

"I'm not at all sure about that," Rita said. "Let me think about how to do this, and in the meantime, I'll call Philip and ask about the Hockney."

"I'm afraid that I don't know Mitzi's father's first name," Stone said.

"It's Mike. She told me."

"Good, I'll leave it with you."

"Are you home? I'll call you back."

"No, we're in a sushi restaurant downtown with Hildy and Sharpe."

"Call me when you get home. I'll be up late."

"Will do." Stone hung up and returned to the table.

"Oh, Stone," Mitzi said, "Derek and Hildy are coming for drinks tomorrow evening."

"How nice," Stone said, very glad that he had called Rita. Then he had a terrifying thought: Had Hildy ever visited Rita's apartment?

They finally wrapped up dinner, and the check came. It sat there. Stone was damned if he was going to pick it up; this had been at least a seven-hundred-dollar dinner, given the wine Sharpe had ordered, and it wasn't Stone's party. He decided to take the bull by the balls. "Thank you so much for dinner, Derek," Stone said, pushing the check across the table. That was very extravagant of you." He thought he saw Sharpe turn pale. He turned to Mitzi. "Shall we go?"

"Yes, let's do," she replied. "Can we drop you?" she asked Hildy and Sharpe.

"We're going to have an after-dinner drink at the bar," Sharpe said. "We'll make our own way home."

Stone hustled Mitzi out of the restaurant and into the car.

"How'd that go?" Tom Rabbit asked.

"Wonderfully well," Mitzi said.

Stone thought she was a little drunk. "You really threw a monkey wrench into the works," Stone said.

"How's that?" She seemed baffled.

"Well, first of all, that business about the Hockney."

Mitzi giggled. "Oh, yes, I forgot about that."

"I spoke to Rita. She's going to borrow a Hockney from Philip Parsons."

"Well, that's all solved, then, isn't it?"

"Not quite. Now we have to deal with your chummy relationship with America's most famous designer, who has personally decorated your apartment."

"Well, it *looks* as though he decorated it," she said innocently.

"And that stuff about your father investing with Lauren years ago."

"Oh, that's perfectly true," she said.

Stone looked at her skeptically. "Are you sure about that? Because that's a loose end that can't be left untied."

"Of course, I'm sure."

"All right, then we're okay on that story about your father and Ralph. What are we going to do if Hildy gets to him and asks if he decorated your apartment?"

"Oh, I'll call Ralph in the morning and square that with him." She turned and took him by a lapel. "Did you really think I would spout all that stuff without being able to back it up?"

"Frankly, yes. I had no idea where that was coming from, and it would have been nice if you had tipped me off before you said it."

"Oh, ye of little faith," she said.

"And what about the Hockney? Did you have that all squared, too?"

"Well, Rita took me to the gallery, and I saw a Hockney there. I figured something could be done."

"Mitzi, if you continue this high-wire act, you're going to give me a coronary," Stone said.

"Yeah," Tom echoed from the front seat, "she gives me coronaries all the time. You'd better get used to it."

"Tell me about your own little monkey wrench," Mitzi said.

"What are you talking about?" Stone asked.

"I'm talking about Carrie Cox," she said. "God, what a scene."

"Well, I had no idea she was going to be there," Stone said lamely. "I hustled her out of there as fast as I could."

"And did you tell her I'm a cop?"

"I had to; she would have blown you on the spot."

"Talk about high-wire acts," Mitzi said, laughing. "You know, I think she actually lent some credibility to our little farce. Even her jealous act helped."

"I hope you're right," Stone said.

"So, you and Carrie are an item," Mitzi said.

"I told you, I've done some legal work for her."

"Well, I guess it was legal," Mitzi replied. "I mean, she is of age, isn't she?"

At 740 Park, Stone walked Mitzi to her door.

She kissed him on the cheek. "By the way," she said, "you acquitted yourself very well yesterday afternoon."

"I must say, that was a surprise," Stone said.

"Judging from the look on your face, I'd say it was a shock!"

"Well . . ."

"Let's do it again sometime."

"Absolutely," Stone tried to say with confidence. He was still a little rattled by the experience.

"And Rita feels the same way," Mitzi said. "Good night." She gave him a little wave and went into the building.

Stone got into the front seat of the Bentley. "That woman is something," he said to Tom.

"You don't know the half of it," Tom replied.

23

The following day Stone went to the stage door of the Del Wood Theater, gave his name to the watchman, introducing himself as Carrie's attorney, and went and stood in the wings.

Carrie was in the middle of what was apparently her big dance number, and Stone was impressed. Paco, from the night before, was her dance partner, and he was trying gamely to keep up and almost making it. The number ended, and the choreographer called Paco over for a chat.

Carrie grabbed a towel and patted her face. When she saw Stone in the wings she came over. "Visitors aren't allowed at rehearsals," she said. "Wait for me in my dressing room." She pointed the way and then walked back onto the stage.

Stone found a door with a star tacked to it and let himself in. It was fairly large, with a big dressing table, a long couch, and a couple of chairs, as well as an en suite bathroom. The decor wasn't much, he thought, but there were a couple of paint cans and some wallpaper rolls in a corner, so he reckoned that would change soon. He settled on the sofa and leafed through a *Variety* from the coffee table.

Carrie came in after a few minutes and slammed the door behind her.

Stone got up to greet her.

"You were very mean to me last night," she said, pouting.

"You were behaving badly," he said, "so I had to be mean. You could have caused a great deal of damage."

"So she really is a police detective?"

"She is."

"That's what Tom, her driver, said."

"Tom is a cop, too. He's Mitzi's partner."

She pushed him onto the sofa and sat beside him. "All right, I want to hear the whole story."

"I'll give you the *Reader's Digest* version," he said, and he managed it in a few sentences. "And you should stay away from Derek Sharpe," he told her.

"I can see that," she said. "Anyway, I hate his stuff. I don't know why anyone would buy it."

"You have excellent taste."

"Yes, I do," she said, getting up and stripping

off her sweater and tights. "I'm going to take a shower," she said. "You want to buy me dinner later?"

"Sure."

"Can we go to Elaine's and see Dino?"

"I'm fairly certain he'll be there; he always is."

She dropped her clothes into a hamper and took off her bra and panties.

Stone was impressed all over again. She had a dancer's body: slim with long muscles and high breasts. She went into the bathroom and turned on the shower without closing the door. Stone was happy to watch. When she came out, drying herself with a towel, she gave him a long look, then locked the door and sat on his lap, facing him.

"Your lips become fuller when you're turned on," Stone said. "That's some kisser you've got there."

She kissed him. "That's what the lips are for," she said, then slid to the floor, unzipped his fly, and showed him how else the kisser could be used.

Afterward, Stone fell asleep, waiting for her to get dressed.

Dino didn't seem surprised to see them. Stone ordered them drinks.

"Dino," Carrie said, "you were very naughty last night not to tell me about Mitzi being a cop and all."

"You aren't supposed to know about that," Dino said, shooting Stone a sharp glance.

"She turned up at Derek Sharpe's studio, unannounced," Stone said in his defense.

"Do I have to tell you everything I do?" Carrie asked, sipping her drink.

"You have to tell me when you decide to go to Atlanta," Stone said.

"I'll do that," she said.

"You didn't do that," he replied.

Her jaw dropped. "How did you find out?"

"Why, it was all over 'Page Six' in the *Post*," Stone said. "'Crazy Dancer/Actress to Visit Her Atlanta Ex-husband, Who Wants to Kill Her.' Didn't you see it?"

She laughed. "It was not."

"Tell me," Stone said, "what was the point of our pulling out all the stops to keep you safe if you're going to go running into his arms at the first opportunity?"

"It's not like that," she said.

"What is it like?"

"A mutual friend has offered to mediate the settlement," Carrie said.

"You told me you already had a settlement."

"There are a few loose ends," she said. "Dear Max has bounced back financially with the help of a Saudi prince, who has a house in Atlanta. I'm told he's actually better off now than he was before."

"I'm told that, too," Stone said. "So you're going to hold him up for more?"

"For more cash. He was strapped a year ago, so I took not very liquid assets."

"There's nothing like cash," Stone said. "It makes a wonderful motive for murder. What makes you so sure Max won't be meeting your flight and taking you for a little ride?"

"I know what would make you feel better about this," Carrie said. "Come with me."

Stone was brought up short. He had no desire to go to Atlanta, but having made a fuss about it, he could hardly say no. "All right," he said.

"I'll book you on the same flight," she said. "And I've already booked a suite at the Ritz-Carlton Buckhead."

"Who else is going to be at this meeting?" Stone asked.

"Max's lawyer and our mutual friend, a lawyer named Ed Garland."

"I know Ed," Stone said. "Had you planned to do this without an attorney of your own?"

"I was going to ask you," she said, "and I would have last night, if you hadn't marched me out of Derek Sharpe's studio."

"I'm sorry I had to do that," Stone said.

"I'm sorry you had to do that, too," she replied. "I apologize for my behavior."

"No need to apologize."

Dino spoke up. "Does anybody want to order dinner? Or do you two want to get a room?"

"Dinner now, room later," Carrie said, shooting Stone a leer. "You owe me." She picked up a menu.

"I do, and I'll pay," Stone promised.

24

Stone was at his desk the following morning when Bill Eggers called.

"Good morning, Bill," Stone said.

"Can you give me a progress report on the Parsons problem?"

"I can," Stone said. "I've arranged for a female police detective to be dangled before Derek Sharpe, pretending to be an heiress from South Carolina. Actually, she's not pretending, because that's what she is."

"Go on."

"The idea is that, having loosened him up with a displayed interest in buying his work, she will attempt to buy drugs from him. If that works, he's off the street."

"I like that," Eggers said, sounding surprised.

"Why do you sound surprised?" Stone asked.

"Well, frankly, I hadn't expected such fast action with the promise of such permanent results."

"This hasn't worked yet, Bill," Stone replied. "Things can go wrong, and the detective is placing herself at some risk."

"I'll keep that in mind. Have you spoken with Philip Parsons about this?"

"He's being kept apprised by a staff member of his gallery."

"And he's happy?"

"I've no reason to think that he's not."

"Good work, Stone. I'm proud of you."

"Thanks, Bill, but be proud when it's done."

"I'll be proud then, too. Good-bye." Eggers hung up.

Carrie, holding the straps of her duffel, appeared in his office. "Our flight is in two hours," she said.

"Where'd you get the clothes?"

"From your closet. Didn't you notice they were there?"

"Nope."

"Where are your clothes?" she asked, her head cocked to one side, hand on hip.

"They're in my closet, too," Stone replied.

"Had you planned to take some with you?"

"What will I need?"

"Something to make you look lawyerly at our meeting and whatever else you need. We'll be flying home tomorrow."

"I'll be right back," Stone said, rising from his desk.

Joan drove them to LaGuardia in Stone's car, and their flight was on time. They were on the airplane before Stone realized that he would rather be flying himself. Well, at least they were in first class.

They were met by a car and driver at Hartsfield International and driven to the Ritz-Carlton.

"What time is our meeting?" Stone asked.

"Four o'clock."

"Why aren't we returning to New York tonight?"

"In case we need a second meeting tomorrow."

They arrived at Ed Garland's office on time and were greeted warmly by Garland, with whom Stone had previously worked on a case, and coolly by Max Long and his attorney. The meeting was called to order, and Stone sat silently while Carrie enumerated her demands. He tried not to hold his breath.

Long's attorney opened his mouth to speak, but Max stopped him. "Yes," he said.

"We'll take yes for an answer," Stone said. "Ed, can I borrow a typist for a moment? We'll get this signed now."

"Sure, Stone."

Half an hour later, both parties signed, and Max

Long wrote a large check. Everyone shook hands and parted.

On the way back to the hotel, Stone handed Carrie her copy of the agreement. "Tell me again why I was at this meeting?" he asked.

"For bodily protection," Carrie said, "and as a prop."

"A prop? Like a stage prop?"

"Exactly. You were the attorney prop."

"You mean you knew that Max would meet your demands?"

"I did."

"How?"

"He knew that if he didn't, I would make his life miserable until he did. I knew that he knew that it would be a whole lot easier for him if he just caved immediately, before I could think of something else to ask for."

"You should have been a divorce lawyer," Stone said.

"I have been, for the past year or so," she said. "I've learned a lot."

"You're a quick study."

"On stage and off."

After dining at the excellent Ritz-Carlton restaurant, they made love until they were exhausted and then fell asleep.

The following morning they were driven to the airport, and as the airplane lifted off the runway,

Stone relaxed. Nobody had tried to kill Carrie, and it appeared that nobody would. He was able to sleep all the way home.

When he got back to the house, there was a phone message from Mitzi Reynolds, time-stamped the afternoon before.

"Our drinks with Sharpe and Hildy have been postponed until tomorrow night," she said. "My place at seven. We're going to dinner afterward."

Stone breathed a sigh of relief; he had completely forgotten their appointment of the evening before.

"I have plans for this evening," he said to Carrie, "so I'm going to put you in a cab home."

"Plans?" she asked.

"In connection with the police operation."

"You're seeing Mitzi, then?"

"I am."

"Do I have to get used to that?"

"You do," he said, "until we pull this thing off."

"I'm going to pout now," she said, pouting.

He kissed her and put her into a cab.

"Call me tomorrow," she said.

He waved her off and went back inside, still tired from his exertions of the past two nights.

When he walked into his office his phone was ringing. He picked it up. "Stone Barrington."

"It's Willie Leahy."

"Hi, Willie."

"You're lucky you're not dead," Willie said.

"Tell me why you think that."

"You were followed from the lawyer's office in Atlanta."

"By whom?"

"Well, after I tapped him on the back of the neck and went through his pockets, he was identified as an Atlanta PI named Wallace Higgs."

"And you think he meant us harm?"

"He was carrying a loaded Glock and a homemade silencer."

"Oh."

"Yeah."

"But we settled everything at the lawyer's office. Max wrote her a check for everything."

"Tell her to cash it quick," Willie said.

"Willie, how was it that you happened to be in Atlanta and happened to be following us?"

"I've been following you since LaGuardia," Willie said. "I was in steerage, while you were drinking champagne up front."

"Why were you doing that?"

"I like the lady. I didn't want her to go to Atlanta, and I didn't want anything to happen to her."

"Willie, you can bill me for that one."

"Don't worry," Willie said, and then hung up.

Stone called Carrie on her cell.

"Hey, Stone. Forget something?"

"Yes. Be sure you deposit that check the moment the bank opens tomorrow and tell them to call the Atlanta bank and ask them to put a hold on the funds."

"Do you know something I don't?"

"Usually," Stone said. "Just do it. Talk to you tomorrow." He hung up and began to go through the mail on his desk.

25

Stone arrived at Rita's apartment fifteen minutes early. The elevator opened directly onto the foyer, and Mitzi met him at the door with an affectionate kiss on the lips. "Please come in," she said.

Stone followed her into the living room and stopped to have a look around. It was a large room with a seating area that would accommodate a dozen people around the fireplace, another seating area at the west end, and a seven-foot Steinway grand piano at the east end, which wasn't in the least crowded.

"What do you think?" Mitzi asked. "Do I have good taste?"

"Well, Ralph Lauren does," Stone said. He nodded toward the painting over the fireplace. "Love the Hockney."

"Isn't it something?"

"I wish I could afford his work," Stone said.

"There were some very nice New York scenes on your bedroom wall," she said.

"My mother's work."

"They're beautiful."

"She thanks you."

"Can I get anybody a drink before I disappear?"

Stone turned to see Rita entering the room. She gave him the same sort of kiss that Mitzi had, one that caused a stirring.

"Sure," Stone said.

Rita poured the drinks from a wet bar concealed behind some paneling.

"It's a beautiful apartment," Stone said, "but you'd better get rid of the photographs on the piano, the ones of you and your parents."

"Oh, God, I forgot about those," Rita said. She scooped them up and put them in a drawer.

Mitzi ran out of the room and came back with an armful of silver frames. "I brought these from home," she said, arranging them on the piano. "My family."

"Good work," Stone said. The phone rang, and Mitzi picked it up. "Yes? Send them up, please." She hung up. "We're on."

"I'll be in my room," Rita said. "I hope I don't hear any shooting." She left the living room.

"Which lamps did dear old Ralph, the family friend, bring over?" Stone asked.

"The pair at each end of the sofa."

"They're not Lauren's—they're antiques," Stone said.

"Ralph has a wonderful eye for antiques," Mitzi replied. "And I called him yesterday and squared things."

"What was his reaction?"

"He was delighted to hear from me, and amused by my situation and happy to help."

The doorbell rang, and Mitzi went to answer it. She came back with Derek Sharpe and Hildy Parsons and another couple, whom Sharpe introduced as Sig and Patti Larsen. Sig looked Swedish; Patti didn't. Drinks were offered and accepted, and a uniformed maid appeared with a tray of hors d'oeuvres.

They arranged themselves before the fireplace.

"Sig is my financial manager," Sharpe said, "and he's very good. Mitzi, I thought you might need some New York help in that line."

Here was an interesting move, Stone thought. If Mitzi bit, then Sharpe would, in no time, have a complete picture of what he could steal from her.

"I'm very well taken care of in that respect," Mitzi said. "My father has three people in his office who do nothing but handle our family's money."

"Perhaps I could meet with them sometime," Sig said.

"They're in Charleston, and they hate New York," Mitzi said.

"You know, I'm going to be in Savannah early next week," Sig said. "Perhaps I could pop up to Charleston and see them."

"I'll ask Daddy," Mitzi said.

"I'm at your disposal," Sig said.

"Where are we dining?" Mitzi asked.

"I've booked us at Sette Mezzo," Sharpe replied. "In half an hour."

This was interesting, Stone thought. Sette Mezzo didn't take credit cards, only cash, unless one had a house account.

Mitzi picked up the phone and dialed a number. "Please be downstairs in twenty minutes," she said into the instrument.

"I love your Hockney," Hildy said, speaking for the first time. "I saw it at my father's gallery, of course."

"Yes, I'm very pleased with it," Mitzi said.

"Oh, by the way," Hildy said, "I ran into Ralph Lauren this morning; he sends his regards."

"That's sweet of him," Mitzi said. "Do you like the lamps?"

"Very much," Hildy said, and Sharpe murmured an assent.

"Ralph found them at one of the Paris flea markets," Mitzi said.

"Wonderful places," Patti Larsen interjected.

"Aren't they?" Mitzi said.

Conversation continued along these lines until they finally made their way downstairs. Stone and Mitzi got into the Bentley, and the other two couples boarded their own black Town Car.

"How did drinks go?" Tom asked from the front seat of the Bentley.

"Just as you'd expect," Mitzi said. "We're all squared away on the Hockney and Ralph Lauren."

"Lexington and Seventy-sixth, please, Tom," Stone said.

Sette Mezzo was, as always, crowded with the voluble, so Stone reckoned their conversation would be subdued at a table for six, since they wouldn't be able to hear one another. They were shown to a corner table, which helped. Sharpe revealed himself as never having been to the restaurant by ordering martinis for everyone. If he had been there before, Stone thought, he would have known that the restaurant served only wine, except for secret bottles of Scotch and vodka kept for more demanding guests. Stone now knew that he would be buying dinner.

Mitzi was seated between Sharpe and Sig Larsen, and Stone between Patti Larsen and Hildy

Parsons. This meant that Stone would have difficulty, in the noisy restaurant, understanding what Sharpe and Larsen were saying to Mitzi, not that she would have any difficulty handling them.

"So, Stone," Patti Larsen said, "what do you do?" Her hand crept onto his knee.

"I'm an attorney," Stone replied. "I sue people."

She removed her hand. "How nice for you."

"Usually," Stone replied.

"Where is your office?"

"I'm of counsel to Woodman & Weld, but I work from offices in my home."

"That's cozy," she said. Her knee was now rubbing against his.

Stone turned to Hildy and made conversation.

When the check came, Stone picked it up and signed it, avoiding a scene where Sharpe and Larsen would be short of cash. What the hell, he thought, Bill Eggers would be getting the bill anyway.

Back in the Bentley, Stone asked Mitzi how it had gone at dinner.

"They were pressing me about Sig giving me financial advice," Mitzi said.

"Was that true about the financial people in your father's office?"

"Yes, but there's only one; I made up the other two."

"Why don't you call him and ask him to make up a fictitious financial statement and stock portfolio?" Stone suggested. "Something that will water Sharpe's mouth?"

"What a good idea," she said. "I'll do it first thing Monday morning. That should thicken the plot."

"I think that, after they see your statement, you should broach the subject of drugs. I'd advise you to tell them the stuff is for friends, not for you. You don't want to get into a situation where you're pressed to actually use something around witnesses. That could blow your case."

"I'm way ahead of you," Mitzi said.

"Believe her," Tom added.

Stone did.

26

Stone got a call from Bob Cantor the next morning. "Hey, Bob."

"Hey, Stone. Willie Leahy thinks he and his brother should be back on Carrie's case."

"Yeah, he told me he followed us to Atlanta."

"And he told you about the PI with the loaded gun and the silencer?"

"Yes."

"Doesn't that make you think the Leahys should be back on the case?"

"But the PI was in Atlanta, not New York."

"Max has already made one stab at her, so to speak, in New York. Why wouldn't he try again?"

"Because Carrie settled everything with him in Atlanta. He even wrote her a check."

"Has the check cleared?"

"We're working on that."

"And why, if it clears, do you think Max would lose interest in hurting her?"

"Well . . ."

"In my experience, guys who hate their ex-wives go right on hating them, even after giving them the money. In fact, they hate them *more* after giving them the money."

"You have a point," Stone admitted.

Joan buzzed him. "Carrie Cox on two."

"Hang on, Bob." Stone put him on hold and pressed the button for line two. "Carrie?"

"Hi. I'm at the bank, and they've put a hold on the funds in Max's account. The check will clear tomorrow."

"That's good news. Hang on a minute, will you?" Stone went back to Cantor. "Bob, let's put them on her for another week."

"It will be done," Cantor said and then hung up.

Stone went back to line two. "I've got some news," he said.

"Good news, I hope."

"No."

"Oh, God, what now?"

"Willie Leahy followed us to Atlanta on Friday, and he caught an Atlanta private investigator following us."

"That doesn't make any sense."

"Bob Cantor makes the point that ex-husbands

hate their ex-wives even more after giving them money, and the PI was carrying a loaded gun and a homemade silencer."

"And what does that mean?"

"It means that he planned to shoot us—or at least, you—quietly, so nobody would notice."

"That doesn't sound like Max."

"Who else hates you?" Stone asked.

"Nobody—at least not enough to actually have me murdered."

"Are you sure about that?"

"Of course, I'm sure."

"Then it's Max. I've put the Leahys back on you; cooperate with them, will you?"

"Oh, Stone!"

"Do you want to make it to opening night? Someone who hates you might love to prevent your dream from coming true."

"Oh," she said. "I see your point. All right, I will welcome Willie and Pete back into my life."

"Give them a nice gift, a necktie maybe."

"I'll give them some new cologne—the one they wear is toxic."

"Good idea."

"Gotta run; I'm due at rehearsal. Dinner tonight?"

"Come over here, and I'll cook you something."

"Done. Seven?"

"Good."

She hung up.

Fifty feet from Carrie Cox's front stoop, Willie Leahy sat in his car surveying the street. He got out of the car and looked both ways, then crossed the street and looked again.

The speaker/microphone for the radio on his belt popped on. "We're ready. Everything okay?"

"Everything okay," Willie replied. He crossed the street, got into the car, and drove up to Carrie's stoop. Peter hustled her into the car. "Where we off to?" Willie asked.

"To Stone Barrington's house," she replied.

"Gotcha." Willie headed for Turtle Bay.

As he turned into Stone's block, he slowed. "A guy I don't like, across the street from Stone's," he said. "Black raincoat."

"Drop me here," Peter replied, "and go around the block."

Willie did so. "Carrie, lie down on the backseat," he said.

"Will do. Are there bad guys?"

"Maybe. We'll know soon." Willie drove slowly past the man and made mental notes: five-eleven, two hundred, suit and tie under the raincoat, forty to forty-five. He drove around the block.

*   *   *

Peter Leahy put his hands in his coat pockets and walked down the block at a normal pace. As he came up to the man in the black raincoat he stopped behind him and whispered in his ear, "Don't turn around."

The man froze.

"The guy who lives in that house doesn't like loiterers," he said.

"It's a free country," the man replied, not moving.

Peter flipped up the lapel of his coat and removed a four-inch-long hat pin that had belonged to his grandmother. He gave the loiterer a quick jab in the ass.

The man cried out and spun around. Then, walking backward, he shoved his hand inside his coat and made his way down the block.

"If you pull that thing on me, you better kill me with the first shot," Peter said.

The man kept his hand inside his coat but didn't draw anything. He turned and now began walking fast, hurrying away.

"And don't come back," Peter called after him. He looked over his shoulder, saw Willie coming, and held up a hand for him to stop. He waited until the watcher had turned the corner before he waved Willie on. They hustled Carrie into the house.

*   *   *

Stone met them at the door. "Any problems?"

"Just one," Peter said. "I sent him on his way."

"How'd you do that?" Stone asked.

Willie showed him the hat pin.

Stone laughed. "I haven't seen one of those things since I was a kid."

"You'd be surprised how useful it can be," Peter said. He turned to Carrie. "Are you staying the night?"

"Yep," she replied.

"Then we'll leave you in Stone's capable hands."

The Leahys departed.

27

Stone walked Carrie down to the kitchen, put her duffel on the dumbwaiter, and sent it upstairs. Then he poured them both a Knob Creek, and they sat down on the large kitchen sofa.

Carrie rested her hand lightly on Stone's crotch. "You know what I like about you?"

"I think I'm getting an idea," Stone said.

"Exactly. And it's always ready to go." She began kneading.

"How could it not be, under the circumstances?"

"Until I met you it had been a long time since I had gotten anywhere near as much sex as I wanted."

"I'm glad to be of service," Stone said.

She unzipped his fly and put her hand inside.

"Men don't really understand how much sex women need," she said.

"I'm beginning to get the picture," Stone said.

She pulled him down on the sofa, took down his trousers, shucked off her slacks, and straddled him, taking him inside her. "How's that?"

"*Mmmmm*," Stone replied.

"Oh, I'm going to come," she said.

"Don't wait for me."

She didn't.

"You're so easy," Stone said. "Again."

"Here I come." And she did. "How about you?"

"I'll save myself for later," he said.

She lay down beside him on the sofa and put her head on his shoulder. "I know I can be a pain in the ass," she said, "but I really appreciate the way you've been protecting me."

"You're paying for it," Stone reminded her.

"Yes, but I never would have arranged it for myself. You've thought of everything."

"I've tried to."

She sat up, pulled her sweater over her head, and undid her bra, freeing her breasts. "I'm dining naked tonight," she said, then started on his clothes.

"I hope you don't mind if I wear an apron while I'm cooking," Stone said. "Gotta watch out for those spatters."

"You do that, sweetie. I'll still get to look at your ass, which is very nice, by the way."

"Same to you, kiddo."

"Did you ever take dance?" she asked him.

"Ballroom, when I was twelve—my mother insisted."

"You've got a dancer's ass," she said. "Muscular and tight."

"Maybe I should start wearing leotards," he suggested.

She laughed.

They dined, naked, on veal chops and risotto.

"This is wonderful," she said, tasting the risotto. "What do you put in it?"

"You watched me make it."

"I was watching your ass," she said.

"Combine some butter and olive oil in a pan; add twelve ounces of Arborio rice, some salt, and the zest of a lemon; and sauté until the rice turns golden. Start adding small cupfuls of hot chicken stock, stirring until each addition is absorbed before adding the next, and continue until a whole carton has been absorbed. Then stir in the zest of another lemon, a couple of fistfuls of Parmigiano-Reggiano, and half a carton of crème fraîche, and serve. Takes a little less than half an hour."

"That's so simple."

"Why do you think I make it?"

She attacked her veal chop, and Stone poured a good Australian Shiraz into their glasses.

When they had finished she sat back and rubbed her naked belly. "God, that was good; I'm almost too full to make love again."

"Would you like some dessert?" he asked. "There's ice cream."

"I think I'll have you for dessert," she said, taking him by the cock and leading him upstairs.

Joan buzzed them at nine, waking them.

Stone picked up the phone. *"Mmmmf."*

"And good morning to you, too," Joan said. "There's a man watching the house."

"Go look out your office window. Do you see the Leahys?"

She put the phone down for a minute, then came back. "They just drove up, and the man ankled it out of here."

"Pete stuck a hat pin in him last night," Stone said. "I guess he didn't want another one."

"And where would Peter Leahy get a hat pin?"

"From his grandmother."

"An heirloom—wonderful."

"Pete's an old-fashioned kind of guy."

"I just thought you'd like to know," Joan said, then hung up.

Carrie was sitting up in bed now. "I've got a

rehearsal in half an hour," she said, climbing out of bed. "I wish I had time to fuck you again." She ran into the bathroom and turned on the shower.

Stone drifted off for a few minutes until she woke him with a kiss.

"Tell Willie and Peter the next time they see that guy, I'd like them to have a chat with him," Stone said. "Find out who he is and see if they can connect him with Max."

"Okay," Carrie replied. "We'll talk later."

"I want the night off," Stone called after her. "I'm exhausted."

"We'll see," she called back over her departing shoulder.

Stone went back to sleep.

28

Stone was wakened by the phone again a little after eleven. "Hello?"

"Hi, it's Mitzi," she said.

"Good morning."

"You don't sound up yet."

"I'm awake—*up* would be too strong a word."

"Rough night?"

"Not exactly."

She gave a low laugh. "I got my fake financial statement from Daddy's office this morning. You'll be happy to know I'm worth thirty million dollars—on paper, at least."

"Whose letterhead is it on?"

"William H. Barrow, CPA."

"Not your father's. Good.

"Should I just give this to Sharpe?"

"Why don't you call him and tell him you'd like to meet with him and Sig Larsen again?"

"Okay."

"Give him your statement and ask how he would handle it."

"Right."

"Does it have individual stocks listed?"

"Yes, about forty of them."

"Good. Tell him you want his plan in writing."

"Wouldn't that put him off?"

"You don't want to be too easy a mark; *that* would put him off. Con men get special satisfaction from screwing smart marks."

"That wasn't quite what I had in mind."

"All right, *fooling* smart marks."

"Actually, I did have that in mind, but with you, not Sig."

"What a nice idea. What's the setup this time?"

"Not a threesome; I'd rather have you to myself."

"I'm a little under the weather," Stone said. "How about later this week?"

"I'll call you," she said.

"And you can give me a full report then."

"I'll give you more than that."

"Bye-bye." Stone hung up and groaned. "When it rains, it pours," he said aloud to himself.

*   *   *

Dino was more cheerful than usual. They had met at P. J. Clarke's for lunch and were having burgers and beers.

"You're in a good mood," Stone said.

"Ben got accepted at Choate," Dino said, speaking of his son.

"Congratulate him for me."

"I will."

"Doesn't this mean you'll see him less often?"

"Well, yeah, but it means I'll have to deal with Mary Ann less often, too. No squabbles about which days I see him or what we do together."

"I'm sure Eduardo will miss him." Eduardo Bianci was Dino's ex-father-in-law, a very rich man who had been—perhaps still was—a major Mafia figure, but who had been very discreet about it, ruling from afar.

"That's true, and I feel for the old man. I'll make sure Ben sees his grandfather when he's home."

"How is Eduardo?"

"Amazingly well. For a man his age, I'd guess you'd say he's in robust good health. I'm sure he'd appreciate a call from you."

"I'll call him today."

"How's it going with Carrie?"

"She's wearing me down," Stone replied. "Literally."

"You lead such a tough existence," Dino said.

"You don't know the half of it. What are you doing for female company since splitting the blanket with Genevieve?"

"Catch as catch can," Dino replied.

"As long as you catch a few."

"There's the desk sergeant at the 19th," Dino said. "We have a nice evening about once every week or two. Keeps the machinery oiled and working."

"She's the one who ended your marriage, isn't she?"

"No. Mary Ann took care of that; Sarge was just the excuse."

"Is that what you call her?"

"In bed as a joke."

"What's her real name?"

"Madge Petrillo."

"Not married, is she?"

"Nah, divorced. I think she may be banging the captain, too, but if so, they're very, very discreet."

"Busy lady."

"You know it. How's the Derek Sharpe operation going?"

"It's going. Mitzi's a smart cop; she's handling it very well. I'm just trying to stay out of the way."

"That doesn't sound like you."

"Well, I've seen Sharpe with her a couple of times, and I give her advice."

"That's very fatherly of you. What else is going on there?"

"Let's not get into that," Stone said, a little embarrassed.

"Oh, so *that*'s what's going on."

"Don't jump to conclusions."

"What, you think I condemn you for sleeping with more than one woman at a time?"

"It's your Catholic upbringing," Stone said.

"I got over that a long time ago," Dino replied.

"Catholics never get over it. I'll bet you still go to confession."

"Every couple of years, maybe. I love shocking the priest."

"I'll bet you do."

"It's a good thing you're not Catholic," Dino said. "At confession, you'd give a priest a heart attack."

"You're right. It's a good thing I'm not Catholic; I'm not sure I could bear the guilt."

"Guilt is very important," Dino said. "It keeps you on the fairly straight and narrow."

"The *fairly* straight and narrow? I like that."

"So do I," Dino said.

They split the check and walked outside, where Dino's unmarked car with driver awaited him.

"You want a lift?" Dino asked.

"No, thanks. I think I'll walk home, get some exercise."

"I thought you were getting lots of exercise," Dino said, laughing.

"Well, the cardiovascular thing is important," Stone said.

"See you later." Dino got into his car and was driven away.

Stone walked home and entered through the outside door to his office.

Joan flagged him down. "Eduardo Bianci's secretary called. He would like you to come to lunch at his home tomorrow at noon."

Eduardo was a mind reader, Stone thought. "Say that I accept with pleasure."

29

Stone drove out to the far reaches of Brooklyn to the elegant Palladian house with a view of the water that was the home of Eduardo Bianci.

Stone's relationship with Eduardo went back some years, to a time that predated even his brief marriage to Eduardo's daughter, Dolce. Dolce was an extraordinarily beautiful woman who turned out to be deeply disturbed, with homicidal tendencies, which were directed mostly at Stone and cost him considerable discomfort, including the pain of a bullet wound. Dolce, now safely ensconced in a suite of rooms in Eduardo's house, was tended by an elderly aunt and professional nursing help. No one but Eduardo had seen her for years.

Stone was admitted to the house by Eduardo's wizened butler, who, according to Dino, previous to—and perhaps after—his employment by Eduardo, had pursued a highly successful career as an assassin, specializing in the Sicilian stiletto. He greeted Stone with a tight smile, or grimace, depending on interpretation, and led him to the rear garden, where Eduardo waited, seated at an umbrella-shaded table near the edge of the pool.

Eduardo, who was unaccustomed to rising for anyone short of the Holy Father, did not rise but extended a slender hand and gave Stone a warm handshake and a broad smile, revealing either amazing teeth or gorgeous dental work, Stone had never figured out which. He was dressed, as usual, in a dark suit, a white silk shirt, and a muted pin-dotted necktie.

"Stone," Eduardo said in his smooth, rich baritone—the voice of a much younger man— "how very good to see you. It has been far too long."

Stone took a seat. "It's good to see you, too, Eduardo. Oddly enough, I was on the point of telephoning you yesterday when I returned from lunch and got your message. You're looking extremely well."

"I am extremely well for a person of my age," Eduardo said, "and I am grateful to my ancestors for the genes passed down to me. My father lived to a hundred and three, and my mother only a year short of that. When she died, my father remarried shortly afterward to a woman of fifty. He told me he had considered a woman of thirty-five but did not wish to be burdened with more children at his age."

Stone laughed. The butler appeared with an ice bucket, opened a bottle of Pinot Grigio, and poured them each a glass. "I hear from Dino that Benito has been accepted to Choate, which is wonderful news."

"Yes, though it means I will see him less often. I think it will be good, though, for him to be out of the city and in the companionship of boys who will grow into leaders in this country."

"I'm sure he will fare well in their midst," Stone replied.

"I have great plans for the boy," Eduardo said.

"Oh? Have you already chosen a profession for him?"

"Not those sorts of plans," Eduardo said, shaking his head. "He will excel at whatever work he chooses. Eventually, he will, with my advice and that of his mother, look after my interests until they become his own."

"What are your interests these days, Eduardo?"

Eduardo permitted himself a small laugh. "You are curious, aren't you, Stone?"

"I confess, I am."

"My interests are broad and deep, ranging from Wall Street, which has been a disappointment lately, to Silicon Valley, with many stops in between."

"Are you still involved in banking?"

Eduardo shook his head slowly. "No. At a board meeting many months ago I heard of this awful bundling of mortgages. I looked into it and immediately resigned from three boards and sold all my bank shares over a period of weeks, well before the crash. A bit later, I moved to cash in the market. Now I have begun to buy again, companies with futures and at very good prices."

Lunch was served: medallions of pork in a garlicky sauce, with tiny, crisp potatoes and perfectly cooked broccoli.

When the plates were taken away, Eduardo leaned back in his chair. "I am given to understand," he said, "that you are involved with two men called Sharpe and Larsen."

Stone was once again astonished at Eduardo's apparent knowledge of everything about everybody. "I met them both recently," Stone said. "Beyond a couple of dinners I am not directly involved with either."

"I must tell you, Stone, that it is dangerous to invest with Mr. Larsen, as I have reason to believe that he has created a Ponzi scheme along the lines of that perpetrated by Bernard Madoff but on a much smaller scale."

"He will not see any of my money," Stone replied, "such as it is."

"Good. And I must tell you that it is dangerous merely to be in the company of Mr. Sharpe."

"How so?"

"The gentleman has ventured into waters that are rather thickly populated by others of more experience and cunning. In addition, he has attracted the attention of the police, and when his business associates learn of this, his existence will become uncertain."

"I will certainly heed your warning," Stone said. "And I will tell you, in confidence, that I have had a hand in pointing the police in his direction."

Eduardo looked surprised, an expression Stone had never seen on his face. "Have you, really? That speaks well of you, Stone."

"I'm afraid that Mr. Sharpe has gained some sway over the soon-to-be-wealthy daughter of a client of Woodman & Weld, and I was asked to see what I could do about it."

"Ah, that would be Miss Parsons, would it not?"

"It would."

"I had heard that she had been seen often in Mr. Sharpe's company, and I was concerned. Her father is a friend of mine, and I have bought a number of artworks from him over the years. I hope that your endeavor will be successful soon, for I fear there is not much time."

Dessert was served, a light, Italian cheesecake. Then, over coffee, Eduardo radically changed the subject.

"Dolce has been feeling much better the past few months," he said.

"I'm glad to hear that," Stone said carefully. Not since the divorce Eduardo had effected for him had he mentioned his daughter's name to Stone.

"She has expressed a desire to see you," Eduardo said.

Stone nearly choked on his coffee. "If, in your judgment, that would be a good idea, then I would be happy to see her."

Eduardo laughed his little laugh again. "That was an artful lie, Stone," he said, "but in my judgment, as you put it, I think it would be good for Dolce to speak with you for a short while." Eduardo turned and looked over his shoulder toward the rear terrace of the house.

Stone followed his gaze and saw Dolce, clad in a pretty, summery dress, standing on the terrace. His heart stopped. Then she began walking slowly toward them.

"If you feel that, then I will redouble my efforts."

30

She looked younger, somehow, than when Stone had last seen her, when she was being hustled into a private ambulance, wearing a straitjacket, frothing at the mouth. She now seemed untroubled, at peace, and not in the least dangerous.

Stone got to his feet. "Hello, Dolce," he said, offering his hand. "It's good to see you."

Dolce took his hand then offered a cheek. "And you, Stone," she said.

Stone moved to kiss the cheek, but she turned her head to place his lips at the corner of her mouth and flicked her tongue snakelike at his. He gave her the chair next to her father, then sat down with her between them. "You're looking very beautiful," he said.

"Thank you, Stone. You were always so gracious."

Why then, he asked himself, did you want so badly to kill me? "Thank you," he said aloud.

"Dolce has taken up painting," Eduardo said, "and she is exhibiting a hitherto unseen talent."

"Oh, I painted as a little girl, Daddy," Dolce replied. "You just don't remember. In those days you were preoccupied with business."

"I suppose I was," Eduardo said. "I was at that time withdrawing from certain activities and moving into others that seemed more . . . inviting."

"You mean more legitimate, don't you?" she asked, giving him a smile.

"If you wish, my dear." Eduardo turned toward Stone. "At that time certain federal agencies were taking too much of an interest in my associates. I had managed never to be in a situation where my conversations might be recorded or my face photographed, but I believed that it would be impossible to continue that way for long. As it turned out my beliefs were confirmed more quickly than I had imagined, but by that time, I had receded into privacy, and my communications with my former associates had become less frequent and more indirect."

"You have always struck me as the most prudent of men," Stone said.

Eduardo shrugged. "I came to the view, earlier than my partners in . . . such activities, that those activities, as the saying goes, did not pay, at least not for long nor in proportion to the risks required. I judged that it was better to be involved in enterprises where good behavior was enforced by law rather than by vengeance."

Stone smiled. "I have had a number of clients who came late to that realization, to their regret."

"Every one of my associates from those days ended up dead by extraordinary means, deported to birthplaces they did not long for, or permanent guests of the federal government."

"Daddy, on the other hand," Dolce said, "ended up lord of all he surveyed and much more."

"My daughter is too impressed with her father," Eduardo said, shooting her a glance.

"Did you know he was offered the Presidential Medal of Freedom but declined?"

"I have never wished to be famous," Eduardo said, "even for a brief moment at the White House."

"Oh, Daddy, you're too modest," Dolce said. "You've been to the White House many times to visit half a dozen presidents."

"But never with television cameras present," Eduardo pointed out.

"Daddy won't even allow his photograph in the annual reports of the companies and charitable institutions on whose boards he sits," she said.

"I admit it, my dear, I am shy," Eduardo replied.

"Now let's turn the conversation back to you." He dusted imaginary crumbs from his suit, a rare gesture of irritation.

Dolce looked over her shoulder, and Stone followed her gaze. A large man in a dark suit stood on the back terrace. He looked at his watch. "Oh," she said, "I'm afraid Alfonzo is becoming impatient. We're going shopping."

Stone was startled to think of Dolce roaming Madison Avenue, a free woman, but perhaps Alfonzo could manage her.

"Dolce needs new clothes," Eduardo explained, "now that she is going out more often."

Dolce stood. "Perhaps Stone would like to tag along with me sometime."

Stone stood, too. "I'm afraid I'm rather occupied with someone who wouldn't understand."

"Yes, I know," she said, leaning forward to kiss him good-bye. This time her tongue momentarily found Stone's ear.

"Good-bye, dear Stone."

"Good-bye, Dolce," Stone managed to say. He watched her walk away, an inviting performance.

"Sit for a moment more," Eduardo said, "until she has made her escape."

Stone sat down, hoping Eduardo did not mean that literally. "She really is looking very well," he said.

"I think her mental state, particularly her anger,

made her seem older," Eduardo said. "Now that she has been relieved of those tensions, it shows in her demeanor."

"I suppose so," Stone said. "How long has she been going out?"

"Only for the past ten days or so," Eduardo replied. "I am being very careful with her, following the advice of her psychiatrist, who is a sensible woman."

"I wish I could have helped her," Stone said.

"No one could have helped her in those days, Stone," Eduardo said. "And I would not wish you to feel that you must try again."

"Thank you, Eduardo," Stone said. "I must go now, but it has been a very great pleasure to see you, and I'm glad that Dolce is making such a good recovery." He stood and took Eduardo's hand again.

"I think seeing you was good for her," Eduardo said, "and I'm glad we had an opportunity to talk about Sharpe and Larsen."

"So am I. I will take your advice to heart." Stone walked back to the terrace and through the house. The butler was there to open the front door for him. He got into his car and began the drive back to Manhattan.

He had calls to make now, after Eduardo's warning about Sharpe. Previously, he had been concerned only about Hildy Parsons with regard to her fortune. Now, it seemed, she was in more immediate danger. So, indeed, was Mitzi Reynolds, above and beyond the call of her duty. Sharpe needed to be shut down quickly and Larsen with him, and not by just a loss of reputation.

Beyond those thoughts, a knot had been forming in Stone's stomach, and he searched for the reason. Then he remembered: Dolce, when told he was seeing someone, had said, "I know."

Stone's heart thudded in his chest, and his hands made the steering wheel slippery.

31

Stone put the car in the garage and went quickly to his office. Several message slips were on his desk, among them one from Brian Doyle at the downtown precinct. He called the number.

"Lieutenant Doyle."

"Brian, it's Stone Barrington."

"Hello, Stone."

"I'm returning your call."

"I had a meeting with Mitzi earlier this afternoon, and she told me how well things are going. She said you have been a big help. 'Invaluable,' was how she put it."

"I'm glad to have helped."

"We're getting to the point where we can set up a purchase and a bust," Brian said.

"Brian . . ."

"We don't think it will have to be too big to get

a conviction: A pound of grass and half a kilo of coke should do it—plenty to charge him with distributing."

"Brian, listen to me."

"Okay, pal, I'm listening. What's up?"

"I have some new information that you're going to have to take into consideration before you decide whether to continue."

"What sort of information?"

"I have it from a very reliable source that Sharpe has stepped on the toes of some pros who take a very proprietary view of their business operations."

"And which pros are these?"

"I don't know, but they are pissed off at having what they consider to be an amateur dipping into their exclusive territories, and they are planning to do something about it."

"And where does this information come from?"

"I'm sorry, but that's completely confidential."

"That's not good enough, pal."

"Then I'm going to have to invoke attorney-client privilege."

"Stone, if you want me to believe you, you're going to have to give me something more than your word."

"Listen, you started this operation on nothing more than my word."

"That's not quite so," Brian said. "There had been rumblings from other quarters."

"What quarters are those, Brian?"

"Sorry, that's confidential—official police business."

"I'm sorry, Brian, but *that*'s not good enough," Stone said.

"That's how it works, Stone: You have to tell me; I don't have to tell you."

"I'm telling you that very soon somebody is going to remove Derek Sharpe from your precinct in a decisive way, and when that occurs anybody who happens to be standing near him is going to be removed, too. That includes Mitzi and, not least of all, Hildy Parsons, on whose behalf I initiated this whole thing."

"I'll worry about Mitzi," Brian said, "but you're going to have to deal with your little rich bitch who got into the sack with the wrong boyfriend."

"I have a responsibility to Mitzi, too," Stone said, "and I'm telling you she is not well enough protected with just Tom watching her back. He's usually waiting in the car while she's dealing with Sharpe and, incidentally, with somebody called Sig Larsen, a financial advisor who's running a Ponzi scheme."

"Well, Mitzi is going to be wearing a wire from

now on, so we'll know who she's talking to and every word they say."

"And you think a wire is going to make her safer? It's more likely to get her killed."

"Stone, a wire these days doesn't mean what it meant back in the olden days, when you were on the force. They're very clever little devices now."

"Brian, if you send Mitzi in there you're going to have to find a way to get her some on-site help. You need somebody at the scene in case things turn bad."

"Well, as it happens, I've got just the guy to go in there with her. He's known to all the participants, and he'll fit right in."

"Good. Who is that?"

"His name is Stone Barrington," Brian said.

"Oh, no you don't," Stone said. "I'm retired, remember?"

"Oh, I think I can get you put on temporary, active status until we're done with this."

"I don't want that, Brian, and in any case, you need a lot more than me. You need guys in black suits and body armor parked in a vegetable truck around the corner, ready to storm the place.

"Speaking of body armor, Mitzi is being fitted out in the latest fashion as we speak. I'm told it will make her even more inviting, that it'll add a couple of inches to her tits."

"Brian, you're not getting this: The biggest threat to Mitzi is not from Sharpe or Larsen, it's from the people who want Sharpe permanently out of business. Mitzi wearing a wire and armor is not going to protect her from a hail of shotgun or automatic weapons fire."

"We do the best we can, Stone," Brian said. "Now, I've already put in an application to the commissioner for your reactivation to the force, and I'm ordering you not to decline any invitations from Sharpe or Mitzi to join them on some occasion."

"*Ordering* me? Where do you come off doing that?"

"Detective Second Grade Barrington, you will comply with the lawful orders of your superiors, including me, Lieutenant Brian Doyle, do you understand me?"

"I'm calling the commissioner myself," Stone said.

"Since when does the commissioner take your phone calls?" Brian asked. "I heard never."

"Then why do you think he would approve active status for me?"

"After speaking with him myself," Brian said, "I think he believes it would be better to have you inside the tent, pissing out, than outside, pissing in. I believe Lyndon Johnson first said that, but it hasn't lost its meaning over the years."

"Oh, God," Stone said.

"By the way, don't leave your house; I've got an officer on the way over there to fit you out with some of today's electronic marvels and your own cute little vest."

"I won't let him in the house," Stone said.

"Oh, yes, you will," Brian said, then hung up.

Stone put down the phone, feeling a little sick at his stomach. First Dolce and now this.

Joan buzzed him. "Willie Leahy on one," she said.

That had been Stone's next call. "Hello, Willie?"

"Yes, Stone."

"What's up? Is Carrie all right?"

"She's still a pain in the ass, but she's fine."

"What's going on?"

"Carrie said you wanted us to have a conversation with the guy staked outside your house."

"Yes, that's right. Is he Max Long's?"

"Apparently not. Never heard of Max, in fact, and he doesn't even know anybody in Atlanta."

"Then what's he doing out there?"

"Watching you."

"For whom?"

"We couldn't get him to say, not even with Peter's hat pin, but *somebody's* paying him well."

"Oh, shit," Stone said.

"A woman. We got that much out of him."

"Shit again," Stone said. "Thanks, Willie. Oh, does he have any instructions to hurt me?"

"He wasn't armed, and I don't think he's the hand-to-hand-combat type."

"Thanks, Willie. Good-bye." Stone hung up. His very pleasant day had just gone to hell.

32

The police officer set a shirt-sized box on Stone's desk. "Take off your shirt," he commanded.

"Go fuck yourself and Brian Doyle, too," Stone replied politely.

The man fished an envelope from a pocket and handed it to Stone. The return address in the corner belonged to the police commissioner. "Read this," he said.

"I'm not touching that," Stone replied.

The man tore open the envelope and extracted a sheet of paper. "I'll read it to you," he said.

"I'm not listening," Stone replied, placing his fingers in his ears.

"Memo to personnel division!" the officer shouted. "'Detective Second Grade Stone Barrington, retired, is hereby restored to active duty

in the First Precinct under the command of Lieutenant Brian Doyle until further notice. Signed, et
cetera, et cetera.' Got it?"

"Stop shouting," Stone said, removing his fingers from his ears. "I can hear you."

The officer dug into another pocket and came
out with a wallet containing a detective's shield
and an ID card with a very old photograph of
Stone. "This is for you. Now take off your shirt.
Orders from Lieutenant Doyle."

"The police commissioner can't draft somebody
into the NYPD," Stone said.

"He can, if you're a retired cop on a pension,"
the officer said. "Read your retirement papers."

"Do they really say that?" Stone asked.

"Read 'em yourself. Now take off your shirt, or
I'll tear it off you."

Stone said a bad word and stood up, unbutton-
ing his shirt. "What's in the box?" he asked.

"The latest in fashion," the cop said, opening
the box and holding up a gray undergarment.
"They say it'll stop anything that doesn't have an
armor-piercing tip."

Stone fingered the garment. "Feels rough."

"I'll be gentle," the cop said. "Turn around."

Stone turned, and the man slipped the thing on
him. "Zip it up," he said.

The garment overlapped, like a double-breasted

jacket, giving double protection for most of the important internal organs.

"A perfect fit," the cop said. "You'll take it."

"Gee, thanks," Stone said.

"Now sit down; I've got to fit you with the earpiece."

"The what?"

The cop held out his hand, and a small bit of soft plastic lay in his palm with a wire protruding from it.

"People will be able to see that," Stone said. "Bad people."

"Nah," the cop said. "It fits too far down in your ear canal. The wire has a hook on the end; that's how you get it out: You hook the end of the wire in right here and just pull it out. My advice is, don't lose the wire." He turned Stone's head to one side, stuck the device into his right ear, removed the hook, and handed it to Stone.

"How do you turn it on?"

"It's on all the time. The battery is good for ten days."

"What do you do after ten days?"

"If you're still alive, I'll bring you a new one."

"Joan!" Stone shouted. "Bring me your makeup mirror!"

Joan came into the room with the mirror and handed it to him. "Cute underwear," she said.

"Oh, shut up." Stone held the mirror in position to look at his ear. "Can you see anything in my ear?"

She took back the mirror. "Yeah, daylight from the other side." She went back to her office.

"Nice lady," the cop said.

"Not always," Stone replied. "Take my advice and stay away from her."

"I heard that!" Joan yelled from her office.

"They heard it downtown," the cop said, tapping his ear. He pulled out a vibrating cell phone. "Yeah? Good deal." He closed the phone. "Like I said, they heard that downtown."

"How do I get the fucking thing out?" Stone asked.

"Use the little wire with the little hook on the end."

Stone began rooting around in his ear with the wire. "What am I supposed to hook it onto?"

"There's a little plastic loop. I showed you, remember?"

Stone made contact and extracted the earpiece.

"It's a good idea to wear it awhile, get used to it," the cop said. He took the thing from Stone and reinserted it. "By the way, if you put a phone to that ear, downtown can hear both ends of the conversation, and they can speak to you."

"That's just great," Stone said without enthusiasm. "It's time for you to go away now."

"Enjoy your badge, vest, and bug," the man said, and with a little wave, he left.

Joan came back into the office. "What's in your ear?" she asked.

"A bug."

"Put your head on your desk; I'll pour some water into your ear, and it'll float out."

"Not that kind of bug," Stone said.

"Oh, you're wired?"

"In a manner of speaking."

"What's the badge?" She picked up the commissioner's letter and read it, then giggled. "You're a cop again? How can you afford to pay me?"

"It isn't funny," Stone said. "Brian Doyle is trying to get me killed."

"What did you do to Brian Doyle?"

"Nothing much. I just handed him a very nice bust on a platter, and now he's pissed off because I made more work for him, so he did this to me."

"This is so much more fun than working in an actual law firm," Joan said.

"This *is* an actual law firm," Stone replied.

"If you say so," Joan said, flouncing back to her office.

"Don't flounce," Stone called down the hall after her.

"I'll flounce if I want to," she called back. "It's not like this is an actual law firm."

Stone tidied his desk, took off the vest, and put

his shirt on. The phone rang. He didn't wait for Joan to answer it; he just picked the phone up. "Hello?"

"It's Dino. Dinner?"

"Sure. See you there."

Another voice spoke on the line. "You boys have a nice evening, now."

"What was that?" Dino asked.

"I'll explain later. Good-bye—and go fuck yourself."

"What?" Dino said.

"That last part was for the other guy on the line."

"Oh."

Stone hung up and started looking for the little wire with the hook.

33

Stone arrived at Elaine's shortly after Dino, and they both ordered drinks.

"What was all that about on the phone earlier today?" Dino asked.

"It's too embarrassing to tell you about."

"Oh, good. Tell me about it."

"Well, first of all, I'm back on the force."

"*What?*"

"No kidding. The commissioner has reactivated me and assigned me to Brian Doyle. I've been drafted."

Dino began to laugh.

"You think this is funny?"

Dino tried to answer but couldn't. He was laughing too hard.

Elaine came over and sat down. "So, what's funny?"

Dino couldn't stop laughing but pointed at Stone.

"Yeah?" Elaine asked. "What about him?"

Stone produced his new badge and ID and showed them to her.

"You gotta be kidding," she said.

"It's only temporary."

"I'm amazed they'd have you back," she said.

"They insisted," Stone replied.

Dino continued to laugh.

"All right," Stone said, "you can shut up now."

Dino gradually got control of himself.

Stone stuck a finger in his right ear. "And they bugged me, too."

"You mean you're wearing a wire?" Dino asked, wiping tears away with his napkin.

"Right this minute."

"Where is it, in your crotch? And why do you have your finger in your ear?"

"It's not in my crotch—it's deep down in my ear, and I've got my finger in it so they can't hear us downtown."

"Why don't you just remove the thing?" Elaine asked.

"Because you need this little wire with a hook on it to get it out, and I lost the wire."

Dino began to laugh again.

"You look kind of silly with your finger in your ear," Elaine said.

"Do you want to be recorded downtown?" Stone asked.

"Not particularly."

"Well, if I take out my finger, they can hear everything you say."

"Okay," she said, "keep your finger in your ear. It's starting to look attractive that way."

Stone took a big slug of his drink. "God, I needed that."

"You know," Dino said, "this is the funniest evening I've ever spent in this joint. I've never laughed so much."

"It's good for you," Elaine said.

Stone looked up to see Mitzi Reynolds walk into the restaurant, and she headed for his table.

She gave him a kiss. "Don't tell me, you've lost the little wire, and you've got your finger in your ear so they can't hear you downtown."

"Drop it," Stone said.

She leaned over and whispered in his left ear. "Rita Gammage is outside in a limo; why don't you and I join her, and we'll go down to your house and have some fun."

"What, with this thing in my ear?"

"I'll show you how to get it out without the wire," she said.

"You're on," Stone replied. "Will you excuse us?" he said to Elaine and Dino before tossing back his drink.

"What, you're not eating?" Elaine said, looking shocked. "You took up a whole table, and you're not eating?"

"Dino's the one taking up the table," Stone said, "and he's eating. Maybe I'll eat later."

"What's going on?" Dino asked.

"Something's come up," Stone replied.

Mitzi leaned over and whispered, "Something's *going* to come up."

They left the restaurant and got into the rear seat of the limo. Rita was there, and she kissed Stone and continued to kiss him as they rode downtown, while Mitzi unzipped his fly and got a hand inside.

"This is working," she said.

Stone still had a finger in his ear. They got to his house and upstairs. "How do I get this thing out?" he asked. Rita was working on his buttons.

"Stand over the bedside table," she said, "with the right side of your head down. Stick your finger in your left ear, hold your nose with your right hand, take a deep breath and blow, but hold your breath in."

Stone followed the instructions and the bug popped out onto the table. "Thank God," he said.

Rita had his shirt off, and Mitzi was getting his trousers down. After another few seconds of the frantic shedding of clothes, the lights were turned off, and they were all naked in bed.

Stone lay on his back while somebody kissed him and somebody else had his penis in her mouth. He couldn't tell which was which in the dark, but it hardly mattered. He did what he could with his hands, then somebody mounted him and somebody else sat on his face. He could not remember such a medley of sensations.

After a while, they all lay in a heap, panting and sweating.

"So, Stone," somebody asked, "how was that?"

Stone was panting too hard to reply.

"Again?" the other voice said.

"You'd better start without me," Stone said, and they did, while he explored their bodies with his fingers, entering here and there. The two girls were talking to each other and to him, issuing instructions while they played; then they both seemed to come again, nearly simultaneously.

"Let's order a pizza," someone, perhaps Mitzi, said.

"What kind?" Rita asked.

"Domino's—Extravaganza, hold the green peppers," Stone said. But nobody could move, and they dozed off.

Stone was jerked awake by the noise the front doorbell was making on the telephone. He picked it up. "Yes?"

"Pizza delivery," a voice said.

"Hang on," Stone replied. He found a robe and some money, then went down to the front door and brought the pizza upstairs. The girls were sitting up in bed, and the light was on.

He handed them the box and got some beer out of the little bar fridge.

Mitzi was looking at him oddly. "I remember talking about pizza," she said, "but I don't remember anybody actually ordering it."

Rita opened the box and held up a slip of paper. "What is this?"

Stone took it and read it aloud. " 'From the guys at the First Precinct. Bravo!' "

"Uh-oh," Mitzi said, pointing at the bedside table.

The little bug sat there where Stone had dropped it, pointing toward the bed.

This time they rested and dozed a little.

34

Stone had never experienced a night quite like it. The pizza had revived them, and after having stuffed the ear bug into his sock drawer, they began again.

Now, at ten in the morning, they were having breakfast in Stone's garden, snug behind the ivy-covered brick walls on either side of them and facing the Turtle Bay Common Garden at the end.

The girls seemed fresh as a daisy—showered, shampooed, coifed, and made up, their clothes freshly pressed with Helene's iron. Stone was freshly showered, shaved, and dressed, too, but despite his having drunk a cup of strong Italian coffee—and he was now drinking his second—he felt tired, sore, and sleepy.

"Do you have any important work to do today, Stone?" Rita asked.

"Nothing that can't wait until tomorrow," he mumbled.

"Then maybe you should go back to bed," she said.

"And maybe we could join you!" Mitzi offered.

Stone held up his hands in a gesture of pleading. "Not today; maybe never again."

"We'll see about that," Mitzi said.

"What I need is a massage," Stone replied.

"I'd love to do that, but I've got a meeting at the precinct."

"Thank God," Stone said.

"And I have to go to work," Rita added.

"And good luck to you."

Mitzi spoke again. "The meeting downtown is about our next step with Derek Sharpe."

"What about Sig Larsen?" Stone asked.

"The feds have taken an interest in him. We're going to give them the recordings that you and I make."

"That you and I make when?" Stone asked.

"Perhaps as early as this evening," Mitzi said, "so you'd better get some rest."

"Has Brian Doyle explained to you how dangerous this is, and why?"

"You mean from Derek's rivals in the drug game?"

"I do."

"I'm not particularly worried about that; we'll be well protected. Still, I'm going to armor up, and you should, too."

Stone nodded.

The girls got up and took turns kissing him.

"And don't forget your ear bug," Mitzi said.

"I think you're going to get a hard time from the guys at your meeting," Stone said.

"Oh, no; they'll save that for you, and it will be mostly admiration. They have no idea who you were with last night."

"I hope not," Stone said, waving good-bye to them.

Later, Stone was so zonked out on the massage table that the masseuse had to turn him over when the time came. He had no memory of it when she finished. She helped him to the bed, and he fell into it, his body an oily overcooked noodle.

It was a little after five when Mitzi called. "We're on for tonight," she said.

"Do we have to go to Sharpe's studio? It's dangerous there."

"No, this is about Sig and my so-called money, so we're meeting at 740 Park at seven. After Sig makes his pitch and we've recorded that for the benefit of the feds, I'll take Derek aside and tell him I need some drugs for a friend."

"Good. Don't tell him you're a user, or he'll make you use some with witnesses around."

"My story is that I use only booze, which is all he's seen me use."

"What are you going to ask him for?"

"Half a pound of marijuana and five ounces of coke."

"Are you going to have cash?"

"I've already signed for it."

"You're not going to get a receipt for the drugs, you know."

"Don't worry, we have a bookkeeping way of keeping track of that."

"You should insist that he give you the drugs in the apartment, too, not at his place and especially not in a car."

"Yeah, yeah, Stone, I know. We've worked all that out. Can you be at the apartment at six thirty?"

"Yes, I guess so."

"We can have dinner afterward," she said.

"Okay. See you then." He hung up.

He had just gotten out of the shower when the phone rang. "Hello?"

"Hey, it's Carrie."

"Good afternoon."

"Dinner tonight?"

"I can't; business."

"Cop business?"

"If I told you, I'd have to kill you."

"How much longer is this going to go on?"

"I hope not much longer."

"Me, too. I've been working hard, and I miss you."

"Same here," he said, but he didn't sound very convincing.

"You sound funny."

"I just had a massage, and I'm half asleep."

"Oh."

"Any movement from Max?"

"Not a peep out of him. Tomorrow's the last day I'm using the Leahys. I really don't feel threatened."

"I would advise you to keep them on for another week, at least."

"They're expensive!"

"You can afford it. Max's check cleared, didn't it?"

"It's already in T-bills," she said.

"Keep them on for another week."

"We'll see. Bye-bye, sweetie." She hung up.

Stone struggled out of bed and into some clothes. He was about to leave his bedroom, but he remembered something. He went to his sock drawer, retrieved the ear bug, and slipped it into the ticket pocket of his jacket.

He arrived at Rita's apartment on time, and Mitzi greeted him with a big kiss. She leaned into his left ear. "You were sensational last night."

"So were you," he said, "but you don't have to whisper; the bug's in my pocket."

"Mine's in my ear," she whispered, "so be careful."

Stone nodded.

Mitzi held out her hand. "Give it to me," she mouthed.

He dug out the bug and handed it to her, and she stuffed it into his right ear and pushed it home with the tip of her little fingernail.

"All set, guys," she said. "They should be along in about twenty minutes," she said to the air. "In the meantime, all you're going to hear is the clink of ice cubes." She went to the bar and poured them each a Knob Creek.

Stone accepted it gratefully, then sat down to rest and wait.

35

At five minutes after the appointed time the phone in Rita's flat rang, and Mitzi picked it up. "Yes, please send them up," she said, then hung up.

"They're not going to like having a lawyer here," Stone said.

"I'll handle it," Mitzi replied. She went to the door and let in Derek Sharpe, Sig Larsen, and Sig's wife, Patti. This time there was no maid to serve, so Mitzi trotted out some pre-prepared hors d'oeuvres from the bar fridge, then handed Stone a bottle of vintage Krug champagne to open.

Stone was stunned that Mitzi would waste such a fine bottle on these people, but he uncorked it and filled their thin crystal flutes.

After some small talk Sig placed his briefcase on the coffee table, snapped it open, and lifted the lid.

"Mitzi, we have some very exciting things to talk with you about," he said, "but do you always have your attorney present at financial meetings?"

"Stone is not my attorney," Mitzi said. "He's just a friend I've been seeing a lot of who happens to be an attorney."

"Still," Larsen said, "I'd be grateful if we could meet alone with you. We'll be discussing some highly confidential information."

"Perhaps a good investment would interest me," Stone said.

"With respect, Stone," Larsen replied smoothly, "I think we're out of your league here."

"Stone," Mitzi said, "would you mind?"

"Not at all," Stone said, rising.

"Patti," Larsen said, "why don't you keep Stone company?"

Stone walked off down a hallway, having no idea where he was going, and Patti trotted along behind him. After a short walk, he emerged into a kitchen, a large room filled with the latest in appliances but decorated as though it were a part of someone's comfortable home. Stone opened a refrigerator door. "Can I get you something, Patti?" he asked.

Patti came over and looked into the fridge, placing her hand on his ass and squeezing. "*Mmmm.* Why don't you open that half bottle of champagne?" she asked.

Stone brought it out then searched the cabinets until he came up with a pair of flutes. He opened the half bottle and poured. There was a sofa in the room, but sexually sated as he was, he didn't want to share it with Patti, who, on their previous evening together, had been very seductive, so he took a kitchen stool at a counter in the center of the room.

Patti used a stool as a ladder that allowed her to sit on the butcher-block countertop beside him. "I'm glad we have a little time together," she said. "Last time we met I didn't see enough of you, so to speak."

Stone glanced at her hiked-up skirt, which hadn't been long to begin with and was now near crotch level. "Well, I'm seeing a lot of you now," he replied.

"Would you like to see more?" she asked playfully, hiking up the skirt until there was nothing between the countertop and her ass. She was not wearing panties, and her wax job was Brazilian.

"Is that the new fashion?" Stone asked. "No underwear?"

"Like it?" she asked.

"What's not to like?" Stone asked. "I'm sure it attracts a lot of attention."

"It attracts the attention of only those I'm attracted to," Patti replied.

"That's very flattering," Stone said. He couldn't

think of anything else to say. Clearly, Patti had been sent by her husband to keep him out of the living room, and she was using every technique at her disposal. "I hope no one suddenly walks in here," he said.

"Oh, no one will," Patti said. "It's obviously the maid's night off, and the others are talking about money, which will hold their attention for some time. I'd say we have at least an hour alone before someone invites us back to the living room."

"Perhaps you're right," Stone said, becoming aroused in spite of himself. He sipped his champagne. "Are you always so free with your favors?"

"When I feel like it," Patti replied, "and I feel like it tonight. In fact, I'm getting wet just thinking about it."

"Then I don't think you need me for a satisfactory resolution to your, ah, condition."

"Oh, I never need a man for that," she said, "but there are times when I'd like one, and this is one of those times."

Stone was short of words again.

"In fact," she said, "all you have to do is stand up. This counter is exactly the right height for you to just sort of walk into me."

"I suppose it is," Stone said.

She reached over and stroked his crotch. "And I can tell you're ready." She squeezed.

Stone twitched involuntarily. God knows, I'm

ready, he thought. He looked for a way out of this without insulting her. "Actually, I was quite active last night, and I'm pretty sore."

"I'll be gentle," she said. She took his arm, pulled him off the stool onto his feet, and kicked the stool away. She put a hand inside his belt and pulled him toward her.

"I really am very uncomfortable with this," Stone said, removing her hand from his belt.

"Then let's free things up," she said, reaching for his zipper.

"Let's not," Stone said, removing her hand again.

"Stone!" a male voice called from the hallway.

Stone turned. "Yes?" he called, trying not to sound relieved. When he turned back, Patti had hopped off the counter and returned her skirt to its full length.

Derek Sharpe walked into the kitchen. "Sig would like you back," he said.

"Sure," Stone replied, and followed Patti, who was following Derek.

She reached back for his crotch, but he evaded her by sidestepping.

Stone concentrated on reducing the bulge in his trousers, but it was difficult. He took a seat. "How can I help?"

"Derek," Mitzi said, "may I speak to you privately for a moment while Stone chats with Sig?"

"Of course," Sharpe replied. He got up and followed Mitzi from the room.

"I've been explaining to Mitzi how profitable it can be to invest in emerging technology," Larsen said.

"What sort of emerging technology did you have in mind?" Stone asked.

"A new software company that's developing software for the iPhone," Larsen replied.

"Lots of people are developing software for the iPhone," Stone said. "What's so different about this one?"

"It's very, very different," Larsen said, "but I'm afraid I can't go into that."

"Did you go into it with Mitzi?" he asked.

"In broad terms. I'm prepared to give her a prospectus, if she's interested, but she wanted your opinion."

"It's hard to have an opinion," Stone said, "when you're talking in generalities." He really wanted to be listening to the conversation between Sharpe and Mitzi, but at least downtown was listening.

"I'll make sure that you see the prospectus," Larsen said.

"Do you have a copy with you?"

"Yes, but that's Mitzi's; I'll send someone to you tomorrow with a copy that you can peruse, then return to me."

"You're being very cautious," Stone said.

"The opportunity is large; I don't want word to get around until I have my investors in this company."

"Good thinking," Stone said. Then it got very quiet. He caught Patti looking at his crotch and involuntarily crossed his legs.

36

Mitzi led Derek Sharpe into the study off the living room, and they sat down on a sofa. She turned to face him. "This is awkward," she said.

Derek placed a hand on her knee. "I don't want you ever to feel awkward with me."

She shifted her position to dislodge the hand. "I have some friends in Charleston who want something that I can't supply them," she said.

"And what would that be?" Sharpe asked.

"Something that I have no experience in obtaining," she said, "since I have no personal need for it."

"Well, if we were in the nineteen-twenties I'd think you were going to ask me where you could buy a case of Scotch."

"That's not a bad analogy," Mitzi said, trying to

seem more nervous than she felt. "It's just that I've been in New York for such a short time that my circle of acquaintance doesn't extend to people who . . . have a wider circle of acquaintance."

"Now it sounds as if you want me to provide you with a porno star for your personal use. Or that of your friends."

"That's not a good analogy," she said. "What they want is unavailable over the counter, so to speak."

"Are we talking about illegal recreational drugs?" Sharpe asked.

Mitzi heaved a big sign of apparent relief. "Yes," she said.

"In what sort of quantity?" he asked.

"Oh, just small stuff," she replied. "They asked me if I could find them half a pound each of marijuana and cocaine."

"Half a pound of either of those is not small stuff," Sharpe replied. "Together, they make a quantity that ordinary dealers might be reluctant to sell you."

"Oh?" Mitzi asked innocently. "Why? Don't they want to sell as much as possible?"

"Yes, but they become uncomfortable when someone asks for a quantity that could subject them to arrest for dealing."

"But that's what they do, isn't it?"

"They do, but the penalties for simple possession of a small amount of drugs for personal use and for possession in sufficient quantity to suggest intent to sell are very different, so they become cautious when such a request is made."

"If it's about money, that's not a problem," Mitzi said.

"It's not about money, Mitzi; it's more about discretion."

"Am I being indiscreet?" she asked, widening her eyes.

"Just a little."

"I'm sorry. I have no experience at this sort of thing," she said. "I apologize. Please forget I asked." She began to rise, but he stopped her.

"It's for that reason that I want to advise you," Sharpe said.

"All right, what is your advice?"

"First, we need to find some place to receive the package," Sharpe said.

"How about right here?" Mitzi asked, waving an arm. "This is not exactly a street corner."

"No, it's not," Sharpe admitted, "and this apartment would be a discreet place for you to accept delivery."

"Oh, good," she said, brightening.

"You understand that you must pay in cash?"

"I wasn't planning to write a check or use my American Express card," she said.

"Good, because you're talking about quite a lot of cash." He quoted a number.

"Goodness, that much?"

"That much."

"Well, it's not my money," she said. "I guess if that's the going rate, they'll have to pay it."

"Do you think they might object to that amount?" Sharpe asked.

"They left it entirely to my discretion, and I leave it entirely to yours, Derek."

"All right. How soon can you have the cash?"

"I already have it," Mitzi said. "I always keep some cash in the safe. I hate ATMs—such small bills!"

"I agree entirely," Sharpe said. "Would you like to give me the money now?"

"I believe I'd prefer cash on delivery," Mitzi said. "That's how my daddy brought me up."

"Well . . ."

"I'm good for it, Derek. I hope you know that."

"Of course I know that, Mitzi. I'll send the man over with it tomorrow morning, if that's all right."

Mitzi shook her head. "I'm perfectly happy to receive the package here," she said, "but I won't have some drug dealer in this apartment. I'd be scared to death."

"Well, suppose I send Hildy Parsons over with it."

Mitzi shook her head again. "I wouldn't ask Hildy to do that," she said. "I hardly know her."

"Oh, she won't know what's she's delivering," Sharpe said.

"I don't care about that. I mean, if she had some sort of accident and got caught with it I'd never forgive myself. I'm surprised you'd let her do such a thing, Derek."

"You want me to deliver it myself?" he asked.

She put her hand on his. "Oh, Derek, would you?"

"Well . . ."

"I'd be your friend forever," she said, squeezing his hand. "I might even buy a picture . . . or two."

Sharpe smiled broadly. "I'd be very happy to help you out," Derek said.

"And if my friends are happy with what they get, could you get them more in the future?"

"I'm sure I could," Derek said. "Tell me, how are they going to get the package back to Charleston?"

"They have their own jet," she said.

"Perfect," Sharpe said. "And you'll have the money ready?"

"Of course. I'll find something to put it in for you."

"That won't be necessary; I'll bring a briefcase."

"Oh, good," Mitzi said, standing up.

Sharpe stood up, too, and made a move toward her.

Mitzi hadn't been expecting it, and suddenly she found his lips on hers. It was a struggle not to grab a letter opener from the desk next to her and plunge it into his neck, but she stood still and let him put his tongue in her mouth for a moment, before pushing him gently away.

"Oh, Derek, you're so impulsive."

"I'll be more deliberate next time," he said.

"What would Hildy say?"

"I think Hildy might find it exciting," he said.

"Please don't bring her with you tomorrow," she said. "I would be embarrassed if she found out what we're doing."

"I'll come alone," he said, rubbing the back of his fingers across her right breast.

"Oh, good," Mitzi said, taking his arm and leading him back into the living room. "Did you say ten tomorrow morning?"

"That's good for me," he replied.

She squeezed his arm. "That's good for me, too."

37

Stone and Mitzi sat sipping bourbon at a front room table at the Park Avenue Café.

"So, it went well?"

"So well I can't believe it," Mitzi said. "Downtown was thrilled with what they got on tape." She smiled. "They enjoyed your tape, too."

"I'm afraid Patti had been given the task of keeping me out of the living room, and she was enjoying her work a little too much." He gave her an account.

Mitzi nearly choked on her Knob Creek. "I'm surprised you didn't succumb!"

"If you and Rita hadn't worn me out last night, I might well have."

"Men have no stamina," Mitzi said.

"I didn't know we were so weak."

She nodded. "One orgasm and you're done."

"Well, with a little time out in between I can sometimes manage a second round."

"Sex renders men unconscious," she said. "Whereas Rita and I could have gone on all night. In fact, we nearly did!"

"But I was unconscious."

"Well, yes."

"Maybe we had the wrong kind of threesome," she said.

"You mean . . ."

"Yes, you and another guy and me, lest you mistake my meaning."

"I have no interest in guys."

"Doesn't matter, as long as you're both interested in me."

"You're a glutton," Stone said.

"Sometimes. I've never seen the harm in getting everything you want."

"Hard to argue with that," Stone agreed.

"I mean, Rita and I gave you everything you wanted, didn't we?"

"Everything my heart desired."

"I rest my case."

Stone took a sip of his drink and tried to think of something to say.

"So," she said, "do you know another guy?"

"Dino is the only single man I know, and as much as I love him, I don't think I'd like to get into bed with him."

"I take your point. I guess I'll have to do my own hunting."

"I'm afraid so." Stone finally thought of something else to say. "By the way, tomorrow morning, you should have your people in place a couple of hours before you expect Derek Sharpe with the goods."

"Good idea."

"You could put one of them in a doorman's uniform."

She shook her head. "The co-op board would be outraged if they thought the NYPD was staging a drug bust in the building."

"Come to think of it, you're not going to need a lot of help to take Derek. You and Tom should be able to handle him; then you can walk him out, and the board will be none the wiser."

"I think that's best," Mitzi said. "I'd hate to get Rita thrown out of the building, especially when she's asked me to move in with her."

Stone almost choked on his bourbon. "You two are getting very chummy, aren't you?"

"Well, you're a witness to that, aren't you?"

"I know you like men, Mitzi, but does Rita?"

"You have to ask? She enjoyed you as much as I did."

"I suppose."

"Women are not embarrassed about being attracted to other women. Men, on the other hand, are worried that someone will think they're gay."

"That's perfectly true," Stone admitted, "but I wouldn't have thought you and Rita . . ."

"Rita and me *sometimes*," Mitzi said. "Anyway, it's nice for a girl to have a roommate, somebody to sit around in pajamas with, eating chocolates."

"And each other."

"That, too. Nothing wrong with a full life."

Stone had nothing further to contribute on the subject. "I suppose Brian is pleased with the way your case is going," he said lamely.

"He'd sure better be," Mitzi said. "When we tag Derek, the tabloids are going to go nuts, and he'll be the guy standing in front of the cameras. He'll get noticed at One Police Plaza."

"I guess he'll enjoy that," Stone said. "Is he bucking for captain?"

"You bet your ass he is," Mitzi said, laughing. "And if this case puts him over the top, I'm never going to let him forget it!"

"What about Sig Larsen?" Stone asked.

"I told you, Brian isn't interested in him. He's got the U.S. Attorney's office on pins and needles, though. After Bernie Madoff they think it's fashionable to bring in financial scam artists."

"Tell Brian I don't think he should mention my name to the U.S. Attorney."

"The beautiful blonde? Why not?"

"Well, a couple of years ago, right after she got the job, we had a little thing that ended up getting us into the papers."

Mitzi looked shocked. "That was *you*? You actually got videotaped in bed with her?"

"Fortunately, my face was out of the frame, but she got recognized. She was the one on top at the time."

Mitzi hooted. "Brian is going to love this!"

"Just tell him it's in his interests not to bring my name into it. By the way, did you keep a copy of Sig's prospectus?"

"No, he wouldn't let me. I read most of it, and it sounds very appetizing, if you've got a lot of money to throw around."

"He said he would send someone to my office with a copy that I could read but not keep."

"I know Brian would love it if you found a way to make a copy," Mitzi said.

"I don't live to make Brian Doyle happy," Stone said.

"He loved it that he got you put back on active duty."

Stone winced. "He loves it that he can use that to give me orders."

"Exactly."

"Don't worry; when he starts doing that, I'll ignore them."

"Don't piss him off, Stone; I've still got to live with him."

"Do you and Brian have something going on?"

"A long time ago," she said, "before he made lieutenant. He was my first partner, assigned to break me in."

"And he did?"

"In a manner of speaking," she said with a sly smile.

38

Stone woke up, exhausted again. He was going to have to get some real rest, he thought, as he swung his legs over the side of the well-mussed bed. He could smell bacon frying.

Mitzi had left him a razor and toothbrush in her bathroom. He shaved, showered, and then looked for his clothes. Nowhere in sight. He found a robe in a closet and walked down to the kitchen. Rita was cooking, and Mitzi was ironing. A woman he didn't know was sitting at the counter having coffee.

"You're up!" Mitzi said.

"Sort of. I'm pretty tired."

Rita laughed. "You'd be even more tired if I'd known you were in the apartment."

"Good morning," Stone said to the attractive young woman at the counter.

"Oh, Stone," Rita said. "This is my friend Emma Suess. She served you canapés the first time you were here, in the maid's uniform?"

"How do you do," Emma said, extending a hand. "I'm not really a maid; I'm an actress. I was playing the role of maid that night."

"I'm pleased to meet you, Emma," Stone said. He wondered what other roles she played around the house.

Mitzi handed him his freshly ironed shorts and shirt. "I'll be done with your suit in a minute."

Stone got into them, then his pants, when she had finished.

"Now don't you feel all fresh and new?" Mitzi asked.

"Fresh, maybe, but not new."

"Tom will be here around nine."

Rita put eggs and bacon on the counter, and they all ate with gusto.

"So," Rita said, "you're going to put away Mr. Derek Sharpe this morning."

"We hope," Stone said.

"For sure," Mitzi interjected.

"Let's not get ahead of ourselves," Stone said.

"We've got the guy boxed, Stone. Why do you sound so discouraged?"

"I'm not discouraged. I just don't know what you and Sharpe said to each other last night and if it's going to translate into a successful prosecution.

One thing drug dealers always have is plenty of cash for the best lawyers."

"Once we nail him with the goods, he'll cop a plea, and we'll put him away for ten years."

"The Rockefeller laws have been repealed," Stone said, "or hadn't you heard about that? A conviction doesn't mean an automatic ten-year sentence anymore; the judge is going to have discretion."

"Are you saying a judge can be bought?"

"That, too," Stone replied.

"I talked to Brian this morning," Mitzi said. "The minute we've got the cuffs on Sharpe they'll be in his building with a search warrant, and we'll find his stash. I'll bet it's a lot."

"I'll bet it's not in the building," Stone said. "Sharpe is not stupid. I think you'd do better to let this morning's arrest slide, then set up another one in a few days and nail him then."

"So why didn't you mention this last night?"

"I was thinking about other things last night."

"That's sweet of you, but since you didn't get your two cents in, we'll have to go with it as it is."

"You can call Brian and suggest a new plan."

"He wouldn't go for it."

"At least you'd have your ass covered if this goes wrong."

"Well," she said, "there's a lot to be said for having your ass covered."

"Call him," Stone said.

Mitzi took her plate and went into another room.

Rita took a sip of her coffee and looked at Stone over the brim of the cup. "Now she's going to be all pissed off," she said. "You're spoiling her party."

"I'm trying to protect her from Brian Doyle," Stone said.

"You think she needs protecting from her boss?"

"Brian is a . . . mercurial guy, and if this goes wrong, he's not going to take the blame."

"And if it goes wrong, what happens to Hildy Parsons?"

"There's that, too," Stone said. "And that's my principal interest in all this."

"Mine, too."

Mitzi came back into the room. "Brian says to go ahead with the buy but not to bust Sharpe, just let him walk out with the money."

"Are the bills marked?"

"If they are, Brian didn't tell me."

"I wouldn't be surprised if Sharpe owns an ultraviolet light," Stone said. "He'll be looking for marks."

"Too late to change plans now," Mitzi said. She went to the big Sub-Zero fridge, opened the freezer, and took out a large plastic bag.

"That's your safe?" Stone asked.

"I've got a real safe," Rita said. "My jewelry's in it, but there's room for that, too."

Stone took the bag and fished out a bundle of hundred-dollar bills. He flipped through them like a deck of cards. "I can't see anything. I don't suppose you have an ultraviolet light?"

"Nope," Rita said.

"Where's the safe?"

"In the study," Rita replied.

"Why don't you put this in the safe and let Sharpe see you take it out? It'll be good for his morale."

"What would be good for his morale is for me to fuck him," Mitzi said. "He's already made a big pass at me, and I'm expecting more of the same this morning."

"Slap him hard across the chops," Stone said.

"I think that would just make him mad."

"Rita, does the phone system in the apartment allow you to call between extensions?"

"Yes."

"What's the extension number for the study?"

"Eleven."

"Okay, Mitzi," Stone said, "I'm going to give you three minutes with Sharpe, then call that extension. Answer it, say, 'Send him up,' and tell Sharpe your driver is on the way up."

"Okay."

"What if she's unable to answer the phone?" Rita asked.

"Then I'll interrupt you," Stone said. "By that time you should have completed the deal. Make sure you do that immediately after he arrives. Tell him you have to be somewhere. Make up something."

"What if Sharpe wants to meet your friends from Charleston?" Rita asked.

"I'll tell him they're just in town for the day and have a full schedule," Mitzi replied.

"I'm sure you can handle anything he throws at you," Stone said.

"I'm moved by your confidence in me, sir," Mitzi said, curtseying.

Rita spoke up. "If he throws his dick at you, there's a large pair of scissors on the desk in the study."

"Always use the right tools," Mitzi said. "That's what my daddy always told me."

The phone rang, and Rita answered. "Send him up," she said.

Stone looked at his watch. "Already?"

"It's Tom," Rita said. "Don't have a heart attack."

"What do you want me to do?" Emma asked.

"Put on your maid's uniform, just in case Sharpe comes to the kitchen."

Emma put down her coffee cup and left the room. "Be right back," she said.

Mitzi looked at Stone. "You're more nervous than I am," she said.

"I have a better imagination than you do," Stone replied. "I can think of a dozen things that can go wrong."

39

Tom arrived and was given a croissant and some coffee. "Are you playing in this game?" he asked Stone.

"Only if I'm needed from the bench," Stone replied.

Emma returned to the kitchen wearing a maid's uniform, but not the one she had worn when she served canapés. The skirt was short, the stockings were black fishnet, and the bodice was tight and featured lots of cleavage.

Stone burst out laughing. "Can you come and play maid at my house?" he asked.

"Emma," Rita said, pointing at the door, "you get out of that garb right now and put on the uniform I gave you. This is not a French farce."

"I don't know about that," Stone said, watching her go.

The phone rang, and Mitzi picked it up. "Send him up," she said, then hung up. "It's Sharpe. He's half an hour early."

"Rita," Stone said, "get that money into the safe and make sure that Mitzi knows how to open it—then get to your room." The two women ran out of the kitchen.

Emma came back wearing a more prosaic maid's uniform.

"Emma," Stone said, "as soon as Rita is back in her room, let Sharpe in, show him to the study, and get back here. You, Tom, and I will be drinking coffee together, should he decide to have a look around."

"Got it," Emma said.

"Okay!" Rita yelled from down the hall just as the doorbell rang.

"You're on," Stone said to Emma, and she started down the hall.

Mitzi sat down at the desk in the study and began writing a letter to her father on Rita's creamy stationery. She heard Emma go to the front door, and a moment later there was a knock on the study door. "Come in," Mitzi said.

Emma opened the door and stepped inside. "Miss Reynolds, Mr. Sharpe is here." She let him in, backed out, and closed the door.

Sharpe stood by the door holding a large briefcase and looking nervous. "You didn't tell me the maid would be here."

"She's here every day," Mitzi said.

"Who else is in the apartment?"

"Just the maid and Stone. He's down the hall in the kitchen having breakfast."

"I don't think you understand how sensitive this transaction is," Sharpe said.

"I don't think you understand that nobody in the kitchen cares what you and I are doing in here," Mitzi said. She stood, slid back a shelf of fake book spines, and started opening the safe. "I'm glad you're early," she said. "I've got things to do this morning. Did you bring the drugs?"

"Do you have the money?"

Mitzi opened the safe, removed a brown envelope, and took out several bundles of bills. "There you are," she said. "Count it, and let's get this done." She left the safe open and kept the desk between them.

Sharpe set his briefcase on the desk, picked up some bills, and began counting them. "It's not that I don't trust you," he said, "but my supplier would take offense if I didn't show up with the correct amount."

"I understand," Mitzi said, sitting down again.

Sharpe continued to count. "So you and Stone are an item, huh?"

"You've seen us together before. I like him a lot."

"Didn't he used to be a cop?"

"He retired years ago, I believe; now he's a lawyer."

"So he's not going to come in here and bust me?"

Mitzi laughed. "No, he is not."

Sharpe finished counting the money. He opened his briefcase and put the bills inside, then closed it.

"And where are the goods?" Mitzi asked.

"You'll get them as soon as I deliver the money," Sharpe said.

"Our deal was cash on delivery," Mitzi said. "You've got the cash, now deliver."

"I'll be back in an hour."

"I won't be here in an hour," Mitzi said. "The deal's off; leave the money on the desk and go."

"Now you listen to me . . ." Sharpe began.

The phone rang, and Mitzi picked it up. "Hello?"

"Everything all right?" Stone asked.

"Yes," she replied. "Send him up, please." She hung up. "My driver is on the way up," she said to Sharpe. "And you're not leaving here with my money."

Sharpe opened the briefcase again and extracted two packages wrapped in opaque plastic and sealed with tape. "I was only joking," he said. "Here are your goods. I'll be going."

"Just a minute," Mitzi said, picking up the large

pair of brass scissors on the desk. She began working on the tape of the larger package.

"I thought you were in a hurry," Sharpe said nervously.

"I am, but I just want to see this stuff." She got the package open and smelled it. "That smells like marijuana," she said.

"The finest stuff, I promise you," Sharpe said.

Mitzi began working on the other package.

There was a knock on the door. "Ms. Reynolds?"

Sharpe looked like a trapped rabbit.

"Tom, please wait in the kitchen," Mitzi called back. "I'll be ready in a minute." She continued to work on the smaller package and finally got it open. "You're supposed to taste this, aren't you?"

"Lick your finger, dip it in, and taste."

Mitzi did so. "What's it supposed to taste like?"

"Exactly what it tastes like."

"Is it pure?"

"Of course not. It would take your head off if it were pure. It's been cut; all cocaine is cut. Don't worry, your friends will love it."

"Okay, if you say so," Mitzi said. She put the two packages in the safe, closed it, and turned the handle. "Thank you very much, Derek," she said. "I believe that concludes our business."

"I believe it does," Sharpe said, still looking as though he might be arrested.

"If you'll excuse me, I have an appointment."

"Sure, let me know if you want more."

"I'll see what my friends think," she said. "Come, I'll show you out." She walked him through the living room and to the front door. "See you soon," she said, giving him a kiss on the cheek.

Sharpe seemed too nervous to kiss her back or grope her. "Bye-bye," he said.

Mitzi closed the door behind him, leaned on it, and heaved a big sigh. Then she walked down the hall to the kitchen, where Tom, Emma, and Stone were waiting.

"He was as nervous as a cat," she said, "and he tried to hold out on me, but we got it done."

"He won't be so nervous next time," Stone said.

40

Derek Sharp started sweating in the elevator, and when he hit the lobby he had to will himself not to run. His car was waiting where he had left it, guarded by the doorman to whom he had given a hundred-dollar bill.

He looked up and down Park Avenue for something that could be an unmarked police car. Across the avenue a garbage truck was loading the trash from another building, and one of the sanitation workers seemed to look at him for a long time. The man wiped his face with his sleeve and seemed to pause for a moment with his wrist to his lips. Was he speaking into a microphone?

Sharpe's hands were shaking, and he had trouble getting the key into the ignition, but he finally got the Mercedes started. He pulled into traffic, and, looking more into the rearview mirror than ahead, he made it down Park a couple of blocks to where the light was just turning red. He floored the car and, tires squealing, made a hard left turn before the uptown traffic could block his progress. Anybody following him would have to wait for the light to change to make that turn.

He drove across town to Second Avenue and turned downtown just as the light changed, still watching his rearview mirror. It seemed safe, but that was what they wanted him to think, wasn't it? Now he would have a ten-block head start, chasing green lights, which were set to a thirty-mile-an-hour speed. He was feeling very pleased with himself until he finally had to stop for a light, and a blue Crown Victoria with two men dressed in business suits in the front seat pulled up beside him. It was an unmarked police car, no doubt about it.

Sharpe contemplated making a left and running, but he was frozen with fear. Then the light changed, and the blue car pulled away from him and continued down Second Avenue. He was startled by a horn from behind him and got the car moving again. He cut across three lanes of traffic and made a right. When he got to Lexington Avenue, he turned downtown again. The cops in that car had probably not been looking for him, he thought; then he started looking down Lex for the car, wondering if they were going to drive across town and cut in front of him.

When he finally got downtown to his building, after suspecting a dozen other vehicles along the way, he drove around the block twice before using the remote control to open the garage door on the ground floor of his building. Only when the steel door had closed behind him did he feel safe.

He took the big lift up to his studio and let himself in. Hildy was stretched out on a sofa at the end of the big room, which covered the width of the building.

"How did your business go?" she asked, yawning.

"Very well," he replied. "Has anyone come to the door?"

"No, it's been very quiet."

"Any phone calls, especially with the caller hanging up?"

"The answering machine took a couple of calls," she said. "Messages were left."

Sharpe went to the machine and replayed the messages, both routine calls from an arts material supplier and a stationer. He walked from the studio into the office, where two middle-aged women worked keeping books and paying bills, then on to the lower level of his apartment.

He went into the kitchen, opened the refrigerator door, grabbed a handle inside, and rolled the big unit away from the wall. Behind it was a cutout in the Sheetrock, with the cutout replaced. He took a small knife from his pocket and pried out the loose area, revealing a large Fort Knox safe. He entered the code into the keypad, spun the wheel, and swung open the double doors. Inside were stacks of tightly packed plastic bags in the lower half and papers and stacks of cash above. He opened his briefcase, removed the brown envelope, and stacked the newly earned money on a shelf. Then he took a ledger from the safe and made a coded entry. He closed the door, replaced the Sheetrock, wheeled the big refrigerator back into its place, and then leaned against it and mopped his brow.

He was getting paranoid, he thought. He had never made such a large delivery so far from his base, and the experience had wrecked him. The thought of the money in the safe made him feel better, though. How could he have thought that Mitzi Reynolds could be a cop?

Sharpe went upstairs and changed into paint-stained work clothes; then he went back to the studio, where he found Sig Larsen seated next to Hildy on the old sofa waiting for him. "Hildy, make yourself scarce," he said to her. "Sig and I have to talk."

Hildy left the room without a word.

Sharpe collapsed on the sofa. "Jesus," he said, mopping his brow again. "I must be getting old."

"What's wrong?" Larsen asked.

"I made that delivery to Mitzi uptown," he said, "and every cell in my body was in alarm mode. Once I was there I thought I'd be busted with all that product. For a minute, I even thought that Mitzi might be a cop."

"That's called paranoia," Larsen said. "If Mitzi is a cop, then I'm Warren Buffett."

"Or maybe Stone, who used to be a cop," Sharpe said. "He was there for the buy, but he was in the kitchen. He must have stayed the night."

"But you got out okay?"

"Yeah, but then I thought every car I saw was the cops."

"Derek, you need to take some time off," Larsen said. "Why don't you take Patti to a hotel and fuck her for a couple of days? She could use it and, apparently, so could you."

"So could Hildy, but it's so boring with her, why bother?"

"When does she come into the money?"

"In a few weeks. She's cagey about when her birthday is, so I don't know exactly."

"I can't wait," Larsen said. "I want her out of our lives."

"So do I," Sharpe replied. "You can't imagine."

"I can imagine. Patti's got to go, too; she's beginning to take being called my wife seriously. If we can scam both Hildy and Mitzi we'll have enough to get out of this town to some place with nice weather and no extradition treaty with the United States."

"And where is that going to be?"

"How does Brazil strike you?"

"I could never learn to speak Portuguese," Sharpe replied.

"How about Spanish?"

"I've got my Tex-Mex from back home; I could get by on that."

"Let me do some research."

"You'd better research some passports for us, too."

"The trick is to leave legally, with our own passports, before the feds or the cops shut us down."

"We've got to move some cash soon," Sharpe said. "The safe is full."

"Sell the product that's in there, and I'll take a couple of suitcases down to the Bahamas and make the hop to the Caymans."

"Not without me, you won't," Sharpe said. "Anyway, the jet charter is cheaper per person, if you have a few people aboard."

"You don't think like an accountant, Derek."

"Have you sent that prospectus to Stone Barrington?" Sharpe asked.

"It's on the way uptown as we speak."

"You think he has any money?"

"Not enough for us to bother with," Larsen said.

41

Stone had made it home and was at his desk when Joan buzzed him.

"A man to see you. He says he's from Sig Larsen," Joan said on the intercom.

"Send him in," Stone replied.

The man did not look like someone from a messenger service; he looked like someone from the Russian mob, tall and thick. "Good morning," he said in unaccented English. He handed Stone an envelope. "Mr. Larsen says you can read this, but you can't copy it; I have to take it back with me."

"Would you like some coffee?" Stone asked.

"Yes, thank you." The man took the offered chair. "Black, please."

Stone buzzed Joan and asked for a large coffee, and she brought it in.

The proposal was forty-one pages long, and Stone began to read every line.

The man finished his coffee and began to look restless.

Stone was on page eight.

"Could I use a restroom?" the man asked.

"Right over there," Stone said, pointing to a door.

The man got up, went to the toilet, and closed the door.

Stone picked up the proposal and ran down the hall to Joan's office. She watched incredulously while he shoved the stack of papers into the Xerox machine and pressed the button. "How many pages a minute does this thing copy?"

"I don't know, maybe twenty-five."

Stone tapped his foot impatiently, and when the last copy came out he grabbed the original and ran back to his office. He had just sat down when the man let himself out of the toilet.

"Sorry this is taking so long," Stone said.

"Take your time," the man replied.

Stone began reading faster, then scanning. Finally, he restacked the sheets and handed them to the man. "Tell Sig thanks," he said.

The man returned the pages to their envelope and left.

Stone called Mitzi.

"Hello?"

"Hi, it's Stone. Sig sent over his proposal, and I read it."

"What was it like?"

"Too good to be true. There is no corporation or company mentioned, no names of the principals, and no audited balance sheet."

"A scam, then?"

"Of course, what did you expect?"

"And you weren't allowed to copy it?"

"I wasn't allowed, but I copied it anyway, while the messenger was in the john."

"Oh, good. Will you fax it to the U.S. Attorney's office?"

"No, but I'll give it to you, and you can fax it to her without mentioning my name in any context."

"Is it really that bad between you and her?"

"I don't know, and I don't want to find out."

"Okay, here's the fax number at the apartment." She gave it to him. "Dinner tonight?"

"Can't tonight."

"Tomorrow?"

"Let me call you; I'm still in recovery."

She laughed. "Poor baby."

"Bye-bye," Stone said. He hung up, gave Joan the fax number, and asked her to send the document to Mitzi.

"Sure," Joan said. "Oh, a delivery arrived for you."

"Bring it in."

Joan came in holding a crystal vase containing at least two dozen red roses. "Here's the card," she said, then stood waiting while he read it.

With fond memories and anticipation

The card didn't need a signature; Stone immediately recognized Dolce's bold, slanted handwriting.

"Who?" Joan asked.

"Will you kindly send these to the nearest hospital or old folks' home?" Stone said.

"I thought so," Joan said. "I saw her across the street yesterday afternoon, looking as if she was trying to decide whether to come over here."

Stone was further alarmed. "Was she alone?"

"There was a large man with her."

"Her keeper," Stone said. "Eduardo is allowing her out of the house for shopping trips."

"Oh, then she must be a lot better," Joan said.

"Don't you believe it," Stone replied. "I saw the look in her eyes: She's still mad dog crazy."

Joan looked worried. "Oh, God, what should I do if I see her out there again?"

Stone thought about that. "I don't know."

"Well, thanks, that's very helpful. Should I call the cops or just shoot her?"

"Neither of those options works for me," Stone said. "Are you on friendly terms with Eduardo's secretary?"

"Well, I imagine her as some sort of Sicilian bat, hanging upside down in his house, but she's civil, in an abrupt sort of way."

"Call her and tell her you didn't want to mention this to me, but Dolce is hanging around my house."

"That's taking yourself out of it very nicely," she said.

"Look, I do *not* want to call Eduardo and tell him his lunatic daughter is stalking me."

"No, you want me to do it."

"No, just mention it to his secretary in the terms I outlined, and I'm sure word will get to Eduardo in the proper manner."

"You know I have a .45 in my desk drawer, don't you?"

"Yes, of course I know it. Have I ever mentioned to you the amount of paperwork and the number of court appearances required to deal with charges of murder and possessing an illegal weapon?"

"It's not illegal; you got me a license, remember? I can even carry it around."

"Getting you that license the way I got it is almost as difficult to deal with as a murder charge," Stone said. "So for God's sake, don't shoot Dolce—or anybody else."

"I'll try not to," Joan said, and flounced out.

"And don't flounce!" Stone called after her.

Joan buzzed again. "Bob Cantor on one."

"Hello, Bob, what's up?"

"I'll tell you what's down," Bob said, "the spirits of the Leahy boys."

"What's the problem?"

"They're bored stiff. They're saying I promised they could shoot somebody, but there's nobody there."

"Gee, I'm sorry they're not being entertained by shooting people. You'd think they would be happy they're not being shot *at*."

"What are you gonna do?"

"All right, tell them to drop the surveillance on Carrie, and tell them to explain carefully to her that they think there's no longer any danger."

"Oh, thank you!" Bob said with a faked sob. "Bye-bye." He hung up.

Stone tried to think of something to do.

42

Stone was having a sandwich in the kitchen when the phone rang. Joan was at lunch, so he picked it up. "Stone Barrington."

"It's Tiffany Baldwin, Stone," said the U.S. Attorney for the Southern District of New York.

"Hello, Tiff," he said warily. "I didn't know you were speaking to me."

"Well, you made up for everything by sending me this very nice fax this morning."

How the hell did she know it came from him? "Which fax was that?"

"The one about this character, Sig Larsen."

"Oh, that one."

"I know you sent it to the NYPD first, but when I got it, it still had your imprint at the top from your fax machine."

"Oh."

"This is a very interesting situation," she said.

"Is it?"

"Yes, it's the first I've heard of it."

"I thought the NYPD had mentioned Larsen's name to you."

"Maybe to a minion, but it didn't float up to my desk until your fax came in."

"I'm happy to be of help."

"Have you actually met this Larsen?"

"Yes, I have."

"What did you think of him?"

"A very slick con man, I thought."

"And he's trying to fleece your client?"

Stone didn't want to pour out everything about Mitzi's undercover work; he didn't know if she had heard about that. "In a manner of speaking," he said.

"I assume it's a she."

"I don't know why you assume that, but she is a she."

"It's always a she with you, isn't it, Stone?"

"Sig Larsen isn't a she."

"And how did you happen across Mr. Larsen?"

"I was looking into an associate of his for a client, when he turned up."

"And who is his associate?"

"A so-called artist named Derek Sharpe."

"I've heard of him. Is he complicit in this scam?"

"He introduced me to Larsen, and he was present when Larsen first mentioned this investment."

"You think Sharpe knows it's a scam?"

"Based on what I've seen and heard of him, I'm prepared to believe the worst about Mr. Sharpe."

"So, I should investigate them both?"

"Tiff, I can't tell you what to investigate; if you like Larsen and Sharpe, go get 'em. I'd be happy to see them both off the street for an extended period."

"You mean your client would be happy?"

"Him, too."

"I thought it was a she."

"There's a he and a she; I don't believe they've met."

"Tell me about the she."

"She's from the South, new in the city, wealthy, and Larsen and Sharpe must think she's vulnerable."

"Is she?"

"Not really."

"Then you're giving her good advice."

"I try."

"What is her name?"

"I can't divulge that without her permission."

"Then get her permission."

"Next time I speak to her I'll ask her if she'd like to be an undercover agent for the federal government."

"You can be smoother than that, Stone."

"I find that when someone wants to embroil my client in what might be a dangerous situation it's better to be blunt about what's wanted of her."

"All right, be blunt with her, but do it quick, all right?"

"I'll do my best."

"Dinner sometime, Stone? Without the cameras, I mean."

"Tiff, I tried to explain that the presence of cameras in my bedroom was unknown to me, but you wouldn't listen."

"My investigation of the event confirmed your claim of innocence, if not *total* innocence."

"I'm relieved to hear it."

"We had some good times," she said. "It might be fun to revisit them."

"Right now, Tiff, I'm embroiled in a number of things that are creating great pressures on my time. Maybe in a few weeks." She might forget about it in a few weeks.

"I'll look forward to it," Tiffany said. "Good-bye."

Stone hung up and dialed Mitzi's cell phone.

"Hello?"

"I've just had a phone call from the U.S. Attorney," he said.

"Oh?"

"Don't play innocent with me. You failed to re-

move my name from that prospectus before you
faxed it to her."

"I asked Brian to do that," she said. "I'm sorry,
if he didn't."

"I might have known," Stone said. "Ms. Baldwin would like you to be an undercover agent for
her in the pursuit of Sig Larsen. What shall I tell
her?"

"Does she know I'm a cop?"

"No."

"I'd better speak to Brian about this, then."

"Do it now; Tiffany is an impatient woman."

"You should know," Mitzi said, with a vocal
leer. "I'll get back to you." She hung up.

Stone went back to his sandwich, which had
grown cold. He nuked it for a few seconds, then
started to eat again. The phone rang.

"Stone Barrington."

"It's Brian Doyle, your commanding officer."

"Go fuck yourself, commander."

"I hear you've got the U.S. Attorney trying to
poach one of my people."

"You sent her the fucking prospectus without
taking my name off it, as requested. That's why she
called me."

"What did you tell her?"

"Nothing. I refused her to give her my client's—
Mitzi's—name. She wants to use her to get at
Larsen."

"I'm using her to get at Sharpe."

"Look, if you'd shown some interest in busting Larsen, this wouldn't have happened. Trust me, Tiffany Baldwin is going to gnaw away at this case until she knows everything, so my advice to you is to call her right now and offer to share the fruits of your investigation and the use of your undercover officer in making a federal case against Larsen. Maybe Sharpe, too. It's an easier way for you to get him off the street."

"But without the credit."

"So work out a credit-sharing plan with Tiff. She'll keep her word if you get it in writing."

"Why did you get me into this shit, Stone?"

"*You* got you into this shit, Brian, and unless you call Ms. Baldwin right now, she's liable to approach you through the commissioner. It would be a lot better if you could tell the commissioner you got the feds involved and worked out a deal with them."

Doyle didn't say anything for a moment.

"Look," Stone said, "if she calls me back, I'm going to have to tell her more."

"Don't threaten me, Stone."

"It's how it is, Brian. Now go deal with it." Stone hung up. His sandwich was cold again.

43

Stone sat at Elaine's with Dino, gulping bourbon.

"What's the matter?" Dino asked.

"What's the matter?" Stone made a moue. "Well, let's see: I've been assigned by Eggers to save a fair damsel from the clutches of an evil fortune plunderer, as a result of which I've become embroiled in an NYPD undercover drug operation; I've been shanghaied back into the department, reporting to Brian Doyle, of all people; I've been fucking his undercover detective and her girlfriend at the same time, all the while trying to protect Carrie Cox from her evil ex-husband while fucking her; Tiffany Baldwin has reared her beautiful but addled head again and wants me to fuck her, and she's going to try to shanghai me into working on *her* undercover operation to bust Sig Larsen. Let's see, did I leave out anything?"

"Well, mostly, it sounds as if you're fucking every woman in sight. What else is new?"

"Two undercover operations."

"They don't sound all that daunting."

"They're plenty daunting, believe me; multiple opportunities to get one or more of these women killed along with myself."

"Wear armor."

"Brian Doyle has thoughtfully provided that along with an ear bug that's hell to get out once it's in. Did I mention that?"

"I don't remember," Dino said. "Have another drink." He waved at a waiter.

"You talked me into it," Stone said, draining his glass and setting it aside to make room for another, which arrived with lightning speed. "It's hot in here," he said to the waiter. "Please make it cooler." He patted his forehead with his napkin. "It's always too hot in here."

"It's the bourbon," Dino said, "and all this talk about sex."

"I used to enjoy sex," Stone said disconsolately.

"Don't you still?"

"There are too many demands being made on me."

"Most guys would be very happy to have those demands made on them."

"Maybe I'll just go up to the Maine house for a while," Stone said. "Nobody would think of looking for me there this time of year."

"That's because you'd freeze your ass off this time of year," Dino pointed out. "You wouldn't enjoy it; you don't like extremes of temperature."

"It seems a small price to pay for a little peace."

Eggers came through the front door and headed for their table.

Stone looked up. "Oh, shit."

Eggers hung up his coat and sat down. "Evening, gentlemen."

"Evening," Dino said.

Stone just stared into his drink.

"What's wrong with him?" Eggers asked Dino.

"He feels put upon," Dino replied.

"Put upon?"

"That's it, put upon."

"I suppose I'm the putter-upon?"

"One of several, I believe," Dino said.

Stone took a gulp of his Knob Creek.

"Has he been drinking like that all evening?" Eggers asked.

"No," Dino replied, "just for the last half hour, but the night is young."

"You didn't return my phone call, Stone," Eggers said.

"What phone call?"

"Don't you ever get your messages? I sent you an e-mail, too."

"I forgot to look at my e-mail."

"What's wrong with you, boy?"

"Too much sex from too many women," Dino offered.

"Good God!" Eggers said. "You haven't been fucking our client's daughter, have you?"

"No!" Stone said. "I haven't laid a hand on her."

"She's the exception to the rule," Dino said.

"Because I don't know how I would explain that to Philip Parsons," Eggers said.

"Since it's not happening, you won't have to explain it," Stone said, looking up from his glass.

"Well, it's a relief to hear that you make an exception now and then. Or is Hildy the first?"

"Hildy is *not* the first," Stone said emphatically. "I have a normal sex life. Normally."

Dino burst out laughing, and so did Eggers.

"Are you people here just to torment me?" Stone asked. "Can't you see I'm in pain?"

"Oh?" Eggers said. "Where does it hurt?"

Dino started laughing again.

"I withdraw the question," Eggers said. "Can we have some menus?" he said to a passing waiter. "You'll feel better, Stone, when you get some food into your stomach to keep the bourbon company."

"I'm not hungry," Stone said.

"We're going to have to force-feed him," Dino said, trying not to laugh.

"Well," Eggers said, "I didn't come here to put any pressure on you."

"Thank you, Bill," Stone said gratefully.

"Now what the hell is going on with Philip's daughter and that so-called artist?"

"Gee, thanks for not putting any pressure on me," Stone said.

"Come on, give me the lowdown."

"An undercover cop has made a buy from Sharpe, and it's on tape," Stone said.

"So he's in jail?"

"No, not yet."

"Why the hell not?"

"They want him to do it again, so it'll be a bigger bust. If he does it twice, maybe he'll get a longer stretch."

"How much did he sell the cop?"

"Half a kilo of coke and a pound of grass."

"Shit, that'll get him at least ten years, no parole."

"The legislature repealed the Rockefeller laws, haven't you heard?"

"Now that you mention it," Eggers said. "What would he get now?"

"Who knows? There's a lot of money at stake; somebody might get to a judge."

"Well, they haven't repealed greedy judges," Eggers said. "When is this business going to get wrapped up, so I can return Hildy Parsons to her father intact?"

"Who knows?" Stone said. "But I wouldn't count on her being intact."

The waiter came, and they ordered. Stone ordered another bourbon. "Did I mention that Dolce is stalking me?" he asked Dino.

"*What*?"

"Don't make me repeat myself."

"Wait a minute," Eggers said, "you're fucking Eduardo Bianci's crazy daughter?"

"No, but she wants me to. She sent me two dozen roses, and she's hanging around outside my house."

"I thought she was locked in a rubber room in Eduardo's house," Dino said.

"Not anymore. She goes out shopping with a minder."

"Now *this* is dangerous," Dino said.

44

Stone opened his eyes and gazed at the ceiling. It was moving around. He held on to the mattress to steady himself and got his feet on the floor. He barely made it to the bathroom before he knelt at the throne and emptied his stomach.

He lay down on the bathroom floor, pressing his hot cheek against the cool marble. From the bedroom came the sound of Joan buzzing him. He struggled to his feet, splashed cold water on his face, staggered back, sat on the bed, and picked up the phone. "What?"

"You sound awful."

"What is it?"

"Shall I call an ambulance?"

"Just skip a step and call an undertaker."

"You're hungover, aren't you?"

"The word doesn't cover it."

"This ought to help: Tiffany Baldwin is on the phone."

"Tell her I'm ill and can't talk."

"That won't work; I've been on the phone with you for too long."

Stone pressed the button. "Hello?"

"Did I wake you?" Tiffany asked.

"No. You can't wake the dead."

She laughed. "You have to be in my office in an hour for a meeting."

"I'm sorry," Stone said. "I thought you said I have to be in your office in an hour."

"You have to be in my office in an hour," she said, "for a meeting."

"Tiffany, I don't have any current business with your office. What is this about?"

"We're all meeting in an hour," she said. "It's a strategy session."

"Can you hold on for just a minute," he said. He pressed the HOLD button, ran into the bathroom, and threw up again. He ran some cold water on a facecloth and went back to the phone, swabbing his face. "I'm sorry, I don't know what you're talking about, and if I did, I wouldn't come."

"Your Lieutenant Doyle requested the meeting," she said.

"He's not *my* Lieutenant Doyle; he's just a cop I know."

"It's my understanding that the commissioner has placed you under his command."

"That's a lie."

"That's not what the commissioner says; I called him."

"Okay, it's not a lie; it's just a perversion of justice."

"Once again, Stone, be in my office in an hour for this meeting. The commissioner will be here, and if you're not, he'll notice." She hung up.

Stone wanted to collapse into bed again, but he got to his feet and threw himself into a cold shower, regretting it immediately. He shaved, cutting himself twice, struggled into some clothes, and went downstairs. He went into Joan's office, poured himself a cup of coffee, and began sipping it.

"You were right," Joan said. "I should have called an undertaker."

"Too late," Stone said. "I have to go downtown to the Federal Building."

"To see Tiffany Baldwin?"

"Among others. She said the commissioner is going to be there, too, but that may have been just to scare me."

"Did it work?"

"Sure did. I don't want him messing with my retirement pay."

"I'm sure that's beneath him."

"It's not beneath Brian Doyle, who hates me because I make more money than he does."

"I'm sure that's not the only reason."

"If I talk about this anymore, I'm going to throw up," he said. "Again. Will you drive me downtown? It seems to be raining outside."

"Oh, all right," she said, putting on her raincoat.

Stone found his trench coat and an umbrella and followed her to the garage.

More than slightly damp, Stone stood in the line at the metal detector and waited while a woman emptied her handbag onto a steel table and then put everything back, one item at a time. He was cold from the heavy rain, and his trench coat was soaked, being very old and no longer waterproof.

He emptied his pockets into the tray, put his umbrella on the conveyer belt into the X-ray machine, and passed through the metal detector. *Beep*. He took off his belt; the large silver buckle must have set it off. *Beep*.

"Take off your shoes," the uniformed woman said. "Sometimes it picks up the nails in the heels."

Stone took off his shoes, put them on the conveyer belt, and stepped through the metal detector again. No beep.

The guard at the X-ray machine pushed his

shoes toward him with the back of his hand. "You always wear two different shoes?" he asked.

Stone stared at his shoes. The man was right: one black and one brown. "Only when it's raining," he said.

He got his shoes back on over socks that were wet from treading in the pool of water that other people had left behind and went upstairs in the elevator. He found the office and presented himself to a receptionist who reported his presence.

"You may go in," she said.

Stone opened one of the double doors that led into a large corner office, furnished in the federal government's best taste plus a few personal touches from Tiffany. She sat with her long legs propped on her huge desk, reading glasses poised on her nose, a thick document in her lap.

"You're ten minutes early," she said.

Stone looked at his wrist, but there was nothing there. "I seem to have forgotten to wear a watch."

She peered at him over her glasses.

"What?"

"The phrase 'death warmed over' comes to mind."

Tiffany got up and led him to a sofa at the other end of the room. "Let's sit here for our meeting." She sat down, crossed her legs, and leaned into him.

The phone on the coffee table buzzed. Saved, Stone thought. He got up and moved to a chair beside the sofa.

"Send them in," Tiffany said into the phone.

The door opened and Brian Doyle entered, accompanied by Mitzi and the loyal Tom.

Tiffany got up and greeted them. "I suppose you all know Stone," she said.

"Yeah, sure," Doyle replied, and Mitzi gave Stone a big smile. They sat down and looked at each other.

"I think we should wait for the commissioner to arrive before we start," she said.

There was a knock at the door, and a secretary opened it and stepped back. "The commissioner," she said.

The commissioner, a fireplug of a man, marched into the office and took a seat at the end of the sofa nearest Stone. He looked at Stone's feet.

"Barrington," he said, "do you always wear two different shoes?"

45

Stone looked at the commissioner. "Only when it rains."

The commissioner didn't laugh, which was like him.

"Let's get this show on the road," he said to Stone.

Stone blinked. "It's not my show."

"Commissioner," Tiffany said smoothly, "we're here to coordinate the investigations into Derek Sharpe and Sig Larsen."

"Who's Larsen?" the commissioner asked, frowning.

"Short for Sigmund, presumably. He's the man who's running some sort of Ponzi scheme."

"Be nice to catch one of these guys *before* he steals everybody's money," the commissioner said.

A secretary came into the room with a tray of

Danish pastries and set them on the coffee table in front of Stone, who became ravenous at the sight of them. Desperately in need of something to get his blood sugar up, he grabbed a cheese Danish and took a big bite of it.

"Barrington," the commissioner said, "as I understand it, you initiated these investigations, so give us a rundown."

Stone, whose mouth had been dry to begin with, chewed faster and tried to swallow some of the cream cheese. He looked desperately for coffee, but none had been brought. He made a shrugging motion to gain time.

"Barrington, are you hearing me?"

Stone nodded and chewed faster. "It's like this," he managed to say, then chewed and swallowed some more. The secretary returned with a coffee jug and cups, and Stone poured himself some. He scalded his tongue taking a big swallow, but most of the Danish went down with it. "It began as a private thing," he said. "A client of the law firm to which I am of counsel asked me to investigate Derek Sharpe, fearing for his daughter's trust fund, which she was about to come into."

Brian Doyle interrupted him. "That's when we got involved," Brian said.

Stone fought back. "Yes, that's when I called Lieutenant Doyle and suggested he might be interested in Sharpe. I don't believe he had heard of him until then."

Doyle turned red. "Sharpe was already on my radar, but we hadn't yet had cause to move." He explained in some detail the involvement of Mitzi and Tom, leaving out Stone whenever possible.

Stone used the opportunity to take a smaller bite of the Danish, which helped cool his tongue. "Then Sig Larsen entered the picture," he said. "I can understand why Lieutenant Doyle wasn't interested in him, and I wasn't surprised to hear that the U.S. Attorney became involved."

"And that's why we're here," the commissioner said. "To coordinate the two investigations."

"Actually," Tiffany said, "I don't want to assign investigative personnel to this matter at this point. Lieutenant Doyle seems to have the situation well in hand."

"Thank you, Ms. Baldwin," Doyle said.

"Then there's nothing to coordinate?" the commissioner asked.

"All we need is your go-ahead to proceed, sir," Doyle said.

"I would have given that on the phone," the commissioner said, rising to his feet and snagging a Danish. He wrapped it in a napkin and put it in his jacket pocket. "Good day to you all," he said, and marched toward the door. But before reaching it he stopped and said, "Barrington, step outside with me."

Stone reluctantly set down his Danish and followed. The sugar was making its way to his brain now, and he was thinking more clearly. He followed the commissioner out of the office and through the reception area into the hallway outside.

"Listen," the commissioner said to Stone. "Has Doyle really got this thing in hand?"

"I'm afraid I don't know," Stone said truthfully. "So far, I've been used as a beard for Detective Reynolds for the most part."

"Not a bad place to be," the commissioner said with a little smirk.

"She's a very competent detective," Stone said, not wishing to mention her other area of expertise.

"I'm going uptown," the commissioner said. "Can I give you a lift?"

"Thank you, sir, yes," Stone said. A detective came out of the office with Stone's coat and umbrella. They took the elevator to the basement garage and got into the commissioner's black Lincoln, which followed a black SUV and led another, and shortly they were motoring through driving rain. Stone kept quiet, knowing that the commissioner didn't like small talk.

"How come you never made detective first grade?" the commissioner asked suddenly.

Stone was surprised he knew that. "I was due for promotion at the time I was retired for medical reasons," Stone said.

"Bullet to the knee, wasn't it?"

"That and a lot of precinct politics," Stone said. "I disagreed with the direction an investigation was taking, and somebody wanted me out. The knee was an excuse."

"Ah, yes, the Nijinsky investigation. I heard some stuff about it at the time," the commissioner said. "I was captain of the First Precinct, and shortly after that I got moved up the ladder. I re-read the file when Doyle wanted you reactivated. I know how to read between the lines. If it's any consolation, I added an addendum, correcting the impression your captain left in it."

"Thank you, sir," Stone said, surprised. "That was very kind of you."

"I hear you've done all right since leaving the department," the commissioner said.

"I can't complain," Stone said.

"You might have done better, if you'd had Brian Doyle's political instincts."

Stone said nothing.

"Doyle will go far," the commissioner said, "but only so far. Somebody will cut him off at the knees before he gets to my office."

"There's usually somebody willing to do that," Stone agreed.

The car came to a halt in front of Stone's house. He had forgotten how fast a police motorcade could move through traffic.

The commissioner shook Stone's hand. "Try not to let anybody get hurt in this investigation," he said, holding on to Stone's hand. "That's not the sort of thing Doyle thinks about."

"I'll do my best," Stone said. "Thank you for the lift."

Stone opened the car door, got his umbrella outside first, and ran for his office door.

Joan looked surprised to see him back. "How'd it go?" she asked.

Stone hung up his wet coat. "Better than I could have hoped," he said. "The commissioner is a better guy than I had thought."

The phone began ringing.

46

Joan handed the call off to Stone. "Hello?"

"It's Mitzi."

"Hi."

"Where did you go?"

"The commissioner wanted to talk to me, and he offered me a ride uptown."

"Brian is livid."

"Because I left his meeting?"

"Because you left with the commissioner."

"Oh."

"Tiffany Baldwin was a little upset, too, but she hid it better. I think she didn't want to share you with the commissioner."

"If you say so," Stone said.

"What did you and the commissioner talk about?"

"He wanted to talk about old times," Stone said.

"You had old times *together*?"

"Not exactly. He apparently followed a case I worked right before I left the department."

"Tell me about it."

"It's a long story."

"Does that mean I'm not supposed to ask?"

"I'll tell you about it when we have more time."

"And when is that going to be?"

"I'm at your beck and call," Stone said. "You tell me."

"I'll have to place another order with Derek Sharpe first," she said.

"And when is that going to happen?"

"We're letting him stew a bit; besides, I don't want to appear too eager."

"If it's any help, I think Sharpe and Larsen are going to decamp."

"Why do you think that?"

"Because they're both involved in enterprises that can't continue forever without their getting caught, and I think they're too smart to wait too long. I think you should see Sharpe for coffee and place a really big order."

"How big?"

"Forget the marijuana. Ask him for ten kilos of cocaine, and imply that the orders could grow. You want to order enough to appeal to his greed; he'll hang around a little longer for a big sale."

"Good idea," she said. "I'll run it by Brian."

"Don't tell him it was my idea; he'll screw it up just to spite me."

"So I get all the credit?"

"And all the blame if it spooks Sharpe."

"You said have coffee with him?"

"Don't go to his studio; he'll rape you."

"Yuck. Coffee it is."

"Some place where Tom can see you from the street."

"Okay."

"When you've got the buy set up, tell Sharpe you want the delivery at your apartment. He ought to be comfortable there now."

"All right. Then after we bust him, you and I will celebrate."

"You're on," Stone said. He hung up, and the phone rang immediately.

"It's Tiffany Baldwin," Joan said.

"Hello?"

"What did you do to get the commissioner to get you out of my meeting?" she asked.

"I think he thought that if I kept eating Danish, he might have to perform the Heimlich maneuver," Stone replied. "Did anything happen after I left?"

"Not a hell of a lot. I don't think I trust Lieutenant Doyle," she said.

"You have good instincts," Stone said. Line two began flashing on his phone. "I've got another call coming in," he said, "so I'm going to have to go."

"Let's get together."

"Maybe after this is over. Bye." Stone hung up and waited for Joan's voice.

"Brian Doyle on two," she said.

"Hello?"

"It's Brian."

"Hi, there."

"What was that you pulled with the commissioner?"

"He offered me a ride home, and it was raining like hell."

"If you think you can pull something behind my back, Stone . . ."

"Didn't you notice that he asked me to step outside? It wasn't my idea."

"All the same . . ."

"What happened at the meeting?"

"We just got our priorities straight with the U.S. Attorney."

"And how do you intend to proceed?"

"I've been thinking about it, and I believe Derek Sharpe and Sig Larson are going to run for it soon."

"Oh? Why do you think that?"

"I think they're too smart to think they can get away with what they're doing forever."

"That's very insightful of you, Brian," Stone said. "You might very well be right."

"Here's what we're going to do," Doyle said. "Mitzi is going to ask Sharpe for ten kilos of coke and forget about the grass. I think he's greedy enough to hang around until the big deal gets done."

"And what do you want me to do?"

"I want you to try to bring the thing with Larsen to a head; get him to commit an actual crime."

"And what would that consist of?"

"It would consist of Mitzi giving him a ten-million-dollar check to invest."

"Like a fake check?"

"No, like a real one."

"Whose money are we playing with?"

"I've got a banking connection who will issue the check and then put a hold on paying it."

"You mean a delay at the bank to keep Larsen in town a little longer?"

"Exactly. I can tell we're on the same page."

"I think you might put somebody on checking out the jet charter services at Teterboro and White Plains airports," Stone said, "because when they run, I think that's how they'll do it."

"Good idea," Doyle said. "I'll get that started today."

"They've probably used the same service before

to move money. And I'd send your guys to the airports to do the inquiry in person. I think that might encourage the charter service to play straight with you."

"I'll keep that in mind," Doyle said. "See ya." He hung up.

The phone rang again immediately.

"Mitzi on line one," Joan said.

"Hello?"

"Are you and Brian on the same page now?" she asked.

"Oh, sure. He told me *his* big idea, and I loved it."

"Brian thinks you're fucking me."

"Now where would he get that idea?" Stone asked.

She was laughing when she hung up.

47

Stone dug out Sig Larsen's card and called the number.

"Larsen Enterprises," a British-accented woman's voice said.

"Sig Larsen, please. It's Stone Barrington calling."

"One moment, please, Mr. Barrington. I'll see if I can find him."

This was apparently designed to create the impression of a large office, Stone thought.

"Just one moment, please, Mr. Barrington. I'm getting him out of the conference room."

Yeah, I'll bet, Stone thought.

"Stone? It's Sig. How are you?"

"Very well, Sig, and you?"

"Just great. What did you think of my prospectus?"

"Well, I had a look at it, and I thought it was a little skimpy on information." Best not to over-enthuse, Stone thought.

"Stone, I hope you appreciate the need for absolute secrecy in this matter; I'm the only person outside the company itself who is privy to this new product, and I've given my word not to disclose the kind of information I think you're talking about. Now if either you or Mitzi isn't comfortable with that level of confidentiality, I'll understand if you don't want to participate."

"Mitzi is more comfortable with it than I am," Stone said, "and she's the boss. She should be in touch with you today about her investment."

"Great, Stone. I'll look forward to hearing from her. Thanks for your help." He hung up.

Stone called Mitzi's cell. "Okay, I've baited the hook with Larsen."

"Terrific."

"How big a bad check are you going to give him?"

"Ten million dollars."

"Whoa! Way too much. Your bogus net worth is only $39,000,000, remember? You'll scare him off."

"How much, then?"

"Five million, tops. What bank will it be on?"

"My Charleston bank, the real one. I've already

talked with my guy there, and he understands and will not pay the check."

"Suppose Larsen has his bank call and put a hold on the funds?"

"I thought of that. My guy will tell them it's against bank policy; they'll have to present the actual check."

"That could work. When are you going to give Larsen the check?"

"Tomorrow morning; we're meeting for coffee at the Carlyle Hotel at ten a.m."

"Will Tom be able to see you?"

"Yes. I'd like it if you could be there, too."

"Participating or just watching?"

"Participating."

"I made a point of sounding as if I have reservations about the investment, and I'll continue that pose at the meeting. The enthusiasm will have to come from you."

"I'll be enthusiastic," Mitzi said.

"All right, I'll meet you there at ten."

"See you then. Dinner tomorrow night?"

"Just the two of us?"

"If you like."

"I think that's best for now."

"I'll try to make up for Rita's absence." She hung up.

*   *   *

Stone met Dino for lunch at P. J. Clarke's, and they both ordered a rare bacon cheeseburger and fries.

"I hear you and the commissioner are getting chummy," Dino said.

"Where the hell did you hear that?"

"You can't keep anything from me."

"No, seriously, how did you know about it?"

"His driver is a buddy of my driver. What did the old man say to you?"

"He asked me why I never made detective first grade."

"And what did you tell him?"

"The truth, what else?"

"You told him it was politics?"

"I did."

"That sounds really lame, you know."

"The commissioner didn't think so. He said that he'd read my file and that he could read between the lines."

"Why the hell would he read your file?"

"He said he read it when Brian asked to have me put on active status."

"Why the hell should the commissioner be interested in you, Stone?"

"I guess he just likes the cut of my jib," Stone said with a smirk.

"Horseshit. He was a captain downtown when all that went down."

"He said he heard about it at the time," Stone replied. "You're beginning to sound jealous of my new relationship with the commissioner, Dino. You want me to put in a good word for you?"

"Yeah, sure," Dino said. "Don't you dare mention my name; I don't want to be associated with you in the commissioner's eyes."

"And why the hell not? What's wrong with being associated with me?"

"Because you're a well-known pain in the ass in the department and a self-important fuckup."

"I am not," Stone said. "I have the reputation of a cop who did his job until he was wounded in the line of duty and given a medical retirement."

"If that's the way you want to think about it, go ahead. Still being in the department, I have a different viewpoint."

"Who the hell said that about me, anyway?"

"Guys who served with us in the squad."

"That crowd? Who gives a shit what they think? They're a bunch of bums. Anyway, most of them are tending bar in Queens by now. I guess the commissioner bases his opinions on better information than squad room gossip."

"You know, there are a lot of guys serving time in uncomfortable precincts who once thought the commissioner had a high opinion of them. He's like that; you can't read him."

"I'm not reading him," Stone said. "I was just

telling you what he said. If you think he's a liar,
fine. Anyway, I'm not subject to a transfer to an
uncomfortable place. This active crap is just a paperwork thing to make Brian Doyle think he's my
boss."

"If you say so."

"I say so," Stone said. Then he looked across
the room and saw Hildy Parsons being seated at a
table alone.

"Excuse me," Stone said. "Somebody I've got
to talk to." He got up and headed toward Hildy.

48

Stone walked up to her table and held out his hand. "Hello, Hildy," he said.

Hildy took his hand. "Oh, hello, Stone."

"May I speak with you for a moment?"

"Sure, please sit down. I'm expecting a friend, but I'm a little early."

"Hildy, I have some information for you, but I'm going to have to ask you to give me your word that you will not discuss this with *any other person*."

"All right."

"I mean, not with your father, not with Derek Sharpe, and not with anyone else."

She looked at him suspiciously. "Are you going to try to talk me out of seeing Derek?"

"I'm not going to try to talk you out of anything. I just have important but highly confidential information to give you."

"All right, I promise I won't discuss it with any-one else."

"I'll trust you to do that."

"Well, what is it?

"How much do you know about Derek?"

"I know that he's from Texas and that he had a hardscrabble childhood."

"Wrong. He's the son of a prosperous junk dealer, and he grew up with money."

"Look, I don't need this from you, Stone. This smacks of something my father would do. Are you working for him?"

"I'm telling you this of my own knowledge," Stone said.

"I don't care whose knowledge it is—I don't want to hear about it. I'm a grown woman, and I can judge people for myself."

"All right, then let me tell you something you don't know that might help you form your own judgment."

She sighed. "All right, and then this conversa-tion will be over."

"If you continue to be close to Derek for so much as another day, it is likely that you will be arrested." That seemed to register with her, so he continued. "And it is very likely that you will end up in prison."

She stared at him wide-eyed but said nothing.

"That's all I have to tell you," Stone said. "If you pass that on to Derek, someone could get killed. I would advise you to absent yourself from Derek for a few days—a death in the family, a sick friend, any excuse."

"Derek and I are about to take a vacation," she said. "Out of the country."

"If you go with him, you will find yourself a fugitive from justice," Stone said. "I tell you this only because I don't want anything bad to happen to you. I hope you understand that."

He started to rise, but she put her hand on his arm, and he sat down again.

"You seem like a trustworthy person," she said, "but so does Derek."

"One of us has ulterior motives," Stone said. "One of us is lying to you. One of us wants your money. If you need a place to go for a few days I have a house in Turtle Bay with guest rooms." He took a card from his coat pocket and handed it to her. "My secretary is there all day. May I tell her to expect you?"

"No, I don't need a place to hide," she replied, but she put the card in her bag.

"My cell phone number is on the back of the card," Stone said. "Call me day or night, but whatever you do, don't go back to Derek's place and don't see him for a few days." He took a key from his pocket. "This will let you into my house." He wrote the security code on another card and gave it to her. "Please, please, make yourself safe by being alone for a few days."

"I'll think about what you've said," Hildy replied, then looked up and waved. "My friend is here."

Stone got up and went back to his table, where Dino had started without him.

"Your cheeseburger is getting cold," Dino said. "Who was that?"

"Her name is Hildy Parsons. She's the reason I got mixed up in this thing with Brian Doyle."

"That looked like a pretty earnest conversation," Dino said.

"I hope she heard me." Stone's cell phone rang. "Hello?"

"It's Mitzi. I wanted you to know that we hit pay dirt at Teterboro," she said. "Larsen and Sharpe have chartered half a dozen times from the same company, every time to the Bahamas or some other island."

"Have they been to the Cayman Islands?" he asked.

"I'm not sure if that's one of them."

"It's probably where they're banking," Stone said. "They would probably go to some other island first and then change planes if they're carrying cash."

"Got it," she said.

Stone wanted to tell her about Hildy Parsons, but he decided not to. "See you tomorrow morning at the Carlyle," he said.

"Sure," she said. "Gotta run." She hung up.

49

Stone arrived at the Carlyle Hotel at Madison and Seventy-sixth at the stroke of ten. He didn't see Mitzi or Tom, but Derek Sharpe and Sig Larsen were sitting at a corner table in the dining room, so he joined them.

"Good morning, gentlemen," Stone said, and hands were shaken. He sat down and looked at his watch.

"Women!" Sharpe said.

"What's that about women?" Mitzi asked, and they all turned to look at her. She was wearing a flaming red suit and carrying a handbag to match. Every head in the dining room had turned to follow her.

Everybody stood up, Larsen held a chair for her. "Would you like something, Mitzi?"

"Yes. I'll order breakfast." A waiter appeared,

and she ordered scrambled eggs, bacon, and toast.

"I'll have the same," Stone said, "with orange juice, coffee later."

The two men seemed surprised that Stone and Mitzi were ordering food.

"Derek and I had breakfast earlier," Larsen said, pouring himself and Derek another cup of coffee from the pot on the table.

There was idle chat for a moment, then Larsen said, "So, Mitzi, what did you think of our investment opportunity?"

"I think it's very exciting," she replied. "Stone is slightly less enthusiastic."

"Not at all," Stone said. "I'm just accustomed to having more information before I advise a client to make an investment."

"As I told Stone," Larsen said, "I am the only person outside the company who has all the facts, and since it's crucial to keep the news of this software a secret until the company is ready to announce it, I simply can't tell anyone anything that isn't in the prospectus, and I promise you, very few people have seen that."

"I understand completely," Mitzi said. "And when do you think the announcement will be made?"

"In no more than ninety days," Larsen said.

"And what would you anticipate the stock price will do at that time?"

"That's when the initial public offering would be made," Larsen said, "and I believe it will at least triple on the first day of the offering. It's going to be the hottest thing since Google."

"Is the software in beta yet?" Stone asked.

"It finished beta testing yesterday," Larsen said, "and the results were fantastic—very few bugs for a brilliant new program. The next three months will be devoted to organizing the IPO and slipping subtle hints to the trade and business press to create a high level of buzz."

"And at what level will the stock be offered?" Stone asked. He turned his head slightly so that his ear bug would capture their voices clearly.

"Somewhere in the fifty to seventy-five range, probably," Larsen replied. "You could make a bundle, Mitzi, by selling on the first day."

"That's what I wanted to hear," Mitzi said.

"And at what level would you like to participate?" Larsen asked.

"I'll take a hundred thousand shares," she replied, removing an alligator checkbook from her handbag and opening it. "At fifty dollars a share. Do you have a pen, Sig?"

Larsen nearly broke an arm extracting a pen from his jacket pocket and handing it to her. "I will get you that price," he said. "I must say, I had expected a cashier's check."

"You think my personal check isn't good, Sig?" Mitzi asked, gazing at him across the table.

"Of course I don't think that, Mitzi; I'll just have to wait until the check clears before having the stock issued to you."

"Well, that will take only a few days," Mitzi said. "To whom shall I make the check?"

"Larsen Enterprises," Sig replied.

"Not directly to the company?"

"I'll have to move your money through my firm and issue my own check to the company, since its name must remain secret. I shouldn't think it would be more than four or five days before I can issue the stock."

Mitzi wrote a check for five million dollars and noted "100,000 shares" on it. "Let's be clear," she said. "This is for shares in the company that you described in the prospectus, not in Larsen Enterprises."

"Of course it is," Sig said, looking at the check. "A Charleston bank?"

"I don't have a New York account yet," Mitzi said. "Perhaps you could suggest a bank here?"

"I work with half a dozen," Larsen said, "mostly small, privately owned banks. I should think that for your purposes one of the big banks, Morgan Chase, perhaps, would be fine. Just pick a branch near your home."

"Thank you. I may do just that," Mitzi replied.

Their eggs arrived, and Mitzi and Stone began to eat.

Conversation seemed to pall, and Larsen and Sharpe seemed a bit antsy.

Larsen consulted his wristwatch. "Oh, Derek and I have another appointment downtown in half an hour," he said. "I hope you don't mind if we leave you to your breakfast." They stood up and hands were shaken. "You're going to be a very happy woman in three months," Larsen said. "Bye, now. Bye, Stone."

"Derek, could I speak to you for a moment before you leave?" Mitzi asked.

Stone put down his fork. "Please excuse me for a moment." He went looking for the men's room.

Sharpe took Stone's seat. "How can I help you, Mitzi?"

"Well, Derek," she said, "my friends from Charleston were very pleased with the quality of the, ah, 'art,' you sold them, and they'd like to make another purchase."

"The same again?"

"No. This time they're less interested in the grassy picture and more interested in the powdery ones."

"All right. How much would they like?"

She leaned forward and whispered, "Ten kilos."

"My goodness," Sharpe said. "Your friends have become more . . . commercial, shall we say!"

"Perhaps. I'm not familiar with their business arrangements."

"Of course not."

"And how soon could you deliver?"

"Two, three days," Sharpe said. "And at the same price per."

"Oh, I should think a volume discount would be in order," Mitzi said.

"I might be able to get you five percent off," Sharp replied.

"Oh, I think ten percent would be more acceptable to my friends," Mitzi said, giving him a brilliant smile.

"Given the quantity, I can do that," Sharpe said.

"We'll do it the same way as last time," Mitzi said. "I'm more comfortable with this sort of transaction in my own home."

"I don't know about that, Mitzi," Sharpe said. "My sources don't like to repeat themselves geographically. I'm sure you understand."

"No, I don't," Mitzi said firmly. "And I'm not going to do this on some street corner. Anywhere else but my home would be a deal breaker."

Sharpe shrugged. "All I can do is try," he said.

"Try hard," Mitzi replied. She shook his hand, and he went to join Larsen in the lobby, just as Stone was returning.

"How'd it go?" Stone asked.

"I got ten percent off!" Mitzi squealed. "He bridled at doing it in the apartment again, but I put my foot down." She looked around. "This is an awfully nice hotel. Why don't we get a room?"

Stone looked at his watch. "I'm afraid you'll have to wait until tonight before I can jump you. Eight thirty at Elaine's?"

"Oh, all right," she said, giving him a luscious kiss.

50

Stone walked home, and as he came through the front door, Joan flagged him down.

"A Brian Doyle is waiting in your office," she said. "He insisted; he showed me a badge."

"Right," Stone said. He tiptoed down the hall to his closed door and put his ear to it. He could hear the sound of drawers being opened and closed. Silently he turned the knob, then threw open the door.

Brian Doyle was caught with a handful of cancelled checks. "What do *you* want?" he demanded, as if Stone had entered his office unannounced.

"I think that's *my* question," Stone replied, "since you're rifling my desk."

"Oh, this?" Doyle tossed the bundle of checks onto the desk. "They were just lying here."

"No. They were at the back of my center

drawer," Stone replied. "You're the one doing the lying."

"I have a perfect right to search your desk," Doyle said, as if he really did.

"I think that's called breaking and entering," Stone said.

"Not if you're my subordinate."

Stone came around the desk, grabbed Doyle's necktie, dragged him to a chair, and pushed him into it. "Let's get something straight, Brian," he said, "once and for all: I am not your subordinate in any sense of the word—intellectually, morally, or sartorially. I am your superior in every department, and if you think your little prank with the badge makes any fucking difference, I'll stick it up your ass sideways."

Doyle held up his hands in a gesture of surrender. "All right, all right, just calm down."

"State your business, then get out," Stone said, glaring down at him.

"I just want to talk about the Sharpe and Larsen bust," he said.

"So, talk."

"I'm concerned about Mitzi's safety," Doyle said.

"So soon? I've been concerned about it from day one."

"Well, me, too. Why do you think I put Tom there to take care of her?"

"Because he's her partner, and it's his responsibility, perhaps?"

"Well, sure, but he's the right guy for the job."

"So, why aren't you talking to Tom instead of to me?"

"Because since we have him set up as her driver, he's not going to be welcome at the buy. You will be, though."

"I'm aware of that," Stone said. "I've just come from a meeting with Sharpe and Larsen where Mitzi proposed the big buy, and Sharpe agreed to the terms."

"I heard that from Mitzi's earpiece," Doyle said. "And why weren't you wearing yours?"

"Because it's a pain in the ass and because I don't want you listening to every word I say," Stone replied. "I'll wear it when it's necessary."

"It's necessary every time you have a meet like that," Doyle said. He was beginning to recover his composure and adopt his superior attitude again. "We've got to have yours as a backup, in case Mitzi's goes on the fritz."

"I'll wear it when it's necessary," Stone repeated.

"I want us to have another meeting with Tiffany Baldwin about the bust," Doyle said, changing the subject.

"You have another meeting with her, not I."

"What, are you afraid of her?"

"If you knew her better," Stone said, "*you'd* be afraid of her. You'd better watch your ass, Brian, because I think even the commissioner is a little afraid of her. Otherwise, he wouldn't have been at the last meeting."

"Why should I be afraid of that bitch?" Doyle asked.

"Because she could destroy you in a heartbeat if she felt like it," Stone explained.

"And how would she do that?"

"Oh, I don't know, how about a federal grand jury indictment?"

"Indictment? For what?"

"Don't you think that if she chose to put a couple of investigators on you she wouldn't find something? You're not exactly squeaky clean; you never have been."

Doyle reddened. "I have nothing to fear from her."

"No? Well, you'd better not screw up the Larsen part of the bust, because if you do she'll come down on you like an Amazon goddess, and she'll hand you your balls."

Doyle pushed his chair back and stood up. "I can see I'm not going to get anywhere with you," he said.

"Finally," Stone said. "Now let me tell you how this bust is going to go down. Mitzi has set it up at the apartment, but you're not going to have anybody in the building except me."

"Why the hell not?"

"Because Mitzi is borrowing the place from a friend of mine, and her neighbors would not take kindly to having a SWAT team in their lobby and elevators. And you can't grab him when he comes out of the building, either. You'll have to put four cars on him and wait until he's well away from there."

"At his place? Why?"

"Probably not at his place."

"Then where?"

"If you want Sharpe and Larsen together, you'd better do it at Teterboro Airport, because they're ready to run."

Doyle shook his head. "I don't want to pull any Jersey cops in on this."

"Then you'd better have some FBI there, hadn't you?"

"That's what I want to talk to Tiffany about," Doyle said. "I don't want them there. This is our bust."

"It's yours because Tiffany allowed you to do it, and she said so in the presence of the commissioner," Stone said. "So you'd better not fuck it up, and that means having a federal presence there."

"I hate the FBI," Doyle said sullenly.

"What cop doesn't?" Stone asked. "You think you've got a monopoly?"

"I don't want to ask her for help."

"She's waiting for you to do just that, and if you don't, then this case is going to fall on you from a great height."

Doyle thought this over. "Teterboro, huh?"

"That's where Sharpe and Larsen have chartered in the past," Stone said, "but you'd better have enough people to cover Westchester Airport if they decide to go there instead."

"You think they might do that?"

"If they have the slightest inkling that you're on to them, they could do anything."

"How many people do you think we'll need?"

"An army," Stone replied. "Go put it together, and ask Tiffany for help."

Doyle got up and left, muttering under his breath.

51

Mitzi looked at Stone over the rim of her glass of Knob Creek. "You seem a little down," she said. "What's wrong?"

"I'm worried about the bust," he said.

Mitzi adjusted her push-up bra. "I thought you liked it."

"Not that bust," Stone said, laughing in spite of himself. "Sharpe and Larsen."

"Sounds like a Dickensian accounting firm, doesn't it?" Mitzi said.

"I wish it were," Stone replied.

"Oh, come on, Stone. It's pretty straightforward, once we cover all our bases."

"We don't even know where all the bases are," Stone said.

"Brian and Tom had a meeting with the U.S.

Attorney this afternoon and asked for some of her people. That should help."

Stone admired her bust again. "Do you have a vest that will protect those?"

"Without looking overweight and dowdy? No."

"Just this once?"

"Maybe, after we make the buy."

"Wear it during the buy."

"You think Derek is going to shoot me in the apartment?"

"I don't know what to think. How are you going to pay for the drugs?"

"I already have, remember?"

"Sharpe is going to want real money, not a bad check."

"Tiffany had a word with Sharpe's bank."

"How do you know which bank he uses?"

"By the deposit stamp on the back of the check."

"You're not going to get a New York banker to tell Sharpe that your check has cleared and the funds are available."

"No. An FBI agent on the banker's phone line will confirm that. The bank isn't liable for what an FBI agent says to Sharpe, especially since they won't know what the agent is telling him."

Stone nodded. "I like that. Whose idea was it?"

"Mine, but I let Brian propose it to Tiffany."

"You shouldn't be so self-effacing," Stone said.

"It won't do you any good. Brian will get all the kudos from the bust, and he'll leave you high and dry."

"Can I trust you with a secret?"

"Sure."

"I passed the lieutenant's exam last week."

"So you think you'll get Brian's job?"

"Only if he gets kicked upstairs," she said. "Otherwise, they'll give me a squad in Staten Island or someplace way out in Queens. But if Brian does get kicked upstairs I'll have a shot, mostly because there's not much competition at the precinct."

"They'll transfer you either way; they're not going to put a woman in charge of a squad of guys she's been working with. Never happen."

"We'll see," Mitzi said.

"Good luck to you," Stone said, raising his glass.

Dino came through the door and shot Stone a questioning glance.

"You mind if Dino joins us?" Stone asked Mitzi.

"You think I didn't expect to have dinner with Dino, too?" she asked.

Stone waved him over.

Dino sat down and ordered a Scotch. "You two still drinking that Kentucky swill?" he asked by way of a greeting.

"I don't trust any booze that has to take a boat

here," Mitzi said. "Also, my daddy once told me he'd disinherit me if I drank un-American."

Dino looked at Stone, then at Mitzi. "What's the matter with him?" he asked her.

"He's worried about the bust," she replied.

"What have you got to be worried about?" he asked Stone. "Let the cops take care of it."

"By 'the cops' you mean Brian Doyle?"

"Oh," Dino said. "I get your point."

Mitzi looked at both of them askance. "What is it with you guys? Brian's not so bad."

"We've known him longer than you have," Dino said. "He's the kind of guy who'll take credit for your work."

"It isn't enough for Brian to take the credit," Stone explained. "For him to feel good about himself, he has to make everybody else look bad."

"Oh, really!" Mitzi laughed. "Why don't you two get him in here, then put 'em on the table and we'll measure."

Dino looked at Stone and shrugged.

"Mitzi," Stone said, "has Brian ever complimented you on your work?"

"Many times," she replied.

"Has he ever said anything good about you to your captain?"

"Well," she said, "I assume he passed it up the line; he said he would."

"Have you ever read your file after a performance review?" Dino asked.

"Yes, I have."

"Has he ever given you a positive review that didn't make it sound like he was responsible for your success?"

Mitzi thought that over.

"Let me guess what he had to say," Dino said. "He said something like, 'This officer has responded well to the training and advice of her commander.'"

Mitzi's brow furrowed, a strange sight. "I think I see what you mean," she said softly.

"Who's your rabbi?" Stone asked. "Not Brian, I trust."

"Not exactly," Mitzi said.

"You don't have a rabbi, do you?" Dino asked.

"Not exactly."

"All you've got is Brian."

"I have other friends in the department," she said uncertainly.

"I'm really glad to hear that," Dino said, as if he didn't entirely believe her.

Nobody spoke again until a waiter came to take their orders.

52

They started fooling around in the cab on the way home, and by the time they had made it upstairs they were leaving a trail of clothing across the bedroom.

Mitzi undid her bra and threw it as far as she could. "Free at last!" she half-shouted. She tackled Stone, and they fell onto the bed, writhing in the mutual pleasure of their naked bodies. In a moment they were conjoined.

"I think this is what they mean by 'one flesh,'" Stone said.

"I like it," Mitzi said, sticking her tongue in his ear.

It was, perhaps, her tongue that kept him from properly hearing the first outburst.

"What?" Stone asked.

Mitzi froze. "That wasn't me," she whispered.

"What was it?"

"Lying scum!" a female voice said.

"You promised not to bring your roommate," Stone said to Mitzi.

"I didn't."

Stone sat up and looked around the darkened room, lit only by a few shafts of moonlight cutting through the venetian blinds. As he squinted, a naked female stepped out of his dressing room.

"Miserable son of a bitch," Carrie Cox said. "And with *her*." She pointed at Mitzi.

"Oh, come on, Carrie," Mitzi said, sitting up on one elbow. "You've got to get over high school."

"Carrie," Stone said. "What are you doing here?" He realized that sounded hollow, but he couldn't think of anything else to say.

"What am *I* doing here? What is *she* doing here?" Carrie pointed again.

"You want to join us, Carrie?" Mitzi asked.

"*What?*"

"Stone's pretty good at threesomes," Mitzi said. "Come to think of it, so am I. And I like your dancer's body."

"Mitzi, please," Stone said. "Let me handle this."

"Okay, handle it," Mitzi replied. "I'll wait here."

"Carrie," Stone said, getting to his feet, "let me get you a cab home."

"Why should *I* leave?" she demanded.

"Carrie," Mitzi said, "I'm trying to make the best of this. Either get into bed or get out of here."

Carrie seemed to be thinking it over, and Stone found himself speechless. Then Carrie disappeared into his dressing room, and a moment later she came out, holding her clothes in her arms.

"I'll get my own cab," she said, stalking out of the room.

Stone made to follow her but found his wrist locked in Mitzi's iron grip.

"She's an actress," Mitzi said. "Don't spoil her exit."

Stone sat down on the bed, and a moment later he heard the front door slam. "I hope she got her clothes on before going outside," he said.

Mitzi knelt on the bed behind him and put her arms around his neck, pressing her breasts into his back. "How did she get in?"

"I seem to remember giving her a key a while back," Stone replied.

"Oh."

"She was in trouble and needed a place to stay."

"She seems to have taken a proprietary interest in the house. And in you."

Stone sighed. "I guess this is my fault."

"Let's talk about it in the morning," Mitzi said, pulling him back onto the bed. "Carrie was always a little crazy, even when she was fourteen." She fondled his penis. "Oh, she frightened it. Poor baby."

Stone did his best to turn his attention to Mitzi again, and his best was pretty good.

Very early in the morning the bedside phone rang. Stone opened an eye and checked the clock. Half past five. He closed his eyes and let the machine pick up on the third ring.

After a short delay it rang again, and the machine picked up again.

"Maybe you'd better get that," Mitzi said, pulling a sheet over her head. "Somebody really wants to talk to you."

When it rang again, Stone picked up the phone. "What?"

"Stone, it's Bob Cantor. Carrie has been shot; she's in the Lenox Hill Hospital ER."

"I'm coming," Stone said, then hung up. He went to his dressing room and started pulling on clothes, noticing that a lacy pair of Carrie's panties still hung from a hook there.

"What's going on?" Mitzi asked, sitting up.

"I'm sorry," Stone said, "a bit of an emergency has come up, and I have to go out."

"At five thirty in the morning?" she asked. "What kind of emergency comes up at this hour?"

"Gotta run," Stone said, grabbing a jacket. "Go

back to sleep, and when you wake up, Helene will fix you some breakfast." He trotted down the stairs and out the front door just as, miraculously, a cab drove by. He stopped it in its tracks with a loud whistle.

At six in the morning the Lenox Hill ER was already getting busy. As Stone strode toward the admitting desk he was intercepted by Willie Leahy.

"Hang on, Stone. They said we can see her in a few minutes." Willie dragged him toward a chair and sat him down.

"What happened?" Stone asked.

"Last night, Carrie left the house and went to your house, walked right past me, and I didn't have time to stop her before she got in the cab. I got the next one and followed her."

"Well, *I* didn't shoot her. How badly is she hurt?"

"I know you didn't shoot her. I got her into my cab after she came out of the house, half naked, and took her home. She was running up her front steps when I heard the shot and saw the guy running away. I didn't even have time to get off a round."

"Willie, tell me: How badly is she hurt?"

"Flesh wound at the top of the shoulder. Went in and out, bled a lot. I got her here as fast as I could."

"Why didn't you call me then?" Stone asked. He thought he must have been banging Mitzi or vice versa when this happened.

"Tell you the truth, I was a little shaken up," Willie said, "and I was covered in blood. Peter brought me a shirt, and after I got cleaned up in the men's room, I called Bob."

"Why didn't you call me?" Stone asked, while grateful that he hadn't.

"Because I work for Bob, remember?"

"Oh, yeah."

A young doctor in blue scrubs came out a door, looked around, and beckoned Willie. Stone followed.

Carrie was lying on an ER bed that had been cranked to a sitting position, her left arm in a sling. "You two," she said, pointing at Willie and Stone. "Get me out of here."

53

Carrie sat, seething, between Stone and Willie Leahy in the back of the cab.

"Carrie," Stone said, "I . . ."

"I'm not speaking to you," she said.

"Now wait a minute . . ."

"And I'm not listening, either."

Willie wisely kept his mouth shut.

"Willie," Stone said, "did you get a look at him?"

"At his back," Willie said. "Tall, slim, black raincoat."

"It was Max," Carrie said.

"Did you see him?"

"I didn't need to see him," she replied. "It was Max."

"Carrie, during rehearsals has anyone shown any animosity toward you?" Stone asked.

"Everyone," she replied.

"Beg pardon?"

"I'm the star; nobody likes the star."

"And you've been behaving like the star?"

"It's my right."

Stone looked at Willie. "I think the list of suspects is growing."

"Yeah," Willie said. "Anybody in the show could have done it; she's been a perfect bitch."

"What?" Carrie screamed. "You're fired!"

"I don't work for you, remember?" Willie seemed to have had enough.

"Stone, fire him this minute."

"He doesn't work for me," Stone said, "and I don't doubt for a minute that Willie is right."

Carrie started to get out of the moving cab, but Stone and Willie held her down.

"You're hurting me!" she shouted.

"No, you're hurting you," Stone said. "Stop it."

Amazingly, she went both limp and silent. The cab arrived, and the three got out.

"I want to go to bed," Carrie said. "I've got a rehearsal at ten."

"You're going to be late," Stone said. "You've got to talk to the police before you can go anywhere."

"The police? Why?"

"Because they take gunshot wounds seriously, and Lenox Hill Hospital has already reported this one to the police. We just happened to get out of the ER before they arrived."

As they reached the top of the steps an unmarked police car pulled up, and two detectives got out. Stone didn't know them.

"Carrie Cox?" one of them asked.

"Come on in, fellas," Stone said, flashing the Brian Doyle badge. "Let's get this done."

Stone left the four of them in the living room and used the kitchen phone.

"Bacchetti."

"It's Stone. Can you get over to Carrie's house?" He gave Dino the address.

"What for?"

"Somebody took a shot at her, only a graze. Probably her ex-husband. She's supposed to open in the big show next week, and we don't want it in the papers."

"Any of our people there?"

"Two. I didn't get their names."

"Gimme fifteen minutes."

Stone went back to the living room and sat down, knowing that Willie would have steered the conversation in his absence.

"You got anything to add?" one of the detectives asked Stone.

"Nope. I wasn't here. I went to the hospital as soon as I heard."

"Why didn't you report this to the police?"

"I am the police," Stone said. "You want to see my badge again?"

"What precinct?"

"The First."

"Who's your boss?"

Stone gritted his teeth. "Lieutenant Doyle. I'm on special assignment."

"What kind of special assignment?"

"If I was allowed to tell you that it wouldn't be special," Stone explained. It went on like this until Dino arrived.

Dino showed his ID. "You two," he said, pointing two fingers at the detectives, "listen up."

The detectives tried to look attentive.

"I'm taking care of this," Dino said. "There's no report to make."

"We gotta make a report, Lieutenant," one of them said softly. Dino was well-known in the department, and they were being appropriately deferential.

"You don't gotta do nothing," Dino said, "except forget this. Mention it to nobody, and if anybody mentions it to you, refer them to me at the Nineteenth. Believe me, you don't want to be involved in this one."

The two detectives looked at each other, then back at Dino. They nodded simultaneously, got up, and left the house.

"Thank you, Dino," Carrie said. "That was sweet of you."

Dino patted her on the head. "Don't you worry

about it, sweetheart." He looked at Stone. "You want a lift?"

"Please," Stone said, getting up.

"You're leaving?" Carrie asked, looking surprised.

"There's nothing more for me to do here," Stone said.

"But plenty for you to do in your bedroom," she said, pouting.

"My bedroom is none of your business," Stone said. "Now shut up and let Dino do his work."

Stone and Dino left the house and walked down the front steps.

"You're sure it's the ex-husband?" Dino asked Stone.

"No. Apparently, Carrie has treated the entire cast of her show like shit. It could be anybody."

"I'll have the airports watched."

"Just Teterboro," Stone said. "The guy flies himself."

"That makes it easier."

"He's off the ground by now, but the tower will have a record of his departure."

"Where does he land in Atlanta?"

"Probably Peachtree DeKalb," Stone replied.

"I'll pull a favor and get him talked to. How long would his flight take?"

"He flies a King Air. Say, three hours. All this happened between five thirty and six. If he went straight to Teterboro, he'd be in the air by seven. You've got a shot at having him met."

"But no evidence."

"Well, there is that."

"What about a bullet?"

"Passed through," Stone said, but he turned and looked at the front of the house. "There," he said, pointing at a brick with a missing chunk. "Ricocheted from there."

They both looked around for the bullet but couldn't find it.

"It'll be distorted anyway," Dino said. "Wouldn't provide any ballistics to check."

They got into Dino's car and left.

54

Stone found Mitzi in the garden, dunking a croissant into her coffee.

"Charleston manners?" Stone asked.

"My mother would turn over in her grave," Mitzi replied, "but I love it this way."

Stone asked Helene for some breakfast and sat down at the garden table.

"So, what was the emergency?" Mitzi asked.

"Somebody took a shot at Carrie," Stone said.

"Hit her?"

"Yes."

"Oh, good."

"Don't gloat; it wasn't that bad. She's going to rehearsal later this morning."

"I'll bet the list of suspects is a long one," Mitzi said.

"How'd you guess?"

Mitzi made a snorting sound. "You could include all the members of her high school class."

"And the cast of her show, apparently, but it was probably her ex-husband. He's been stalking her."

"You think he meant to kill her? I mean, he missed."

"Most people are lousy shots," Stone said. "The untrained just point in the general direction and yank the trigger."

"More people should train," Mitzi said.

"If they did, we'd just have a lot more successful shootings."

"Good point. Do you suppose we could persuade the NRA to support training shooters badly?"

Stone laughed. "Probably not."

"You were good last night," Mitzi said. "There are times when I'm so discouraged with men that I think about becoming a card-carrying lesbian. You've restored my faith in men."

"Really?"

"Well, mostly; a lot of them are still shits. Women are more empathetic."

"Am I a shit?"

"Never," Mitzi said, "at least, not on purpose."

"Well, I guess that's a compliment."

"A higher one than you might think."

"You said you took the lieutenant's exam?"

"Right."

"I thought you were a detective first grade."

"I made sergeant two years ago. I don't talk about it much; three members of my squad flunked the sergeant's exam."

"All the more reason for the brass to transfer you if you get the promotion."

"I have other things going for me," she said. "Some of them might offset male cop jealousy."

"Has the department come that far since I retired?"

"Ask me after a few dozen more cops retire or die."

"You think Brian will get bumped upstairs?" Stone asked.

"I don't think he'll be where he is much longer," she replied.

"Not even if this bust is a big success?"

"If it is, it won't be Brian's fault. I think enough people in the department know that."

"I hope you're right," Stone said.

Helene came into the garden from the kitchen, carrying Stone's breakfast and the cordless phone. She handed it to Stone. "For you." She went back to the kitchen.

"Hello?"

"It's Tiffany."

"Good morning."

"Are you alone?"

Stone thought about this before he answered. "Yes," he said finally.

"Let's have dinner tonight."

Stone didn't hesitate. "I don't think that's a good idea until this bust is over. Let's not get talked about right now."

Mitzi's eyebrows went up. She mouthed, "Tiffany?"

Stone nodded. "There's something else I want to talk to you about, though."

"What's that?" Tiffany asked.

"I think we need a chopper to cover this bust."

"Why?"

"We're dealing with two experienced and very tricky con men, and I'm worried about being thin on the ground."

"Why can't the NYPD furnish the chopper?"

"The demand for their air fleet is heavy; yours is lighter."

"Should I speak to the commissioner about this?"

"I don't think that's necessary," Stone replied. "All I want is to be able to make a cell phone call and get something in the air instantly."

"You worry too much."

"I think it's best to worry too much before the bust than afterward."

"Oh, all right, I'll make the call, but you owe me for this one."

"Yes, I owe you."

Tiffany hung up without saying good-bye.

"That's interesting," Mitzi said.

"Asking for a helicopter?"

"Yes, that, too, but more that Tiffany is calling you."

"You know we have some history."

"Everybody who reads 'Page Six' in the *Post* knows you have some history."

"That was speculation; I didn't appear in the photographs, and they couldn't prove that the woman was Tiffany."

"Sorry, I should have Mirandized you before I asked about that. But why is Tiffany calling you?"

"She wants to have dinner."

"She wants a second chance to become infamous?"

"That's an interesting way to put it," Stone said. "I never considered that dining with me carried the risk of infamy."

"I shouldn't think it would do either of you any good. It's obviously a toxic relationship."

"Mitzi, you don't have to talk me out of it; I don't want to have dinner with her."

"Well, you did put her off, didn't you?"

"I thought it best."

"I'm glad," she said, leaning over and kissing him on the forehead.

Stone rolled his eyes upward. "Do I have lipstick on my forehead now?"

"It's very becoming," Mitzi said, patting his cheek.

Stone resisted the urge to wipe it off with his napkin.

Mitzi put down her napkin and stood up. "Well, I have to go to work."

Stone stood, too. "Have you heard anything from Derek about the buy?"

"Not yet. Don't worry; he'll call. He's on the hook."

"I hope we can keep him there," Stone said. He walked her to the front door and let her out, then went down to his office.

Joan walked in with the mail, took one look at him, and burst out laughing.

"What?" Stone asked, mystified.

She put the mail on his desk. "Oh, nothing," she said; then she went back to her office, chortling.

55

Dino was uncharacteristically late for dinner at Elaine's. Stone and Elaine were sitting together, chatting, waiting for him to show. Stone ordered a second Knob Creek.

"You're looking better," Elaine said. "You didn't look so hot last night."

"I'm feeling better," Stone admitted.

"You got laid last night, huh?"

"In a manner of speaking. You know Carrie, the actress?"

"Sure. From what I hear on the grapevine, everybody's going to know her next week."

"Right."

"You weren't with her last night; you were with Mitzi."

"Right again. I had to go to the hospital very

early this morning, because Carrie's ex took a shot at her."

"She's dead?"

Stone shook his head. "Barely wounded. She'll make opening night."

"Somebody ought to lock that guy up."

"Dino's working on it."

At the mention of his name, Dino walked through the front door and headed for his table. A waiter saw him and ordered his usual Scotch. He sat down at the table, and Elaine pinched his cheek.

"Aw, come on, Elaine," Dino said. "Everybody's watching."

"You two enjoy," Elaine said and moved to another table.

"Yeah, I know," Dino said to Stone. "I'm late."

"What happened in Atlanta?" Stone asked.

"You mind if I get a drink first?" A drink appeared before him, and he took a tug at it.

"So?"

"Don't rush me."

"Me rush you?"

"All the time."

Stone sighed, sat back, sipped his bourbon, and waited for Dino to speak.

Dino took another tug at his Scotch. "Okay," he

said, "two Atlanta PD detectives met your man at the airport. He denied being in New York and showed them a flight plan from Charleston."

"Anybody can run off a flight plan on a computer," Stone said. "That doesn't mean he flew it."

"They called the FAA, but there was some screwup. Apparently, he did fly from Charleston, but they weren't able to figure out when he got there."

"And I'll bet he has a Charleston alibi."

"You got it," Dino said. "And since we don't have any evidence against the guy—no ID, no bullet—he can't be touched."

"So that's why you were late?"

"No. I was at a meeting with Brian Doyle and the commissioner."

"Subject?"

"Your pending bust."

"It's not *my* pending bust. It's Brian's; he owns it."

"Yeah, I know, and that's what worries me. I hear you got Tiffany to give you a chopper."

"Shit! Was that mentioned at the meeting?"

"No, but I have other sources."

"I think we need it."

"I think you're right," Dino replied. "If there's a way to fuck this up, Brian will find it. He's a walking, framed copy of Murphy's Law."

"How did he ever make lieutenant?" Stone asked.

"You mean, whose cock was he . . .?"

"Exactly."

"I think he did whatever was necessary."

"It doesn't speak well of the NYPD that they would promote the guy."

"Look, you and I could name a dozen guys who got promoted above their level of competence," Dino said.

"Yeah, we could. I just wish we didn't have one of them running this bust."

"All right, tell me who you're worried about," Dino said.

"Mitzi," Stone replied, "and Hildy Parsons."

"Oh, that's right. Hildy is why you're in this."

"Exactly. But I've come to feel a lot for Mitzi, and she could get hurt."

"You want me to be around when it goes down?"

"Yes, please. I'd like you at Rita Gammage's apartment when the buy is made, and we'll take it from there."

"When?"

"I don't know yet; we're waiting for a call from Derek Sharpe to tell us he has the goods. Mitzi will see that we have some notice, though."

"Okay, I'm available."

"Do me a favor?"

"What is it this time?"

"I need you to call the NYPD flight department and inquire about a helicopter pad somewhere in the vicinity of Park and Seventy-second Street."

"Okay, I can do that."

"I think that's all I need until the bust goes down," Stone said. His cell phone vibrated on his belt, and he dug it out of its holster. "Hello?"

"It's Mitzi."

"Hello, there."

"The buy is tomorrow morning, eleven a.m., at the apartment."

"Gotcha. Dino and I will be there early."

"Great."

"Something I'd like to know about the apartment."

"What?"

"The windows, the ones overlooking Park Avenue, do they open?"

"You mean, are they not sealed shut?"

"Exactly."

"Hang on."

Stone waited until she came back.

"Yes, they open," she said.

"Thanks. See you tomorrow." He hung up. "We're on," he said to Dino. "Eleven a.m. tomorrow."

"Good."

"You still have your old .22 target pistol?" Stone asked.

"Yeah, it's in my safe."

"Bring it."

"Why?"

"Just bring it."

Dinner arrived, and they dug in.

In spite of the bourbon and the good food, Stone was nervous again. He didn't like being nervous; something bad usually happened when he was nervous.

56

Stone woke early, shaved, showered, and got to Rita's apartment at eight. Dino met him on the sidewalk.

"I didn't get breakfast," Dino said.

"Neither did I," Stone replied, ushering him into the building, "but we will." He gave the doorman their names and waited until they were allowed upstairs. Before they went to the elevator, Stone pulled the doorman to the front door and pointed. "See that parking space?"

"Yes, sir."

Stone put a hundred-dollar bill in his hand. "Please make sure no one parks there but a Mr. Sharpe. He drives a black Mercedes, and he'll be here around eleven. Tell him that Miss Mitzi reserved it for him."

"I'll put a couple of cones out and watch for him," the doorman said.

Mitzi answered the door in a silk dressing gown, and it looked as though she was wearing nothing under it. The sight stirred Stone, but there wasn't time.

"You want some breakfast?" she asked.

"You betcha," Stone said.

She led Dino down the hall toward the kitchen, but Stone went to a front window and made sure it would open; then he went to the kitchen and sat down at the table with Mitzi, Rita, and Dino. Moments later they were eating omelets and croissants, Mitzi dunking hers.

They lingered at the table, chatting, until after ten; then the women went to dress. Stone walked to the big stainless-steel refrigerator, took two eggs from the door shelf, and slipped them into his jacket pocket. Then he went into the living room and began reading the *Times*.

Dino joined him and took the Business section.

"Since when did you start reading about business?" Stone asked, surprised.

"When I got my hands on some money." Dino had received a generous settlement when he was divorced.

"So now you're a capitalist?"

"You bet your ass."

"You brought the .22 pistol?" Dino had won a department championship with that pistol.

"It's on my belt," Dino said, not bothering to show him. "Are you armed?"

"I am," Stone said.

"Not that you could hit anything."

"Why do you think I asked you to bring the target pistol?" Stone said. He didn't argue with Dino's opinion of his marksmanship.

At ten thirty Dino used his cell phone to check on the status of the bust, then he hung up.

"Everything set?" Stone asked.

"Yep."

"Oh, what did you find out about a helicopter pad?"

"There's a tennis club a couple of doors from the corner of Seventy-ninth that's being renovated. They're taking down the nets and posts on the rooftop courts. My car is parked a block from here; my driver will run us there."

"How many courts on the roof?"

"Four, stacked."

Stone called the number Tiffany had given him for the helicopter pilot.

"Hello."

"This is Stone Barrington."

"Right, Mr. Barrington. We're all set."

"How long a flight from your position to the corner of Seventy-second and Park?"

"Two minutes."

"At eleven a.m. sharp, start your engines and be ready." He explained about the tennis club.

"I know the place; I've seen it from the air. The space is plenty big."

"See you there," Stone said.

At ten minutes to eleven the buzzer rang from the doorman, and Mitzi answered it. "Send Mr. Sharpe up," she said, then hung up. "He's on his way; you two had better get into the kitchen."

Stone went to the window and opened it. The black Mercedes was parked, nine stories down. He leaned out the window, aimed carefully, and dropped an egg. "Bull's-eye!" he said.

"What the fuck are you doing?" Dino asked.

Stone didn't reply but aimed the second egg. "Hah!" he shouted. "Let's get to the kitchen."

They ran down the hallway just as the doorbell rang.

Mitzi opened the door and let Sharpe in. He was carrying two catalogue cases.

"Who else is here?" he asked.

"Just the maid," Mitzi said. "You're not going to get all paranoid on me again, are you?"

"Let's get this done," Sharpe said. He knew the way to the study.

Mitzi sat him down, and he opened both catalogue cases and began removing one-kilo bricks of cocaine.

"Do you promise me that this cocaine is just as good as the first shipment you sold me?"

"If anything, it's better," Sharpe said.

"Okay, put the bricks back into the cases," she said, and Sharpe did so.

"I assume my check cleared or you wouldn't be here," Mitzi said.

"You're absolutely right," Sharpe replied. "I've already wire-transferred it out of the country."

"We're done, then?"

Sharpe stood up. "We are. Take care of yourself, Mitzi."

"You sound like you're going somewhere."

"Just a little vacation. I'll be back in a couple of weeks to supply your friends again, if they're still in business."

"They'll still be in business," she said. She showed him to the door and let him out. Then she turned, leaned against the door, and heaved a great sigh. She went to the phone and pressed the PAGE button. "He's gone," she said. "Let's get moving."

Stone and Dino ran down the hall and into the living room, and Stone continued to the window. "Any problems?"

"Not a one," Mitzi said.

Stone looked out the window. "There he goes."

Dino called for his car, while Stone called his

helicopter, and then they both ran to the elevator.

When they emerged from the apartment building they found Dino's car waiting for them at the
curb. They hopped in and, after making a quick
U-turn, raced up Park Avenue and around the corner of Seventy-ninth Street.

As they turned the corner, Stone saw the helicopter approaching the building and inside a cop who
was holding an elevator that would take them up.
They emerged from the top floor fire door onto the
roof just as the aircraft landed on the tennis courts,
jumped in, and buckled their seat belts.

Stone took the left seat, next to the pilot, and
put on his headset. "Okay," he said, "we're looking for a black sedan that's been marked with two
raw eggs."

"How'd you do that?" the pilot asked.

"From a great height," Stone replied.

57

Stone spoke into the headset microphone. "Let's stay as low as possible, until we spot the car. When we do, let's go higher, so as not to worry our man."

"Shall we try Park Avenue first?" the pilot asked.

"Affirmative," Stone said.

The helicopter rose vertically from the tennis courts for a couple of hundred feet; then the pilot executed a ninety-degree turn toward Park Avenue and pointed the machine downtown. They had moved only a few blocks when Stone looked down and saw the egg-decorated Mercedes.

"There," he said, "in that traffic backup by the construction site."

Derek Sharpe sat in the traffic jam and began to sweat. He wasn't worried about Sig Larsen leaving without him, since it took both of them to withdraw or transfer funds from their offshore account, but he was anxious to have this over and done with. He longed for a beach and a drink with an umbrella in it.

Finally, traffic edged forward, and he broke loose of the jam and headed downtown at a good speed.

Stone watched as the Mercedes moved quickly down Park Avenue. "He's going to turn west toward the Lincoln Tunnel," he said to the pilot.

"I'm ready," the man replied.

At Forty-seventh Street, the Mercedes made its turn and began the slow process of driving west on a crosstown Manhattan street. The pilot hung back a block or so, keeping the black car in sight.

"He'll turn left on Eleventh Avenue," Stone said. "Then we'll pick him up on the other side of the Hudson when he comes out of the tunnel."

"Got it," the pilot said as the Mercedes turned left on Eleventh Avenue. "Shall we cross the Hudson now and get ahead of him?"

"Sure," Stone said.

The pilot turned right and headed toward the river. "Did you see that guy put the Airbus down in the river?" he asked Stone.

"I saw it a dozen times on TV, and I'm still

amazed that everybody walked away from that one," Stone replied. "The pilot said he was just doing what he'd been trained to do, but he did it awfully well, didn't he?"

"Sure did," the pilot said. "Here comes the other end of the tunnel."

"Let's gain some altitude," Stone said. "I don't want him to spot us when he emerges."

The pilot flew the machine a little way south and hovered at five hundred feet looking back at the tunnel. "Traffic's moving well at this hour of the day," he said. "He'll pop out of there soon."

A black Mercedes appeared. "There," Stone said, pointing.

"Not unless he stopped at a car wash," the pilot said. "No egg on that car."

"You're right. Cars are pouring out of the tunnel; he should be out of there by now."

They hovered for another couple of minutes.

"Something's wrong," the pilot said.

Sharpe had bypassed the tunnel entrance, just in case he was being watched, then turned downtown on Ninth Avenue. Just a few more blocks, he told himself. He joined the West Side Highway at Thirty-ninth Street and headed downtown. Nearly there. He left the highway at the West Side Heliport and parked the car next to it. He could see the chopper on the ground with Larsen standing next to it. The rotor was already turning, and Hildy and Larsen's "wife" would be inside.

Sharpe had nothing in the car he needed to take with him. He hated to abandon such a nice car, but the lease was up in a couple of months, so what the hell? He jogged toward the waiting helicopter.

Larsen was holding the door for him, and he jumped in and gave Hildy a big kiss. The chopper rose, rotated a hundred and eighty degrees and began to fly north along the Hudson VFR corridor.

Larsen was pointing down. "What's that on top of your car?" he asked.

Sharpe looked down and saw the egg splatter on the car's roof. "I don't know," he said. "Vandals, I guess."

"He's not coming out of this tunnel," the pilot said, "because he didn't go into it."

"You're right," Stone said. "We've been had." Then he looked across the river and saw a helicopter take off from the West Side Heliport. "Uh-oh," he said, pointing. "Head over there."

The pilot turned the machine and started toward the Hudson. "There's one that just took off," he said, pointing at a helicopter making its way north.

"I want to see the parking lot," Stone said; then he pointed. "There's the Mercedes with the egg on top."

"The chopper going north is the only one I see in the air," the pilot said.

"Follow it," Stone said. "He's headed for Westchester Airport."

The pilot made the turn north. "Well," he said, "I hope it's the right helicopter."

"So do I," Stone said.

"Is the airplane going to be waiting?" Sharpe asked Larsen.

"It's already there," Larsen replied. "I'll call him when we're five minutes out and tell him to start the engines."

"Man, oh, man," Larsen said. "This is really happening."

"What's happening?" Hildy asked. "We're just going to the Bahamas, right?"

"You'll see when we get there," Sharpe said.

Dino tapped Stone on the shoulder and spoke through his headset from the rear seat. "What the fuck is happening?"

Stone turned toward the rear seats. "They took a helicopter from the West Side Heliport," Stone replied, "and they're headed for Westchester. Just enjoy the view of the Hudson."

Mitzi spoke up. "Should I call Brian?"

"I guess you'd better," Stone said. "Tell him to alert the team at Westchester that Sharpe and Larsen are headed there in a helicopter and to arrest them on sight."

"Will do," Mitzi said.

Stone turned back and looked north. "I don't see the chopper," he said.

"I was just about to mention that," the pilot replied. "I don't see him, either. He was there; then I looked at my chart for a couple of seconds and when I looked up, he was gone."

"I heard that," Dino said. "Now what?"

58

Stone was anxiously looking up and down both shores of the Hudson River. The George Washington Bridge was coming up and the pilot climbed another hundred feet to clear it.

"I don't get it," Stone said. "How could a helicopter just vanish?"

"He's low over land somewhere," the pilot replied. "It's hard to spot a helicopter from above when it's flying low.

Stone began concentrating on looking down. "There . . . No, that's a car."

"See what I mean?"

"Well, it doesn't matter how low he flies if he's going to Westchester," Stone said. "We've got that covered, and they'll see the chopper when it lands."

"What if he's not going to Westchester?" the pilot asked.

"What are the alternatives?" Stone asked.

"I don't know—Albany? Hartford? Bridgeport?"

Stone remembered something. "When I was getting my instrument rating, I flew some approaches at Oxford, Connecticut."

"That's worth a try," the pilot said, flipping through his airport guide. "Five-thousand-foot runway—that's plenty for a corporate jet. If you've got Westchester covered, they won't miss us."

"It's on the way to Hartford," Stone said. "Let's at least take a look at it."

The pilot put the airport's identifier, OXC, into his GPS and swung right, following the needle.

"How long?" Stone asked.

"Twelve minutes," the pilot replied.

In the other helicopter the pilot turned and addressed Larsen. "Five minutes," he said.

"I'll call the airplane," Larsen said to Sharpe. He tapped a speed-dial key on his cell phone and listened. "I'm not getting through," he said.

"We may be moving too fast for the cell phone to capture a tower," Sharpe said. "It doesn't matter—we'll be there in five minutes."

"Six minutes," Stone's pilot said.

"Has this thing got any more speed?" Stone asked.

"I'll push it," the pilot said. Then, a moment

later, "Four minutes." He looked up. "Can you see the airport?" he asked.

Stone looked hard. "No. We're too low; it just looks like countryside."

The pilot climbed another two hundred feet. "There," he said. "Twelve o'clock and five miles."

"There's the other chopper," Stone said, "setting down now, and I can see what looks like a Citation on the ramp." He turned toward the rear. "Looks like we've got 'em, Dino," he said.

Dino reached into his jacket and produced a Colt .45, 1911 model, and checked it. Mitzi was checking her weapon, too.

"You are wearing your vest, aren't you?"

She pretended not to be able to hear him.

Stone turned back to the pilot. "Set this thing down right in front of the jet, and keep the rotor turning. He won't be able to taxi."

"Got it," the pilot said, and started to descend fast. He called Oxford tower and announced his intentions.

Stone watched as people began to get out of the helicopter and hand baggage to a uniformed pilot. He turned back to Mitzi. "As soon as your cell phone works, get hold of Brian and tell him we're at Oxford, Connecticut." He made cell phone motions.

Mitzi nodded and began trying her cell.

"What's your plan?" Dino asked. "As if you had one."

"We're going to set down in front of the Citation so that he can't taxi, jump out, arrest anybody who moves, shoot anybody who produces a gun."

They were half a mile out now.

"Why did you want me to bring the .22 target pistol?"

Stone looked at him. "I want you to shoot Hildy Parsons."

"What?"

"Don't kill her, but make sure she's not able to run for the jet."

"You're crazy. I'm not shooting her!"

"Don't let her get on that airplane, Dino!" Stone turned back just in time to see them set down twenty yards from the Citation. Dino was already getting out of the copter, followed by Mitzi.

Stone unbuckled his belt and started moving toward the door. "Oh, shit," he said aloud, "we're not close enough to the jet."

By the time he made it onto the tarmac everybody on the other copter was running toward the Citation. Sig Larsen produced a pistol and got off a couple rounds. Somebody—Dino or Mitzi—shot him, and he fell to one knee. Derek Sharpe grabbed his arm and started pulling him toward the Citation. Hildy had gone back to the other helicopter

for her purse and was not yet running toward the
Citation, which had its engines running and was
making a sharp turn to the right to clear the helicopter's blades.

"Shoot Hildy!" Stone shouted to Dino, who
was closer to the airplane, then pulled his own gun
and began firing at the nosewheel of the Citation,
missing on the first two shots.

Out of the corner of his eye, he saw Hildy go
down. Then he aimed again at the Citation's nosewheel and saw it go flat. Sharpe had dragged Larsen aboard the airplane and was trying to close the
door. Hildy was screaming at him from the tarmac
and trying to drag herself toward the airplane,
which was still moving, even with the flattened
nosewheel.

Stone ran to the airplane, jerked the half-closed
door open, got hold of Sharpe's jacket lapel, and
jerked him off the airplane, spilling Larsen out as
well. The airplane stopped moving, and the engines began to spool down. Dino produced hand-
cuffs and went to work. Stone looked around.
Where was Mitzi?

Stone turned and looked back. Mitzi was lying
on her back, propped up on one elbow. "Oh,
God!" he shouted and began to run toward her.
He got a glimpse of Hildy and saw blood on her
skirt. Dino had put a .22 slug into her ass.

Stone reached Mitzi, got an arm around her,

and pulled her into a sitting position. He realized immediately that she wasn't wearing a vest. "Where are you hit?" he shouted over the noise of the helicopter, whose rotor was still turning.

"I'm not hit!" she cried. "I broke a heel and fell!"

Stone looked at her feet and saw the shoe with the missing heel. He helped her to her feet. "Call 911 and get an ambulance; we've got two down, Larsen and Hildy. Then call Brian again."

She grabbed her phone and began dialing while Stone ran to help Dino.

"Well, you finally hit the nosewheel," Dino said, snapping cuffs onto Sharpe. "How many rounds did that take?"

"One," Stone replied. "The first two were practice."

59

Stone was back at his desk late that afternoon when the phone buzzed.

"Bill Eggers on one," Joan said.

"Hello, Bill?"

"You *shot* Hildy Parsons?" Eggers said with outrage in his voice.

"Certainly not," Stone said. "There were bullets flying everywhere, and if you'd like to check the bullet that struck her against my gun, you're welcome to."

"Were you carrying a .22?"

"Of course not. You're not going to stop anybody with a .22. I was carrying a 9mm."

"Hildy Parsons was shot with a .22. Cops don't carry .22s."

"My point exactly," Stone replied.

"Then who shot her?"

"Maybe some hunter in the woods. It's a rural area, you know; lots of hunters up there."

"What would a hunter shoot with a .22?"

"Squirrels? Rabbits? Probably some kid."

"Philip Parsons is livid."

"Hildy Parsons is alive."

"But wounded."

"If she hadn't been wounded she might have made it to that jet, and Philip Parsons wouldn't have a daughter anymore. You might explain to Parsons that Sharpe and Larsen were carrying a couple of million in drugs and that much more in cash, and if they had made it, his daughter would have been a fugitive from justice, and he would be spending millions fighting her extradition. As it is, she was just an innocent bystander. I've seen to that."

Eggers thought that over. "Did you hear that, Philip?"

"Yes, Bill, I did."

"I didn't know I was on a conference call, Philip," Stone said, "or I would have been more politic in my statements. Maybe."

"I'm glad you were blunt, Stone," Parsons said.

"How is Hildy?"

"They're keeping her in the hospital tonight for observation. She'll be home tomorrow."

"Have the police questioned her yet?"

"No, it was smart of you to have her taken to New York Hospital."

"It might be a good idea if I have a conversation with her before she goes home," Stone said.

"Now would be a good time," Larkin said. "I'm with her."

"I'll be right there," Stone said.

Stone took a cab to the hospital and found the room. There were two bored-looking detectives sitting in the waiting room.

"Come in, Stone," Philip Larkin said.

Hildy was propped up in bed in a large, sunny room overlooking the East River, and there were flowers everywhere.

"I don't want to speak to him," she said to her father, pointing at Stone.

"Shut up, Hildy," Philip replied.

Stone stood by the bed. "You don't have to talk to me," he said. "In fact, it's better if you don't. You just have to listen." He dragged up a chair and sat down. "You're up to your neck in this, Hildy, and the only way you can get out of it is if you do exactly as I say. There are two police detectives waiting outside to see you . . ."

"I'm *not* going to talk to the police."

"Shut up, Hildy," her father said, "and listen."

Stone continued. "You're going to tell them that you've been seeing Derek Sharpe socially and that you hardly know Sig Larsen. You're going to tell them that you have no idea what happened earlier today, that you had been invited to go to the Bahamas for a few days, and then people started shooting."

"That is exactly what I thought," Hildy said.

"Good, then you won't have to remember a story. You believed Derek Sharpe to be an artist and nothing more. You had no idea that he might be involved in any sort of illegal activity, and you are shocked at the allegations. Got that?"

Hildy folded her arms and looked down at her knees. "Yes," she said softly.

"As soon as the police have finished questioning you, you are going on a vacation, somewhere out of the country. You will not return for Sharpe's trial, and you will not speak of him to any person in this country or abroad. You will carry a cell phone, so that the authorities will be able to reach you if necessary. If you have told them what I asked you to they will not call you as a witness, since you have no knowledge of Sharpe's extralegal activities. Is all that perfectly clear?"

"Yes," she said. "But, Daddy, I don't want to go on a vacation."

"You will go to the house in Tuscany as soon as your doctor says you're well enough to travel," Philip Parsons said. "Once there, you may invite friends to join you. You will not come back until

Derek Sharpe has been tried and convicted, no matter how long that takes."

"Well," she said sheepishly, "Italy is very nice this time of year."

When Stone returned home there was a hand-delivered envelope on his desk. He ripped it open and found a single ticket to the opening night of Carrie's show. There was no note.

60

Stone met Dino at Elaine's at eight thirty. "You're off the hook for shooting Hildy," he said.

"What do you mean, 'off the hook'?" Dino said. "I was never on the hook."

"You're just lucky no one searched you and found the .22."

"There was no luck involved. The Connecticut State Police were not going to search an NYPD lieutenant."

"That's why you're off the hook. I spoke with her father this afternoon, and he's good with it, too. I think he suspects something, but he got his daughter back, so he's not going to make a fuss."

"Is Hildy going to get nailed for her part in this thing?" Dino asked.

"No. I sat in on her questioning this afternoon. She played dumb and innocent, too."

"But she had to know something about what Sharpe was doing."

"Maybe, but she doesn't now, so she's not going to have to testify against him." Stone picked up a menu. "You ready to order?"

"I'm expecting a guest," Dino said. "Let's wait."

The waiter brought them both another drink, and Dino kept checking his wristwatch.

Finally, the door opened, and the commissioner entered, preceded by Mitzi, who looked smashing in a red dress.

Stone stood up, shook her hand, then the commissioner's. "Good evening, sir," he said. "I didn't know you frequented Elaine's."

"I have been coming here since Giuliani was mayor," the commissioner replied, looking around. He turned to the waiter. "You got any single malts?"

The waiter recited the list, and the commissioner chose one. "The lady will have a Beefeater's martini with a twist, not too dry," he said.

Stone shot a glance at Mitzi, but she was not looking at him. However, she delivered a sharp kick to his ankle under the table.

The drinks came, and the commissioner raised his glass. "To successful operations," he said, "and to those who carry them out, even when unexpected circumstances occur."

They all drank, and then they ordered dinner.

"Aren't we missing the, ah, leader of the operation?" Stone asked.

"Oh, Lieutenant Doyle is home studying, I expect," the commissioner said.

"Studying?" Stone asked, puzzled.

"He has been promoted to inspector, and tomorrow he starts his new job as lecturer on tactics at the police academy, his reward for a job well done."

Stone nearly choked on his Knob Creek.

"That said, I think we should raise our glasses to Mitzi," the commissioner said. "This afternoon she was promoted to lieutenant, and tomorrow she will command the detective squad at the First Precinct."

Stone's mouth dropped open, and Mitzi reached over, placed a finger under his chin, and closed it. "Congratulations," he managed to say.

Dino spoke up. "I heard there were some transfers from that squad," he said, "to new assignments in Brooklyn."

"Yes," the commissioner replied, "all promotions. Mitzi will pick her own people."

"All of them women," Mitzi said.

The commissioner looked at her. "*All* of them women?"

She regarded him evenly. "Yes, *sir.*"

Dinner was served. When they were done, the commissioner stood up, followed by Mitzi. "We have to be going," he said. "Barrington, give me your badge," he said.

Stone fished out his Doyle-provided badge and handed it over.

The commissioner placed a small velvet box on the table. "Open it," he said.

Stone picked up the box and opened it. Inside was a retirement badge for a Detective First Grade. From its weight, he judged it to be not plated but solid gold.

The commissioner handed him an envelope. "Here are your retirement papers," he said, "at your new grade." He shook everyone's hand and left, taking Mitzi with him.

Stone sat down.

"You look stunned," Dino said.

"I am."

"You should be. By the way, I'm your date for the theater tomorrow night."

Stone looked at him. "You?"

"You were hoping Mitzi? Not going to happen. Carrie sent me a single ticket, too, for the seat next to yours. In fact, I don't think you're going to be seeing as much of Mitzi in the future."

"What's going on, Dino?"

"Word is, the commissioner is retiring."

"What's that got to do with Mitzi?"

"Word is, he's getting married, too."

Stone stared at him. "You wouldn't kid me?"

"I kid you not."

"I need another drink," Stone said.

61

Dino picked up Stone in his department car and drove him to the theater.

"Is this a kosher use of the car?" Stone asked as they got out.

"I'm on duty," Dino said.

"What are you talking about?"

Dino saw someone he knew and turned to shake hands. The lights were flashing, and they hurried inside to take their seats, which were fourth row on the center aisle.

"Not bad seats, huh?" Dino said.

"What was that about being on duty?" Stone asked, but his question was drowned out by a flood of music from the orchestra pit.

Stone and Dino watched as the curtain went up on a nearly bare stage—only a park bench and a lamppost. The backdrop was an autumnal view of Central Park.

Carrie moved onstage, holding the hand of a young man, and they began to dance. After a moment Carrie began to sing.

Stone relaxed and enjoyed it.

When the first-act curtain came down, the audience roared and wouldn't stop until Carrie and other members of the cast came back for a curtain call. Stone had never seen a first-act curtain call, and the critics sitting near him were on their feet, too.

"Have you ever seen anything like this?" Stone asked.

"Nope," Dino said. Then, as the curtain was being slowly lowered for the intermission, a single gunshot rang out.

Stone and Dino turned and looked toward the rear of the theater, where they saw a scuffle going on in the dress circle. A woman screamed, and a second shot was fired, bringing down a drizzle of plaster from above.

"Stay here," Dino said, and he ran up the aisle, pushing people out of his way.

As Stone stood watching the scuffle in the dress circle, he thought he saw Willie Leahy there. Dino joined the group, and someone was dragged up the stairs and out of the theater. The crowd now moved toward the lobby for intermission.

Stone was sipping a glass of champagne at the bar when Dino returned.

"There appears to be something you didn't tell me," Stone said to him.

"I told you I was on duty," Dino said.

"Was that Max Long doing the shooting?"

"Carrie's ex? One and the same."

"How did this come about?"

"I had a tip from Atlanta. Max took off in his King Air this afternoon and, surprise, surprise, turned up at Teterboro. He's been followed ever since by my guys."

"And how did Willie Leahy get involved?"

"Willie took a personal interest in the events," Dino replied. "We got him a seat behind Max."

"And you didn't tell me any of this?"

"I didn't want to concern you," Dino said. "Now let's go enjoy the rest of the show."

Before the curtain went up, Del Wood walked to center stage and held up his hands for silence. "Ladies and gentlemen," he said, "I wish to apologize for the small disturbance at the end of the first act. It appears that someone wasn't enjoying my show as much as you were and wished to register a protest. He has been relocated and will not disturb us further. Please enjoy the rest of the show.

Thank you." He walked off the stage to a rousing hand.

And enjoy the rest of the show Stone and Dino did, along with the rest of the audience. There were eighteen curtain calls, and the stage was flooded with flowers. The critics rushed up the aisle while the audience was still standing and beating their hands together.

"I'd say it's going to run," Dino said.

Afterward, Stone and Dino went to Sardi's for the opening night party to wait for the reviews with the other invited guests.

Somebody rushed in with stacks of the papers around midnight, and someone else stood on a table and read them aloud, a series of raves, particularly for the show's star.

Stone stood with Dino at the edge of the crowd, watching Carrie accept the congratulations of everyone. At no time did she let go of the hand of her handsome young costar, who was wearing almost as much of her lipstick as she was.

There was a tiny moment when Carrie spotted Stone and gave him a small wave, as if to say good-bye.

Stone and Dino walked into the cool night air and got into Dino's car.

"Elaine's," Dino said to his driver.

"Right," Stone said.

Later, Stone returned home, let himself in, and went upstairs to his bedroom. There was a note on his pillow from Joan.

> Stone, I haven't wanted to mention this but something strange has been going on. I've noticed from my office window that a woman has been standing across the street from the house for periods of two hours or more for the past three days. She is accompanied by a large man who seems concerned for her welfare, but she does nothing but stare at the house. Finally, the man seems to persuade her to leave, but she always returns. I thought you should know about this.

Stone sat down on the bed, put his face in his hands, and made a low, moaning noise.

AUTHOR'S NOTE

I am happy to hear from readers, but you should know that if you write to me in care of my publisher, three to six months will pass before I receive your letter, and when it finally arrives it will be one among many, and I will not be able to reply.

However, if you have access to the Internet, you may visit my website at www.stuartwoods.com, where there is a button for sending me e-mail. So far, I have been able to reply to all my e-mail, and I will continue to try to do so.

If you send me an e-mail and do not receive a reply, it is probably because you are among an alarming number of people who have entered their e-mail address incorrectly in their mail software. I have many of my replies returned as undeliverable.

Remember: e-mail, reply; snail mail, no reply.

When you e-mail, please do not send attachments, as I never open these. They can take twenty minutes to download, and they often contain viruses.

Please do not place me on your mailing lists for funny stories, prayers, political causes, charitable fund-raising, petitions, or sentimental claptrap. I get enough of that from people I already know. Generally speaking, when I get e-mail addressed to a large number of people, I immediately delete it without reading it.

Please do not send me your ideas for a book, as I have a policy of writing only what I myself invent. If you send me story ideas, I will immediately delete them without reading them. If you have a good idea for a book, write it yourself, but I will not be able to advise you on how to get it published. Buy a copy of *Writer's Market* at any bookstore; that will tell you how.

Anyone with a request concerning events or appearances may e-mail it to me or send it to: Publicity Department, Penguin Group (USA) LLC, 375 Hudson Street, New York, NY 10014.

Those ambitious folk who wish to buy film, dramatic, or television rights to my books should contact Matthew Snyder, Creative Artists Agency, 9830 Wilshire Boulevard, Beverly Hills, CA 98212-1825.

Those who wish to make offers for rights of a literary nature should contact Anne Sibbald, Janklow & Nesbit, 445 Park Avenue, New York, NY 10022. (Note: This is not an invitation for you to send her your manuscript or to solicit her to be your agent.)

If you want to know if I will be signing books in your city, please visit my website, www.stuartwoods .com, where the tour schedule will be published a month or so in advance. If you wish me to do a book signing in your locality, ask your favorite bookseller to contact his Penguin representative or the Penguin publicity department with the request.

If you find typographical or editorial errors in my book and feel an irresistible urge to tell someone, please write to Sara Minnich at Penguin's address above. Do not e-mail your discoveries to me, as I will already have learned about them from others.

A list of my published works appears in the front of this book and on my website. All the novels are still in print in paperback and can be found at or ordered from any bookstore. If you wish to obtain hardcover copies of earlier novels or of the two nonfiction books, a good used-book store or one of the online bookstores can help you find them. Otherwise, you will have to go to a great many garage sales.

E laine's, late.

Stone Barrington and Dino Bacchetti sat at their usual table, eating penne with shrimp and vodka sauce, when a young man named Herbert Fisher walked in with a tall young woman.

Stone ignored him. Herbie Fisher was the nephew of Bob Cantor, a retired cop with whom Stone had worked many times. Bob Cantor was Herbie's only connection with reality. Herbie Fisher, in Stone's experience, was a walking catastrophe.

Herbie seated his girl at a table to the rear, then walked back and took a chair at Stone's table. "Hi, Stone," he said. "Hi, Dino."

"Dino," Stone said, "you are a police officer, are you not?"

"I am," said Dino, spearing a shrimp.

"I wish to make a complaint."

"Go right ahead," Dino said.

"What's going on, Stone?" Herbie asked.

Stone ignored him. "There is an intruder at my table. I wish to have him removed."

"Remove him yourself," Dino said. "I'm eating penne with shrimp and vodka sauce."

"You are a duly constituted officer of the law, are you not?" Stone asked.

"Once again, I am."

"Then it is your duty to respond to the complaint of an upstanding citizen."

"What kind of citizen?"

"Upstanding."

"I'm not at all sure that the word describes you, Stone."

Herbie, whose head was following the conversation as if he were seated in the first row at Wimbledon, said, "No kidding, Stone. What's going on?"

Stone continued to ignore him. "Dino, am I to understand that you are ignoring a citizen's complaint?"

"You are to understand that," Dino said, mopping up some vodka sauce with a slice of bread. "Do your own dirty work."

"Stone," Herbie said, "I'm rich."

"That's rich," Dino replied.

"No kidding, I'm rich. I won the lottery."

"How much?" Dino asked.

"Don't encourage him," Stone said.

"Thirty million dollars," Herbie replied.

"How much you got left after taxes and paying off your bookie and your loan shark?" Dino asked.

"I'm warning you," Stone said, "don't encourage him. He's dangerous."

"Approximately fourteen million two," Herbie replied. "I want to hire you as my lawyer, Stone," he continued.

"Why do you need a lawyer?" Dino asked.

"All rich people need lawyers," Herbie said.

"Could you be more specific?" Dino asked.

"Dino," Stone said, "Stop this; stop it right now; he's sucking you in."

"Prove you're rich, Herbie," Dino said.

"I'll be right back," Herbie said. He got up, walked back to where the girl sat, picked up her large handbag, came back to Stone's table and sat down. He opened the handbag wide, displaying the contents to Stone and Dino. "What do you think that is?" he asked.

"Well," Dino said, gazing into the purse, "that would appear to be approximately twenty bundles, of one hundred hundred-dollar bills each, or two million dollars."

"Absolutely correct," Herbie said.

"Do you always walk around with that much money, Herbie?" Dino asked.

"Only since I got rich."

"Oh."

"Stone, I want to retain you as my lawyer. I'll pay you a one-million-dollar retainer in cash, right now."

Stone stopped eating. "Dino, have you had any recent training at recognizing counterfeit bills?"

"Funny you should mention that," Dino said. "We had a guy in from Treasury the day before yesterday who gave us a slide-show presentation on that very subject."

"Would you examine the bills in the bag, please?"

Dino dipped into the bag and came out with a hundred-dollar bill. He held it up to the light, snapped it a couple of times and laid it on the table. "Entirely genuine," Dino said; then he turned to Herbie. "They don't hand out millions in cash at the lottery office, you know. Where did you get it?"

"I cashed a check," Herbie replied.

Stone flagged down a passing waiter. "David," he said, "would you please go and find me a good-sized paper bag?"

"Sure," David replied. He went into the kitchen and came back with a plastic shopping bag. "No paper bags. Will this do?"

"Yes," Stone said, accepting the bag and handing it to Dino. "Will you please put one million dollars of Herbie's money into this bag, Dino?"

"That okay with you, Herbie?"

"Sure, go ahead," Herbie replied.

Dino held the plastic bag close to the purse and counted out ten of the bundles. He handed the bag to Stone. "There you go."

"Just put it on the floor beside me," Stone said, and Dino did so. Stone looked at Herbie for the first time. "All right, you've got my attention; I'll listen for one minute."

"They're trying to kill me," Herbie said.

"Who is trying to kill you?"

"People who want my money."

"Are these people aware that you walk around with two million dollars of it in a woman's hand-bag?"

Herbie shrugged. "Maybe."

"Herbie, you've been flashing this money around, haven't you?"

"Well, sort of."

"The hooker must know about the money, since it's in her handbag."

"What hooker?"

"The one you walked in here with."

"She's not a hooker."

Herbie, she's with you; she is, ipso facto, a hooker."

"Part-time, maybe," Herbie admitted.

"Who do hookers work for, Herbie?"

"Me?"

"Besides you?"

"Madams? Pimps?"

"And who do madams and pimps work for, Herbie?"

"They're self-employed, aren't they?"

"They work for or associate with bad people, Herbie. "If a hooker knows you've got two million dollars in her handbag, then her madam and her pimp know it, too, and if they've had a moment, they've already sold that information to someone who wants to take it from you."

"Sheila wouldn't do that," Herbie said. "She loves me."

At that moment, as if for punctuation at the end of Herbie's sentence, a fist-sized hole appeared in the front window of Elaine's, and a loud report rent the air. This was quickly followed by two more shots.

Everybody hit the floor.

Stone raised his head an inch. "Are you sure Sheila loves you, Herbie?"

STUART WOODS

"Addictive . . . Pick it up at your peril.
You can get hooked."
—*Lincoln Journal Star*

For a complete list of titles and to sign up for our
newsletter, please visit prh.com/StuartWoods